CROSSED SPACES

Crossed Spaces

Edited by Lynne Stringer and R. A. Stephens 2021

Published by Rhiza Edge, 2021
An imprint of Rhiza Press
PO Box 302
Chinchilla QLD 4413
Australia
www.rhizaedge.com.au

Cover design by Rhiza Press
Layout by Rhiza Press

A catalogue record for this book is available from the National Library of Australia

CROSSED SPACES

CONTENTS

FOREWORD

When COVID-19 suddenly became what everyone was talking about, I found myself watching students, adults, family and friends confined to their houses. It inspired me to create an opportunity for something to do—to write! I wanted to use creativity to not only escape but extend one's imagination in a time we all needed it. This collection was created by calling for submissions and the resulting collection of stories is an outstanding series of out of world and slightly unusual stories.

One of my favourite things to do is give opportunities to as many people as possible. I am so pleased each of these authors could be included in this collection and love the interesting connections made in each as well as the places our imaginations went in 2020.

I hope you enjoy them as much as we did.

R. A. Stephens

***

When I first heard of the idea for the *Crossed Spaces* anthology, I was intrigued by the possibilities it presented. Not only that, I felt it was an appropriate time for this kind of journey. Why not escape the difficulties of a global pandemic by crossing into other worlds?

I was privileged to read all the manuscripts that were submitted and delighted at the high calibre of so many of them. Some were authors I knew well, others, people I hadn't encountered before.

That's always the most exciting thing about anthologies—it gives you access to a number of new authors to enthral you.

The 16 stories in *Crossed Spaces* all took the brief in different directions, showing just how many worlds we can access in our imaginations. Some of the stories are set on Earth in a world that looks fairly familiar, maybe with a paranormal or steampunk twist. There are others that branch off into our planet's future, exploring what that could look like, with some frightening scenarios presented. Others still are set in worlds unknown, in the vastness of space, or in a land that bears no resemblance to anything seen before.

All of them show a depth of imagination and exploration that crossed into other worlds in search of new adventures, lost loves and discoveries that could set us free. I'm so happy for the opportunity to be involved in this anthology.

Lynne Stringer

TRAITOR

Geraldine Borella

All five members of the EAB tribunal filed in and took their seats on the panel, ready for day three of testimony. I sat in the front row with my fellow crewmembers of *Peregrine IR*, interested to hear Captain Tate's statement. Would his match all those that had come before?

'State your name,' said Major Erlandson, peering over the top of his half-glasses. An imposing figure, the major had been enlisted by Earth and Beyond to lead the review into our failed exploratory mission—we'd been sent to POLI1, the closest habitable exoplanet, to determine its potential to support human life—and I smirked to watch Tate squirm. Recruited as the onboard scientist, I'd found myself butting heads with him from the moment we launched.

'Captain Brenthon Tate, sir,' said the young captain. He sat ramrod straight in the chair in front, facing the bench where the panel sat. I winced to see him present himself as a competent and reliable operative, his even tone belying the aggressive meathead I'd come to know onboard. I swear, if Tate were a dog, he'd have cocked his leg in every corner of that Interstellar Ramjet Spacecraft and the *Peregrine* would've been soaked and stinking.

'Begin your report, Captain,' said Major Erlandson. The major had a good fifty years on the seventeen-year-old captain but addressed him with the respect due to his rank. 'We will interject as required.'

It must've been strange for the major given the age of the captain and his crew, but interstellar travel demanded youth. Due to our age, our body compositions were able to withstand and recover from the rigours of near speed-of-light transit. We'd be retired from the job at twenty, though—a sad reality for an ambitious space-explorer like me.

'Sir,' said Tate, with a quick nod. He sat up even straighter in his chair and began his report. 'Our transit to POLI1 was without incident, each crewmember settling into their respective roles.'

Rubbish! I held in a snort and glared at the back of his block head. There'd been plenty of incidents on *Peregrine*, the onboard atmosphere toxic, fanned by Tate himself. I'd been ridiculed relentlessly in front of his team, being a civvy scientist and not military, and he'd revelled in the bullying that followed.

'We set down on POLI1,' continued Tate, 'our flight officers making a first-rate landing given the rocky, uneven terrain.'

Well, that's true, at least. FOs Templeton and Strafe had done an exceptional job navigating *Peregrine IR*, finding a spot close enough to an oceanic body that needed investigation, but far enough away to protect from an unexpected tidal flood. Our set-down had landed us in a rocky, barren landscape with little to recommend itself and, at first glance, it seemed unlikely any life could exist on POLI1.

The captain continued. 'I commanded my military crew to take turns escorting our onboard scientist, Callan Sorensen, on his exploratory mission.'

Utter crap! I coughed to prevent my mouth from switching to autopilot. Tate had done nothing of the sort. In fact, once we'd landed on POLI1 and I'd determined the outside atmosphere suitable, he and his crew had spent their time partying and loafing about. It became clear he was there to relax and have a good old galactic holiday.

POLI1 sat well within the Goldilocks zone, at a safe enough

distance from a Red Dwarf to warm the planet without boiling it. And given each hot day was equal to ten days on Earth, life on POLI1 was a summer vacation on steroids.

So Tate and his cronies stuck up a tent to play beer pong, having smuggled cases of beer on board. They wrestled, blasted rocks with laser pulses, pumped iron and set each other stupid challenges, like seeing who could pull the first POLI1 all-nighter. Of course, no one did. Who could possibly stay awake *that* long?

Flight Officer Templeton had been the only crewmember to speak up, offering to accompany me, but was swiftly commanded by Tate to stay put.

'You can check the *Peregrine* over instead,' Tate had said. 'To make sure it'll get us back home.'

'But what if Sorensen comes to harm?' argued Templeton. 'Surely it'd be safer if he had a buddy.'

'You reckon there are aliens out there, do ya, Tempo?' scoffed Tate. He placed his hands over his mouth and opened his eyes wide, mock-terrified, and Sergeants Lowe, Best and Renwick burst out laughing. Templeton flashed a fake smile and attempted to laugh along with them.

'I just …' She shrugged. 'What if Sorensen falls and gets hurt? Breaks a leg?'

Tate snorted. 'Einstein's clumsy, I'll grant you that, but surely he can put one foot in front of the other. After all, he *is* the brains trust.' He'd gestured crudely with his right hand, branding me a total flog. Lowe, Best and Renwick sniggered again, and Templeton gave me a pointed look, which said, *Sorry, Cal. I tried.*

'And what *did* Sorensen find?' asked Major Erlandson, bringing me back to the tribunal.

This ought to be good. Tate had absolutely *no* idea what I'd found, and I couldn't wait to hear his answer.

'Ah …' Tate cleared his throat. 'Sorensen surveyed the area for around—'

'*Around?* snapped Colonel Bullen, situated on the far right of the panel. He leaned back and patted the fingers of both hands against his rotund belly. Lifting his chin, he looked down on the captain. 'We don't deal in approximates, Captain Tate. Please be specific.'

'Yes, ah, my apologies, Colonel,' he said, almost stuttering. 'I'll be sure to do so.' Tate squirmed in his seat and started over. 'I believe it was a total of three POLI1 days, which equates to thirty days on Earth, that Sorensen—'

'Hold up, hold up!' said Colonel Bullen as he raised his hands and shook his bald head. Glaring at Tate, his bushy black eyebrows drew together. 'You *believe* or you know this to be true?'

'No, I … I know this to be true,' asserted Tate, with a decisive nod.

Well, it's close enough to the truth. I'd explored for three and a half POLI1 days, every one of them solo. But what's half a POLI1 day here or there when you're sleeping off a massive hangover?

By the end of the first planetary day, I'd found little of significance and it was beyond disappointing. I'd wanted to return home triumphant, with a definitive answer to Earth's ongoing struggles—our overpopulation, dwindling resources, bad pollution and impending social chaos. The EAB project I'd signed up to had thrilled in scale and possibility. Our task—find an exoplanet close enough to our solar system for the youth of Earth to call their own. I suppose I'd had stars in my eyes, literally and metaphorically.

'And what did Sorensen find, please, Captain Tate?' asked Colonel Smart.

The backs of Tate's ears glowed red. Was it because he had to report to a female superior or because he had no freakin' idea *what* I found?

'That the planet was inhospitable and unsuitable for sustaining life, ma'am.'

Not true, not in the slightest.

POLI1 was more than suitable for sustaining life; I'd found signs of it on day two. And man, did it fire me up! Because where there's life, there's water. Admittedly, it was only a small specimen, like a fine lichen pressed against some rocks, but it was pale green and alive and had what looked like roots.

So I tracked them, digging and digging, following a circuitous path under the layers of dust and rock until I reached an underground tunnel. It had taken ages to find—one full POLI1 day; ten Earth days—but worth every minute of the work invested. I could hardly believe what I saw. The tunnel wasn't carved naturally by the elements—by wind, storm, water, or lava. It had been purpose-built. By someone or some*thing.* I'd shivered with excitement and trepidation because I knew right then we weren't alone. There was life on POLI1 after all, and it wasn't just vegetable matter.

By POLI1 day three, I'd begun to explore tunnels that led further down underground to a deep, cavernous water source. At least I *thought* it was water. The depths were a luminescent blue, bright and almost artificial-looking and I wondered at the curious mix of minerals that would cause it to glow like that. I knelt and tossed a rock in—no steam, no acid burn—so I retrieved the water-quality monitor from my backpack. The liquid was neither too alkaline nor acidic to cause concern. I dipped a finger in. It was cool to the touch and seemed harmless enough, so I cupped my hand and collected some to drink. Probably a stupid thing to do, but I'm a scientist. We take risks. It's what we do.

That's when the strangest thing happened. An inner glow, emanating from my stomach and projecting out, began to suffuse my entire body. Every tissue and sinew, every nerve fibre and atom. I was connected, *plugged in.* I could hear them—existing, growing, communing. I should have been scared. Whatever lay ahead could harm or kill, yet all I felt was a gentle sense of curiosity.

As I followed the sound-trail, I came upon a vast valley filled with what I could only describe as being like the polyps of giant jellyfish attached to the rock walls. The yellow, leathery capsules were of similar size to me, lifeforms at various metamorphotic stages well protected inside. I wasn't afraid. There was no reason to be. They assured me of it. And I believed them.

A humanoid figure emerged from the tunnel at the end of the valley and walked towards me. I call her a 'she', but even then, I understood that classifying gender was irrelevant. Reaching out to take hold of my hands, she welcomed me. Her beautiful green eyes with thick dark lashes, chocolate brown skin and long black hair instantly reminded me of my girlfriend, Najeela. Dressed simply in a light tunic, the ethereal being was barefoot.

'*This is me, but not me,*' she said without speaking, her thoughts reaching into my mind, and I understood what she meant. She'd appeared as something familiar, a human figure so as not to alarm, one I was particularly attracted to.

'*What do you really look like?*' I wondered.

'*In time you will know.*' She gestured at the surrounding rock walls. '*I see you've found our valley of youth.*'

'*They're fascinating. Truly a miracle.*' It *was* a miracle. I'd never seen large creatures grow in such a way. Quite remarkable. I only wished I could have examined them in more detail.

'*They are beautiful and precious, each and every one, for they are our future.*'

'*Yes, I understand.*'

'*And you have come to co-exist with us,*' she remarked, matter-of-factly. It was as though she knew all, saw all, sensed all.

'*We are looking to colonise, yes.*'

'*And you think you could do so harmoniously.*' It wasn't a question, more a statement, but it raised serious doubts in my mind, doubts I couldn't conceal.

'*It's possible.*' Even as I thought that I knew it to be untrue. How could we co-exist with these peaceful beings? Human behaviour was unpredictable, oftentimes inflammatory. With people like Captain

Tate in positions of authority, how could I, in all good conscience, promise peace and harmony?

She stared at me for quite some time, as though reading my every betraying thought. Highly intelligent, these being were undoubtedly far more evolved than humans.

'*But you will need our resources, especially our water.*'

'*That's true.*'

With a decisive nod, she grabbed my hand and led me from the valley of youth into another tunnel. I followed for a long time until we came to a small cave, where a deep pool of luminescent blue water, the same I'd seen before, took up most of the floor area.

The being opened a door to her thoughts; I could see this was where she spent most of her day and that the pool was connected to a massive underground watercourse which spanned the entire planet. She was amphibious, spending time in water and on land, but mostly in water.

'*You will stay here until I speak to the others.*'

I nodded and she dived into the pool.

While waiting, I ate some of the food I'd brought and scribbled in my journal. I wrote for hours, noting all I had recently discovered.

When she returned, she emerged from the pool as her true self, vaguely humanoid yet so alien I couldn't make sense of her. I swallowed my knee-jerk jolt of fear, reminding myself she meant me no harm. She was pale, pearlescent, bipedal, without eyes or mouth and with membranous appendages connected by strands of pulsating netting. Her torso was covered with sensor-like receptors that blinked and shimmered. What functions did they serve? I could only speculate.

She towered over me and, in that moment, I knew exactly what the aliens had decided.

'*You'd best go,*' she suggested, '*but don't be afraid.*'

'Captain Tate!' barked Major Erlandson. Tate turned his attention from Colonel Smart to the head of the tribunal. 'Please continue.'

On familiar ground, Tate resumed his confident air. 'Yes, sir. On day three, thirty Earth days in, dust storms engulfed us—fierce, catastrophic dust storms, hurling rock directly at the *Peregrine.* I was concerned we'd sustain serious damage if they continued for too long or got any worse. Atmospheric radiation spiked, reaching alarming levels, and enormous tidal waves rose like walls of concrete upon the distant shore.'

'I asked Sorensen if he had anything significant to report, as I believed our window of opportunity to respond was closing fast. I knew I'd need to either move the *Peregrine* or set course for home. Sorensen reported, as I've previously stated, that the planet was inhospitable and unsuitable for sustaining life.'

'So you returned to Earth,' finished the major.

'That's correct, sir.'

'Right,' said Major Erlandson, leaning back in his chair and steepling his fingers. 'I think that's about it. You may resume your seat, Captain.'

The major scanned the audience and fixed his steely gaze upon me. 'And we will now hear from scientist, Callan Sorensen.'

Captain Tate rose out of his chair and knocked my shoulder as we passed in the aisle.

'All yours, dipstick,' he whispered.

I straightened my shoulders, brushing off his remark, and took my turn in the hot seat. Within fifteen minutes, I'd confirmed everyone else's reports, not word for word, but close enough to satisfy the members of the tribunal and allow the review to be closed.

***

When I returned to my quarters, I burned my journal, watching the pages curl and crisp, catch flame and turn to ash. I couldn't chance it being discovered; if the truth came out, I'd be branded a traitor.

None of what Captain Tate reported had happened. There'd been no damaging dust storms or spiking radiation, and the distant shores had remained flat and calm. In fact, the truth was far more bizarre.

When I returned to the *Peregrine*, I found the crew acting strangely. They weren't altogether there. It was as though they'd been placed in some sort of hypnotic trance, awake but not awake. Their eyelids were half-closed, yet they acted with urgency, responding to unseen, troubling events.

I watched them dart about and attend to various tasks as Tate shouted commands. Renwick secured the craft for take-off and clipped herself into her seat while Sergeant Best kept a vigilant watch on the far-off ocean, reporting the presence of non-existent tidal waves to Tate. Sergeant Lowe measured atmospheric conditions and external parameters and shouted about the possibility of wind-flung rocks damaging solar panels and rocket boosters. Yet the atmospheric conditions were stable and a quick view outside showed no dust storm. Templeton watched the radiation meter, conferring with fellow flight officer, Strafe, both looking worried. I checked over their shoulders. External radiation was well within normal range.

Confused, I logged onto the ship's computer to check the vital signs of each crewmember. They were all fine, albeit in deep sleep, their brains locked firmly in theta wave mode.

Tate saw me and marched over. 'What did you find out there, dipstick?' Even in a hypnotic trance, he was a jerk.

I wavered, then said, 'Nothing, no signs of life that would lead me to believe POLI1 is habitable.'

'Knew it.' He darted off to issue further commands, preparing the *Peregrine* for launch.

Well out of range of POLI1, I noticed the crew returning to normal. I'd expected confusion and questions, even a dazed kind of wondering. But none of that happened. Everyone just went about their business, continuing to monitor the spacecraft in flight.

To this day, I have no idea how the aliens did it. I can only assume they put the crew in some sort of hypnotic state and implanted fake memories, each crewmember reporting a steadfast recollection of catastrophic dust storms, spiking radiation and rising tidal waves. Yet I had none of those memories. So why was *I* spared?

I left the Earth and Beyond program soon after, unable to sleep soundly since my return home. Had I done the right thing, not reporting alien existence to Captain Tate or the tribunal? Had I betrayed my own kind? Should I report it now? Throw myself at the mercy of the men in uniform? I tortured myself for weeks, going back and forth, asking the same questions over and over, until finally finding peace with my decision.

If we colonised POLI1, made it Earth Mark 2, we'd only be jumping from one dysfunctional relationship into another, destroying another planet for our own selfish purposes. No, I refused to believe myself a traitor to humanity, at least not to the people we'd become. The aliens could have killed us, swiftly and with ease. Instead, they chose a peaceful solution. I'm not so sure we would have done the same.

ENDYMION

Jonathan E. Furneaux

The *Endymion* hurtled silently through space and, aside from the occasional jostle from what we hypothesised were solar winds, it had been a relatively uneventful voyage between galaxies. Uneventful and maddening. I'd read the reports from previous officers who'd navigated *Endymion* before me. Tens of thousands of officers had sat in my seat. Same story.

'We would have been better off sailing down the River Styx,' Krill said. His face was almost the same shade of red as his hair. It was genetic, rather than sunburn.

'Quit being so morbid,' I said, chewing on my brown, greasy hair. 'It makes it worse when you keep going on about it.'

'I'm being realistic, Leah,' Krill shot back. He sat up in his control chair and pushed a lever to make it swivel. A motor spun him around to face me. 'I haven't had a proper sleep in months because of Hana.'

'We *both* have to carry her load.' I turned to face the bulkhead, instead of him. A dense jungle was projected onto it, an almost-perfect illusion. Monkeys swung from the canopy. I'd never seen a monkey in real life. In fact, I only knew that they were called monkeys because a previous navigation officer had forgotten their encyclopedia of animals and left it on the navigation station.

The illusion hid my reflection, and I was thankful for that. If the bulkhead were left blank, I would have been forced to examine my own sunken blue eyes, gaunt cheeks and chapped lips.

I pressed the button to change the landscape that surrounded us. It became a rolling vista of the ocean, complete with waves that threw themselves around us and against the rocks.

'I hate this one,' Krill said. His red face grew pale and sickly as he watched the ebb and flow of water around him.

'We've already spent a week in the jungle,' I replied. 'Besides, Hana doesn't like monkeys.'

A replica moon appeared on the bulkhead, drifting above the digital ocean—the signal for our rest period.

***

I dreamt of my boyfriend again. We had met at the polluted seaside. I'd slipped on the basalt rock pools and he'd come running over—a hairy boy one year older than me, with a tiny dog in one arm. The other arm had gently supported me as I'd limped back towards the shore.

We were inseparable after that, spending our days together in the dark alleyways and backstreets of a crumbling Sydney. I was giddy with the sheer thrill of it all. The independence we'd had. We would stroll between the immense corporate buildings that blotted out the sun, walking through the squelching puddles of mud and chunks of decaying concrete, arm in arm, like we were at the seaside again.

Even in my dream, I could still taste the steely excitement when we'd decided to rob a child who'd taken a shortcut through our backstreets. I had gritted my teeth so tightly that they squeaked. My fists had trembled as they held a long splinter of glass, wrapped in cloth. People listen to you when you have a blade. The child handed over his unleavened bread and bank stick. My boyfriend had made the items disappear into his duster jacket. We sent the kid on his way with a kick on the rump from him and a fist to the back of his neck from my boyfriend. Then the pure adrenaline hit us—a rasping laughter of relief when we realised how easy it all was. We'd managed to squeeze ten or twenty children, just like that.

The dream turned. I saw the day when the Imperial Guard caught us. They had spilled into the dim walkways and catwalks, where they found us patting down another victim, the tip of my glass shiv drawing a prick of blood as I held it against the kid's neck. There had been too many of them, each carrying a shrink-wrap gun. I was thrown against a mouldy brick wall and glued there before my brain even registered that they'd fired. When they'd searched me, they'd found the ring my boyfriend had made for me from coiled copper wire. We hadn't been serious about it. It was just a promise. A silly little promise we'd made one night without thinking. The government didn't see it that way. It was labelled an illegal engagement. That had added another two years to my four-year sentence.

I was allowed to leave prison on parole a year later, on the condition that I spent the remainder of my years doing community service. It was when I was on parole that I saw the floating billboards for the Free Ticket program. One particular billboard was of a strong woman planting corn. She was using a gravity plough to till the blue soil of an alien planet. I'd seen a piece of myself inside that young woman—working the land and planting the first crops with the other colonists. Real frontier stuff. A fresh start. The last ship off-world was scheduled on a journey towards a mostly habitable M-Class planet nicknamed 'Fin' because it was the final planet Earth could afford to colonise. I had stood in a muddy line with the other miserable souls who couldn't pay for a trip off-world.

Earth was doomed; that much was certain. The scientists who were interviewed on the web looked terrified. Many of them shrugged hopelessly when asked what could be done to save the planet. A plate of meat was rare, expensive and usually radioactive. Each day new satellites, armed with nuclear missiles, were launched into orbit by opposing nations. The promise of one final, global war loomed over every soul.

The enrolment officer had barely glanced at my record before offering me a spot in the program. I looked at that billboard again. It was the final day for enrolment.

The Free Ticket program was a gift from fate. One that I'd never get again. My boyfriend had a month left of his prison sentence, followed by a difficult life with a record that would prevent him from owning land or a business. I felt numb as I signed my name on the contract. There was no future on Earth, or with him. There was only the Free Ticket program.

I climbed aboard the recruitment shuttle and left Earth without saying goodbye.

***

The *Endymion*'s imaginary sun rose above me. We got to work at our control stations. I checked our flight path for the millionth time, ensuring that there were no gravitation anomalies, asteroids, or other hazards. Each day when the fake sun rose, a the ship's distorted voice spoke.

'Awaken, Free Ticket,' it cooed. 'You are another day closer to your fresh start.'

A fresh start. That's also how the enrolment officer on Earth had described it. The *Endymion* was a sleeper vessel, carrying frozen colonists to Fin. The Free Ticket program effectively erased my criminal record. There was one catch. Free Tickets passengers went into a raffle. Krill, Hana, and I had been selected via the ship's lottery for a year-long shift.

'A one-in-five-hundred chance,' Krill hissed. 'With only a decade to go until we reach Fin!'

'Stop it.'

'There's two million free ticket passengers aboard this vessel, and *we* got selected to do a year-long shift right before the end? I never thought I'd actually *get* chosen!'

'We were unlucky. Focus on your work.'

Krill spun his chair away from the controls. Behind him, the internal system controls showed the veins of oxygen and fluids that criss-crossed an immense diagram of the ship. He slammed a fist into his palm. The nutrient tube attached to his wrist whipped back and forth.

'The devil's lottery is what it is! I should've just crawled back into my cryogenic bed.'

'That'd be a breach of contract, and treason.'

Krill made a guttural groan. It seemed to calm him down. 'They should give us the option to quit early.'

'If every Free Ticket chickened out of the hard work, then eventually the Paid Tickets would have to do a year shift as well. Or, heaven forbid, some Free Ticket might get woken up for a second year of work.'

The blood drained from Krill's face at the thought. He kicked his thin legs in the air in frustration. Krill hadn't left his chair for a month, and his legs were covered in red sores.

'Did you feed Hana?' I asked.

'It's your turn.' He spun back to face his controls. 'This thing never works. How am I supposed to do my job?'

I stood up from my station. My legs buckled, but I caught myself. Charts, ledgers and printed logs spilled onto the floor.

'Why do you keep all that garbage?' Krill asked, staring at the mountains of crusted, brown paper.

'It's a good backup,' I explained. 'Sometimes I read the logs of past crews. Several of the ship's systems stopped being reliable three hundred years ago. Copper circuitry erodes, you know.'

An earlier navigation officer must have made paper copies of the ship's systems. It had become a collection of artefacts that each retiring navigator handed down to the next before they went back to cryogenic sleep.

I hobbled over to Hana on my pathetic legs and checked her nutrient dispenser. The ship knew that her controls weren't being used, so the nutrient drip attached to her wrist had slowed down to almost nothing. I skimmed through the list of sleepers, checking their vitals for her.

The scale of *Endymion* boggled the mind. There were two million Free Tickets who could be awoken from their sleep to act as the crew, and eight million Paid Tickets who were exempt.

I should have been on my recreation shift, but Hana needed me. She'd starve if someone didn't carry out her duties.

'How's the vegetable, Leah?' Krill asked.

'Don't call her that.'

Hana's head was forever tucked between her knees. She was rocking in her chair. At the start of our year-long shift together, Hana had been animated and excitable, always singing. The monotony of the job had gotten to her. Checking the brain activity of the sleepers each day had worn her down to nothingness. It was the nature of bridge duty. I could feel my own mind peeling away each day.

'Stupid fluid sensors,' Krill said.

'Go fix them, then.'

'I'd have no idea where to look. Besides, I don't want to end up like …' Krill looked up at the domed ceiling above, searching for the end of his sentence. 'What was his name?'

'He didn't say. Just went by his designation—XRD-902.'

'I'm not following his lead. He's been gone for, what, six months?'

The ship was clever, but its designers hadn't anticipated problems like insanity or strange disappearances. XRD was our maintenance guy. A thousand kilometres of space vessel, and one maintenance guy. It was laughable, even with the ship's automated repair systems.

'He must be dead by now,' Krill said.

'He'll be back.'

'What makes you so sure?'

'The computer tracks our brain activity through Hana's console. If someone dies, the ship will automatically wake up a Free Ticket to replace him.'

'Then he's managed to get himself lost forever.'

A loud hiss erupted from behind us. We turned. Standing in the cycling airlock was a tall man.

He ripped a rebreather off his face with a gasp. 'Whoa! This air tastes so much better.'

The skin underneath his rebreather was smooth ebony, but the flesh where the plastic breathing apparatus hadn't protected him was blistered and burned away to pink tissue. His eyes were sunken black orbs—two beaded pins pushed into a cushion.

'How …' he coughed and took a swill of something from a leather skin that hung around his waist. I saw the coiled muscles that wound themselves across his legs and realised how gaunt we'd all become.

'Hell, look at you,' he said, and I realised it was XRD-902. 'You've all wasted away up here.'

'What happened to your face?' Krill asked.

'I saw a star,' XRD replied, 'the one we're heading towards, in fact. Watched it for ten or twenty minutes through a hole at the edge of the ship. Nothing between it and me except the reinforced plastic window of an airlock. Beautiful. Didn't know that was a bad idea until my face started dripping off.'

'Why didn't you come back here for help?' I asked.

XRD unfastened the straps of his bag. He let his pack fall to the ground, exposing the scabbed and calloused skin underneath. 'I got lost.'

The ship's logs were full of similar stories. Maintenance workers who had lost their maps, misread them, lost their frame of reference, gone blind from an accident or starved out there before finding a nutrient dispenser.

It didn't help that most of the ship's internal signposts had faded to blankness. The painted gangways had flaked in the oscillating heat and cold. There were no more buckets of paint. The emergency rations left in safety boxes had all been emptied.

'With each year and with each new maintenance worker, the job becomes harder,' XRD said. He kicked off the thin sandals of rubber on his feet and massaged his toes. When he had departed six months ago, his feet had been furnished in steel-capped boots. 'The previous gent taught me a few tricks of the trade before he went back on the ice. Wait, what's wrong with Hana?'

'She isn't feeling well,' I explained.

'Cracked under the pressure,' Krill added. He rubbed his hands together. 'The ship should be waking our replacements any day now. Then we'll all go back under the ice until we reach Fin.'

'Contracts completed,' I said, and felt my shoulders begin to loosen after a year of mind-numbing work.

'Ah, there's a problem,' XRD said. He stretched forward to touch his toes. His fingers had been broken and then healed in a crooked fashion.

'Did I miscount?' Krill asked. 'Is it next week instead? I've lost track of time here.'

I unplugged my nutrient feed from my arm with a wet, popping sound and approached XRD on unsteady feet. 'What's happened? What did you see?'

'On the way back here, I stopped by an old Free Ticket cryogenics chamber. Everyone was gone.'

'Gone?' Krill asked. 'Gone where?'

***

We spent the better part of an hour questioning the ship's systems and subroutines.

'There might be unknown mechanisms that move sleepers around,' Krill said. He paced back and forth like a toddler, holding onto his chair for support. 'The ship could be trying to prevent radiation poisoning or something. You have your turn near the outside, then swap for the centre where it's safe.'

'Like penguins huddled together?' I asked, thinking back to an entry from the encyclopedia.

Krill's eyebrows knitted together. 'What the hell is a penguin?'

'It didn't look like a simple case of moving them about,' XRD said.

'An impact, then,' Krill suggested. 'Something hit the ship and obliterated the area.'

XRD lay with his head resting against his backpack for comfort. He looked for all the world like he was on vacation. 'There'd be rubble or a breached airlock. This looked nice and clean.'

I moved Hana's chair to the side so I could work on her controls unimpeded. I tried to ignore the nutrients gathering in the transparent chamber above her chair and the scarce fluid inside my own. 'Are you certain there was no one inside?'

'I saw that star through the airlock door, didn't I?' XRD said. 'No mistaking it. Entire chamber was gone.'

I scrolled through the list of Free Tickets. 'Computer says they're sleeping peacefully. No abnormalities.'

'The computer's wrong then,' XRD replied. 'There's only vacuum where those people should be.'

'Let's circle back to my impact idea,' Krill said. His words had become a slur of panic.

I stood up from the controls and put my fists into the small of my back. My spine cracked in several places. 'We're travelling at nearly a hundred kilometres per second. If something collided with us head-on it would be catastrophic. We would know about it. There'd be something in the ship's logs.'

The sensors lit up in a brilliant blue. Krill gasped and pressed a button on his controls. Through the void of space, a low voice crackled from the control panel.

'Contacting vessel. Do you …' there was a burst of static, '… me? Repeat, do you read me?'

Beads of sweat fell from Krill's face. He pecked at the controls with index fingers. 'We're being contacted by another vessel.'

'That's impossible,' I said. 'No other ship was sent along this velocity.'

'We read you,' Krill said. His voice echoed across the bridge. 'Please identify.'

'This is Captain Tsubaz of the colony ship *Discovery.* We are en route to the Fin star system on this trajectory and have picked up your ship's signature.' The voice belonged to a lady. Judging by the command and confidence she exuded, Captain Tsubaz was most likely upper-class. Her accent was clipped, however, and unlike anything I'd heard before.

I elbowed Krill away from the controls. 'We are the sleeper vessel *Endymion.* Leah Martinez speaking. Did Earth reroute a colony ship to this sector? I don't recall your ship's name in any of the records.'

'… check again for me?' The voice returned, mid-conversation. '*Endymion,* our computer suggests you are one of the sleeper vessels launched across the galaxy twelve thousand years ago?'

'That is correct. *Endymion* was the last vessel scheduled to leave Earth,' I replied.

'I see. How fascinating. My great-grandmother was from Earth.'

'I don't understand, Earth should have been destroyed centuries ago.'

'I'm sorry,' came Tsubaz's apologetic voice. 'That might have been the way things seemed when you left, but it's no longer the case. The people who were stranded on Earth launched new satellites. They dismantled the Old War missiles lying in orbit. They built a laser network to clear the sky of debris. They developed photo-sensors that could spot underground water on planets that were previously thought to be desolate.'

'When was this?' I demanded. 'What year?'

'Oh,' Tsubaz sounded sheepish. 'I was not a very good student of history. I will ask Richter.'

The static resumed and XRD placed a hand on my shoulder. 'Leah, are you okay?'

I realised my throat was hoarse. I wiped a tear away. 'I gambled everything on a trip to escape Earth. I left my boyfriend.'

'We all thought it was the end for Earth,' XRD said softly.

The *Discovery* cut through the static once more. 'Richter informs me that the Old War ended in 3744.'

'That was over eleven thousand years ago.' I bit my lip. 'Earth became peaceful a thousand years after we left?'

'Yes,' Tsubaz replied. 'A lot has happened. We were surprised to find you, actually. The consensus from my colony was that all the sleeper vessels would have erupted in mutiny. We only know of one other vessel, like yours, but it was flown into a star by the Free Tickets controlling it.'

Krill made a gurgling sound in his throat. 'Why would the Free Tickets do something like that? Why throw away their fresh start?'

'It's not my place to say.' There was a pause. Captain Tsubaz sounded uncomfortable. 'I should get the counsellor to speak to you.'

'Tell us,' I said.

'I am not a counsellor. You really should be speaking with them about—'

'Do you know where the bodies went?' XRD said. 'We're missing many Free Tickets. An entire bay of them is empty and our instruments aren't reporting on them correctly.'

'Yes, I'm afraid that is by design. The sleeper vessels, like the one you are on, were quickly outlawed on Earth and the other colonies. Their design was clearly unethical. Modern vessels no longer use systems of slavery, such as the Free Ticket system.'

The fake ocean surrounding us continued to crash. Sea foam sizzled on the black rocks as the saltwater receded, only to be absorbed again by the next spray.

'We aren't slaves,' I replied. 'We're working for passage to the new colony.'

'Yes, but unfortunately you will never make it there.' Her voice was patient, like a teacher gently instructing a student who had fouled. 'The paying passengers will certainly make it to the planet. The Free Tickets, however, will not. You are not being offered a fresh start, Leah. When you climb back into your cryogenic beds, you will be jettisoned from the rear of the ship.'

It felt as though the ship had lurched beneath me. I caught the edge of Krill's station to steady myself. 'But why? We chose to work instead of paying.' My voice sounded far away, disbelieving.

'The records of the sleepers are false,' the lady replied. 'This has been documented clearly in textbooks. When I was twelve, I did a persuasive speech about how propaganda techniques were used on you to—'

'What's really going on then?' Krill said. His voice rose and filled the room. His fists were pale and clenched by his sides. 'Why are we here killing ourselves? What's going on?'

'I'm sorry,' the lady replied. She didn't sound sorry, however. Her voice began to betray a hard edge. 'On each ship, a complement of criminals was hired and given Free Tickets. You were always going to be picked for this shift. There was no lottery. There was no chance involved at all. Earth's prisons were too full, so this is your punishment.'

'Punishment,' XRD said. In the reflection of the bridge's walls, I could see tears streaking his face. 'They don't want us to have a fresh start. They want us to die protecting the real colonists.'

'We adjusted our course when we found your thin trail of jettisoned bodies,' the lady said. 'We followed them to you like breadcrumbs.'

'So, what are we supposed to do now?' Krill asked. He gripped the edge of his control station, white-knuckled. Saliva formed at the edges of his mouth. 'Save us! Take us aboard your ship and save us!'

'I wish I could. Unfortunately, I do not have capacity for everyone aboard your vessel. We are much smaller and sleeker, you see. Our ship can make it to Fin in a thousandth of the time.'

'Absurd,' I said. My head ached. 'You'd have to be travelling at the speed of light.'

'Just below it,' Tsubaz replied. 'We had to slow ourselves to match your velocity. You must understand, this is a freak coincidence that we ran into you. Humanity has now colonised hundreds of planets. We've had thousands of years to improve our transport technology. To give you some perspective, the *Discovery* is not an Earth vessel. It was built on the colony Utopia. In fact, we just celebrated our two hundredth year as a planet.'

'Please.' I could feel a pressure building inside my chest, crushing me. 'You must have the technology to help. You don't need *all* the colonists to come aboard. Just take the four of us who are awake and who know the truth.'

Captain Tsubaz's voice changed. It was now unsheathed, like an iron blade. 'I appreciate your plight, I really do, but examine the situation from where I am. We have stumbled on a time capsule of human history, a chapter that is not remembered fondly. You have been poorly treated, I understand. But I cannot allow criminals aboard my vessel.'

'I stole bread and money to feed myself.' I could barely choke the words out.

'We cannot be certain that you are telling the truth,' she replied. 'What if we let a murderer aboard? Or a terrorist? Besides, it would be extremely difficult to dock with your vessel. We do not have docking clamps.'

'Send for help,' I said, 'another ship could be here in no time.'

'Our communication relays have not been established this far out yet. That is our first task, in fact, after we land on the newly terraformed planet.'

'You've already terraformed?' I asked. I blinked, but my vision was blurry. The image of myself as the frontier woman tilling the soil came back to me. I pushed it away. A burning rage filled the space that remained.

'We sent an army of robots ahead of us to plant crops,' the lady said. A muffled voice came over the channel, speaking to her. 'I am afraid we will have to end the pleasantries here. This temporary deceleration has added a month to our journey. We look forward to welcoming your ship's occupants to our colony in ten years. The anthropologists will be very excited.'

'You're going to kill us!' Krill screamed. 'We have to climb back into our beds and die at the end of the year.'

'There is little I can do to help,' the lady said, 'but I will make sure to build a monument in your memory.'

The voice cut off and we were left with the deafening static.

'I think I'll go for a walk,' XRD said. He turned, leaving his shoes, bag and rebreather on the floor, and headed for the door.

'You forgot your survival gear,' I said, but XRD exited the bridge without looking back.

'I'm not getting back in that bed,' Krill said. 'I'll find where the nutrients are made and live off them directly until we make it to the planet.'

He stood on wobbly legs and stooped down to pick up the gear that XRD had left behind. 'I need you to assign me lots of repair jobs from here, things I can do quickly, so the ship will leave nutrient packs in the maintenance boxes for me.'

I could see the glint of adventure in his eyes. I was completely overwhelmed. If Krill left, I'd be solely responsible for the ship. 'You don't know where the nutrients are even made,' I said.

'I'll make my way to the service tunnels above the bridge,' he replied. 'I'll just follow the nutrient tubes from there.'

'They run to the sleeper beds as well. It'll be a labyrinth of tubes.'

'I'll follow all of them, then. I'll find where the food is made.'

He turned and exited the bridge. As I watched him leave, I saw something in Krill's posture that I hadn't seen before. There was a grim purpose in his step. His head was raised high.

On Krill's controls, the blip that represented the *Discovery* followed in our slipstream. The navigator must have been showing off. They were matching our speed easily and gaining on us. As I watched, the navigator ducked close below *Endymion* and I remembered how the glass shiv had felt in my hands, all those years ago. I felt the tingle of nervous energy run through my fingertips like electricity.

I sat at my controls. We needed a slight course correction. An emergency adjustment. I entered the command. 'A bunch of criminals. Not worth saving, are we?'

Endymion fired the emergency thrusters along its topside, forcing it to drop several hundred kilometres in a single minute. Far below me, I felt our vessel collide with the very sleek, very fancy, and very delicate *Discovery*.

The controls lit up bright red. A hundred maintenance items began to populate across Krill's screen as the ship listed every system and subsystem that had been critically damaged by the impact. *There you go, Krill.*

His console lit up with emergency transmissions from the other ship, confused questions from dying lips. I waited. The blip that represented the *Discovery* vanished from the sensors and was replaced by an icon that represented a cloud of debris.

I sat alone on the bridge. That wasn't strictly true. Hana was still staring at the ocean. She hadn't moved position since this morning. Her eyes were wide with delight as the imaginary waves leapt towards us.

A small smile sat in the corner of her mouth.

I guided my chair over to sit beside her. Together, we watched the waves roll in.

ARROGANCE IS DEATH

Lynne Stringer

'You'll never get anywhere unless you take risks.'

I could hear the words so clearly in my head as I snapped the glow stick in half, the light sputtering and crackling. I watched as it grew until it dispersed on the ceiling, spreading to each corner.

The room was dark for this, my memorial for Jenna. She deserved to be remembered, even if we hadn't always agreed.

As the light faded and the gloom closed in, I thought of her last moments. She'd laughed as she'd stepped into the time stream. Then her face had faltered. The last thing I'd seen was her bewildered expression before she'd been sucked into the zone space. Her scream had echoed through the streaming station long after she'd disappeared.

My door opened and light flooded in from the outside, the simple white corridor creating a bright slash in the darkness. It was Islin. 'Alma, come on. It's time for our next session. Why do you have the light off?'

He waved his hand over the globe and I squinted in the brightness. He looked around my scant room with its small bed, desk and chair. It was no different from anyone else's room, except for the trinkets displayed on my desk, souvenirs from my streams—a rubber ball, a rock, a glitter tube.

He scowled as he looked at the glow stick, his eyebrows pulling together under his thick black hair. Islin was eighteen, only a year older than me, but sometimes he looked as old as Cannair. 'What are you doing? Not memorialising …' He rolled his eyes. 'Jenna was careless.'

'That doesn't mean we shouldn't remember her.' I scrambled to my feet, a wisp of my blonde hair blowing into my face. I quickly pushed it back. Jenna hadn't had many friends. I wondered if anyone else would memorialise her.

Islin wouldn't. 'Come on, Cannair's waiting for us.'

The learning station was two corridors away, past rows of rooms with identical doors to mine. Other streamers-in-training emerged, smoothing out their grey uniforms. Grey was ideal for blending in when we were in a stream.

Cannair was pacing the learning station when all twenty of us entered. She walked across in the broad room, standing in front of the lecture screen. There were five streaks of grey through her dark hair now, a testament to how many times she'd streamed. The lines on her face, which had looked hard when I'd first arrived, now seemed gentle. Was it because of Jenna's fate?

Her first words promptly dismissed that notion. 'I'm sure you've all heard about Jenna. Waste no time mourning her.'

Islin nudged me as Cannair began pacing again. 'Streaming is a serious business. Without it, we can't retrieve the goods we need to survive. It's no easy task. A lapse in concentration can mean the end. What's our catchcry?'

As one, we all recited, 'Arrogance is death.'

'Correct.' She continued her march back and forth. 'Jenna assumed because she came from a family of skilled streamers that it would be easy. Guard against that kind of thinking. One wrong step and you'll be sucked into the zone space.'

'Yes, Cannair,' we chorused.

She nodded, and the shadows in her expression eased. 'The majority of you have finished your training, so missions will start.'

I could see all heads rise, all eyes brighten. This was what we'd been waiting for.

'This time, you will be required to follow strict scheduling and bring back specific items. Each of you will be allocated an experienced streamer for your first few attempts. I've sent information to your workboards.' She nodded to the boards, beamed onto the wall to our right.

'Remember, you will go into the past of our world, where there is deception and terror. Do only what you are assigned to do and return. Dismissed.'

Islin and I went over to the workboards. 'Who've you got?' he asked.

'Um ... Posao.' I didn't know him. 'You?'

'Sommer.' He shrugged. 'I've met her once. She's okay.'

'What about Posao?'

It looked like he was choking back laughter. 'Well, you won't need to talk much.'

***

I'd been told to report to the streaming station by hour six. I knew better than to be late.

Not many people were around as I walked down the corridor. No windows lined its sides; it was rare to encounter a window anywhere in our learning station. The sight of our wasted world was only used to remind us of the dangers of venturing out onto its broken ground, black craters and smoky skies. Steel girders were scattered around, pointing erratic fingers at the darkness. Occasional shafts of light came through the blackness, only to highlight the useless dirt—no nutrients; nothing grew on our world anymore. That's why we streamed.

I passed through the gateway from the learning station into a funnel that led to the streaming station. This area still bore marks of the disaster. The walls were streaked with soot and grime. I passed some old communication boards, which were silent, their screens blank and empty. The floor beneath my feet had been repaired, more or less, but I still had to be careful not to trip over the uneven tiles.

At the end of the funnel, a metal door clanged open as I approached. Inside, I could see stream control on a platform to the side of the next funnel. Although the control desk was relatively new, the corruption in the environment had affected it already—stains covered the controls and seepage from the ceiling dripped onto screens. The two technicians ignored it as they prepared for our stream.

I looked up as a man approached. 'Posao?'

He nodded. The two streaks of grey in his hair stood out against the red colouring; he was a veteran, although he didn't look much older than me.

He gave me an appraising look. 'Who are you again?'

'Alma.'

'Well, Alma,' his light blue eyes glittered as he circled me, 'I hope you're ready. If you've trained under Cannair you should be. But discordant elements can always creep in.'

Then his face was right by my ear, leaning in from behind. 'And what do you need to remember?'

I tried not to start. 'I follow instructions. I pay attention at all times. I speak to no one but other streamers. We get what we need and depart.'

'What else?'

'Arrogance is death.'

'Remember that.' He nodded at stream control before turning back to me. 'Ready?'

A green stream appeared in the funnel beside me, the throb from the electronics rising as it solidified. Through it, I could see the mirror image of the platform I stood on. The throb from the control panel intensified to a groan as it tried to solidify our destination. I looked into the stream—not so much one singular tube of green, but a thousand different ones close together, creating the illusion of cohesion, although each led to an alternative past for this very station.

Only one could be held steady by stream control so we could arrive there. Step into one of the others by mistake and I would slip into the zone space between the streams, never to be seen again.

Posao leapt, his long stride taking him to the other side. As I leapt through the stream, it pulled at me, trying to drag me into the zone space. I kept steady so my foot connected with the platform on the other side. The drag throbbed through my body, pulsing in my head. I ignored it, as I'd been trained.

Then I was through and standing on the platform next to Posao. The stream dissipated.

My previous streams had been to solitary locations where I had grabbed a souvenir and returned. This was different. I looked around at the world, *our* world from the past. The platform gleamed white, all the tiles even and matching. The funnel was clean and I could hear transports echoing down them as they sped to other platforms to pick up travellers.

Posao went to a section of the wall and applied pressure in the corner of a tile. It slid aside. 'This way.'

There was another funnel on the other side. We passed some

information boards flashing the latest news and advertising bright, colourful things that filled me with desire—creams, clothes, food, in all imaginable colours and textures.

Soon locals rushed by on their way in and out of the stations. I tried not to stare at them—their clothes, which were so varied in colour, texture and style, the things they held in their hands, travelling cases and bags, the things they were eating. I'd heard legends of delicious drinks full of sweetness, exotic-tasting fruits and tangy bars, so different from the maize dishes we had every day.

Posao marched forward. I tried to keep my mind on what we were there to do, but it was hard with so many delights demanding my attention. I wondered if he would let me take something as a souvenir.

Probably not.

He approached a moving stairway and we jumped on, rising to the city. I squinted at the light that came in, brighter than any globe I'd ever seen.

At the top, we were *outside*. I couldn't believe the smells, sights and sounds. And the sky! The light was coming from there. It was *real*. It was hard to look at for long, which was probably a good thing, as Posao kept moving.

The thoroughfare was filled with people, information boards and places that looked to be *selling* things! Treats and devices that people could buy just because they wanted them, not because they needed them to survive.

I thumped into Posao's back.

He glared at me. 'Remember what we're here to do. Remember what this world becomes. Keep your eyes off the temptations.' He strode on.

As we continued down the thoroughfare, I saw something that sobered me. A man stood to the side, shouting at people passing by.

'We must do something *now.* Things are not what they seem. We must stand up and fight or it will be too late!'

Our leaders are corrupt trailed back and forth across an electronic board he held.

He knew the truth! We'd been told no one had figured it out, that when our government's mismanagement had caused the blast that had destroyed our world, no one had been ready for it.

I raced up to Posao and grabbed him. 'That man—'

'Ignore him.'

I pulled him to a stop. 'But he *knows.* We have to help him!'

He turned and looked at me. The scowl deepened on his face. 'Why are we here?'

'To get supplies, but—'

'And do we *ever* deviate from our assignment?'

'But—'

'No buts. Follow me.'

I couldn't understand his attitude. Here was a man who *knew* something was wrong. Why didn't we help him? Why didn't we concentrate our resources on increasing the reach of his voice, so others understood too? It could prevent catastrophe. Did our rulers know about this? Surely they mustn't or something would have been done.

When Posao leapt onto a travel-cart, I followed and we shoved our way into a corner, holding a rail above us. The conveyance trundled along on its hover mechanism, people of all shapes and sizes looking at devices, chatting or staring out the window.

I was so distracted I nearly missed Posao jumping off. He'd given me no indication we were about to disembark, or had he?

We'd left the more populated areas of the city by then and reached its outskirts. The buildings were old, dingy and tired, as were the few straggling people. The sky seemed darker too, or maybe it was the way the structures leant in, as though they weren't far from toppling over.

This was more like home—rundown, overused, discarded.

We passed a few streets, our feet kicking up dust and dirt, and rounded another corner where I saw three people. I could tell they were from home, even without the streaks in their hair. Their clothes were slightly newer and cleaner, but the grey colour spoke of our world rather than the brightness of this one.

They were unloading a small hover. There were bags of maize on the back, a container filled with electrical wiring that had been stripped from somewhere and a jumble of parts that I knew would be put to use at home.

The man on the hover looked up as we reached them. 'Posao.'

He had two streaks of grey in his hair, the rest a charcoal colour. His hefty arms heaved another bag of maize over the side into the arms of the man waiting there. He was a one-streaker, the mark making a slash across his ebony hair.

Posao turned to the woman, who was marking something off on her noteboard. 'Linden,' he said.

'Posao.' She turned her eyes on me, their green taking me by surprise. The colour of her hair was so pale it was difficult to tell how many streaks she had. 'Who's this?'

'Alma. First-timer.'

She eyed me coldly. 'How many did you lose this time?'

'Seven.'

She looked me over again. 'There'll be more.'

Did she think I was going to misstep? 'I'm sure I'll be streaming as long as you.'

The green stare was levelled at me before she turned back to Posao. 'She won't last.'

The two men came to join us, looking me up and down. I

couldn't keep quiet. 'I'm not a quitter.'

Linden turned back to Posao. 'You're taking a bag of maize and the parts?'

He looked at the other bags. 'If I'd known you had so much I would have brought a conveyance.'

'It's all right. We're expecting other streamers.' She gestured to the one-streak man. 'Enie has to get back to make a report, so he'll take a bag and travel with you.'

I thought Posao might object but he hefted the bag of maize onto his back, putting the straps around his shoulders. Enie grabbed a bag as well and I put my arms through the straps for the box of parts.

Posao turned and walked off. I didn't try to talk to Enie, and no words passed between him and Posao—barely even a look.

We walked the opposite way this time, heading to another travel cart. It didn't look any different from the one we'd taken earlier, but it took longer. We passed through more derelict streets, then into a suburban area. I could see children playing on the streets. I envied their freedom to play in the light.

As we headed back towards the city, the buildings became more streamlined. Their gleaming smooth walls and bright display boards flashed through coloured images of so many things.

Posao nodded as we approached our stop. I leapt off just after he and Enie did.

The city was just as attractive as it had been earlier, with its open storefronts and tempting devices, foods, colours and textures.

As I scouted for a souvenir, I saw the same man we'd passed earlier; the one with the board. He was no longer shouting at the passers-by. He'd been joined by a group, all holding electronic boards shouting slogans about the corruption of the government.

This group had a different leader, a tall man with dark hair and eyes, his voice bold and forthright. 'You think this life is safe and secure, but it's going to come crashing down unless you join us. The government must be stopped. They are experimenting with our lives and it will mean the end of civilisation!'

Surely the people around him would see the truth. Surely they would realise … But everyone hurried past, paying no attention.

They needed proof. I knew we could supply it. His prediction was history to me.

'We've got to give him what he needs.' I turned but couldn't see Posao at first. Then I saw him with Enie. They hadn't even stopped.

I raced after them, standing in front of Posao. He only looked irritated.

'Didn't you hear what he was saying? They know what's going to happen!'

'We need to get back to the streaming station.'

I nodded. 'Yes, we need to get home so they can give us the information they need. If we give them proof, this could change everything.'

Enie rolled his eyes as Posao's face turned to fury. 'We will do no such thing.' He jabbed his finger in my face. 'We need to get these resources back. That's what we came here for.'

'But—'

He turned and marched away, Enie following.

Didn't they understand? What if we could stop everything from happening? What if our world wasn't decimated?

I knew what I'd been trained to do—when you went in a stream, you completed your assignment and then returned. I was to follow instructions. I was to watch for deception. But this was different. This group was talking about *reality*. I couldn't just leave.

I turned back to the group, still waving their signs and chanting doom at people walking by. *This* was my duty. What could be more important than averting this disaster?

I marched up to the leader. 'You're right, you know. Everything you're saying is true. You need to tell people. I can help you.'

He looked down at me, the ebony in his eyes bottomless. 'What do you know?'

'I know what you're saying is true.' I could feel the rest of his group gathering around to listen. 'Disaster is coming. You need to make changes now to avoid it. Please, let me help you.'

The group pressed in even closer. 'Where are you from?' the leader asked.

'Um …' That was difficult to explain.

An emotionless smile spread across his face. 'Won't you tell me?'

'It's a little tricky.'

'Is it?'

I felt hands on my arms. I shrugged them off, only to find they held fast. Two men on either side pinned them behind my back. 'What are you doing? I'm trying to help!'

'Bring her,' the leader said as he turned away.

I pushed my heels into the ground and tried to twist out of their grasp. Bucking back and forth, I pulled away from them, using all my strength to escape.

The rest of the group dispersed, leaving me imprisoned by the two men as they followed the leader.

They led me into an alley. An armed group dressed in black waited there with a covered conveyance, its rear door opened to take me.

I kicked out at the men, struggling with everything I had. I didn't dare yell Posao's name. He'd probably left me for dead anyway. I screamed, kicking my legs.

The black-clad force raised their weapons, pointing them at me. Before they could fire, one fell to the ground, his hand going to his neck. I heard a *ping-ping-ping*. The men holding me pointed their armaments at the tops of the buildings and dove for cover, their grip loosening.

I wrenched myself out of their hands and bolted back the way we'd come. I weaved in and out of passers-by, doing my best to lose any pursuers.

I felt a hand grab my arm and turned to fight, realising it was Posao. His eyes blazed with fire, his hand tightening around my arm. He dragged me between two nearby buildings. 'I told you to stay away and you didn't listen!'

My heart leapt into my throat as I heard a thump beside us. It was Enie. He had a small armament in his hand. 'We need to move *now*,' he said, looking back at the way I'd come.

They ran down the laneway in front of us. I followed, hoping they knew where they were going as I was lost.

I heard the sound of feet behind us and didn't dare turn. It was only as I felt puffs of air around my head that I realised they were shooting at us.

'Just keep running!' Posao panted.

We reached the end of the laneway and darted to the right. A motion to the left caught my eye—it was those people, led by the dark-haired man. They raised armaments and fired at us. I felt something jab into my leg. 'I'm hit!'

Posao and Enie didn't even look around. I ran faster, even as I felt my toes growing numb.

We were in a backway behind a group of buildings. Each one had another laneway beside it, and as we passed them, a glance confirmed that more were pursuing us. I couldn't feel my left foot.

Posao reached back and grabbed my arm, launching me ahead of him. I sobbed in relief when I saw the side of the transport building. Enie reached a panel, pressing a corner. It sprang aside and all three of us dived in. He slammed it shut behind us and I heard the sound of a dozen shots hitting the other side.

We gasped for breath, the two of them pulling out some darts that had pierced their clothes. 'Move.' Posao's voice was low and he was slurring his words.

How were we going to stream like this?

There was only room to crawl in the narrow vent we were in. It was probably a good thing, given my leg.

'This way,' Posao said, as we finally reached another panel. He touched the smooth surface and it slid aside.

We were in an empty corridor that looked familiar. He hobbled along, dragging one leg and arm behind him. Enie bent double and wobble-walked behind us. I wasn't much better, my left foot sliding along the floor.

We reached the streaming station, but as we stepped up to the platform, we heard the sound of pursuit. Posao triggered the activator on the side of the funnel and the stream stood before us.

There was no time to think about what we were doing. I could see the shadows of our pursuers just around the corner. But how could we stream when we were half-paralysed?

What choice did we have?

All three of us leapt at once, the stream dragging at my useless leg, trying to pull me into the zone space. I reached towards the landing platform, groaning as I tried to pull myself through. I *had* to make it. But the streams tangled around my leg. I shrieked against the weight and threw myself forwards. With a jolt, my leg came free and I went flying across the room.

Dazed, I looked up from where I lay to see Posao and Enie both come through safely. Posao screamed for them to shut the stream down.

The station operators raced up to us. 'Are you all right? What happened?'

'Hirelings attacked,' Posao panted. 'Shut this station permanently. We need to find a new one.'

As they called for medical aid, I felt his gaze land heavily on me. There would be repercussions for my actions, I was sure.

***

I picked at my uniform as I waited for Cannair to see me, trying to neaten it. I had to look my best; anything to ensure I wasn't dismissed from the streaming squad.

I shook my leg again. Even three days later, it still tingled. I was lucky I'd only been struck once. Enie had five wounds and was still recovering. Posao refused to come anywhere near me.

'Enter,' came Cannair's voice.

The door slid open and I walked into her office. I had expected austerity, but while the desk and chair were the standard serviceable design, she had several shelves lined with all kinds of artifacts—shiny wrappers, image cards, sparkling stones.

She noticed my interest and raised her eyebrows. I flushed apologetically. 'I'm sorry, ma'am, I didn't realise you kept souvenirs.'

She left her chair and picked up one of the image cards, holding it out to me. 'We all keep things. Things to remind us of what was. Of what our world should be.'

I looked at the card. It had an image of what I knew was a mountain, with a body of water cascading down its side. It was surrounded by colourful foliage. 'It's beautiful.'

'Yes, it was.'

Once she was back at her desk, I felt her probing gaze. I knew I had to speak. 'I'm sorry. I didn't mean to jeopardise our assignment.'

She steepled her fingers. 'Alma, the rules are there for a reason.'

I hadn't meant to make excuses, but I had to ask. 'Why weren't we told about those people? Surely it would have been better to warn us?'

Her gaze hardened. 'Streaming is a privilege. Everyone who signs up for this knows the risks and promises *unquestioning* obedience.'

'But who were they?'

'Government agents trying to discover discordant elements and silence them.'

I started. 'So there *are* discordant elements? They're not just after us?' Surely that meant … 'These other elements are working with us?'

She pursed her lips. 'No.'

My heart leapt. 'Then we must contact them. We must work with them!' They at least suspected the truth.

Her gaze remained steady. 'No.'

'Why? We could see this world righted.' I snatched up the image card. 'We could make the world like this again. *Our* world. Don't you want that?'

She slammed her hands on her desk and rose, anger pulling at her eyebrows.

I stepped back. What had I done? This was my leader and I was lecturing her? 'I'm … I'm so sorry.'

Her expression cooled. 'Let me show you something.' She pressed a control on the desk and instantly we were surrounded by memorial cards. Holograms of different faces confronted me. I didn't recognise any of them but assumed they were streamers who had died. I expected to see Jenna peering back at me, but she was nowhere to be seen.

'These faces.' She waved her hand at them. 'All streamers that we've lost. All were careful where they stepped. All respected the privilege to stream.'

I nodded. 'Not arrogant.'

She gave a dark chuckle. 'And yet they were. Each knew their instructions. Each knew what they should do, but faced with the greatest temptation, they couldn't resist.'

She took the image card between her fingers. 'They wanted this back. They thought they could achieve it. They thought they saw something the thousands who'd gone before them had missed.'

Her hand moved over the console again and a new set of memorial cards appeared. These faces were more senior, some dressed in military uniforms. 'These are officials from our society, our brightest minds. Some you would have heard of.'

She sat down at the desk, looking weary. 'When we first started streaming, they all wanted to save our world and thought that returning to the past was the way to do it. Each went back, convinced, even as others failed, that they could make people see. That their plans, their way, their persuasion would make the difference. They all died. Every one of them.' Cannair sniffed. 'And even as the number of dead increased, still more went.'

She looked up at me, away from the mesmerising images. 'Alma, I want that world back. I would do anything to achieve that. But the people of the past don't want to change. They have made it clear over and over again.'

I couldn't believe it. There had to be something we could do. 'But if we just—'

She nodded at the holograms. 'Every single one of them said that. What makes you think *you'll* be any different?'

I opened my mouth but swallowed the words. What had I been about to say? *But …*

But what? It would be different? Why? Because it was me? Because I knew better? I looked again at the faces hanging suspended around me. Our greatest minds. What could I add that would make a difference?

I lowered my head as I realised that my arrogance had nearly killed me. 'Then there is no hope?'

Her voice became strangely lighter. 'No, there *is* hope. We take what we can from the past and use it to rebuild. The past can't be saved. It doesn't want to listen. It doesn't want to change.' She came around her desk and took my hands. 'They won't hear. They won't accept the truth we know.'

'The truth?'

'That arrogance is death. They believe they know everything. They believe they have all the answers. But we know that's not true. We steal wherever we can, and maybe someday we'll make this world new again, but until then, we must always remember ...'

I nodded. 'That arrogance is death.'

'That's right. We must learn from the past and keep from repeating their mistakes.' She sighed and walked back to sit down. 'It's all we can do.'

She was silent then, reviewing the documents that slid across her desk. I waited for my dismissal, the one I expected—dismissal from the streaming squad.

But she said nothing. Eventually, I broke the silence. 'Cannair, am I to be punished?'

She didn't look up. 'Have you listened?'

'Yes.'

'Have you learnt?'

I had definitely learnt to follow instructions. I would need to keep my head down on assignments in future and wait before leaping into action myself. It was as dangerous as Jenna's stream had been. 'Yes.'

'What have you learnt?'

'That arrogance is death.'

She looked up and nodded. 'That's what I needed to hear. Go back to your duties.'

EBENEZER'S CAFE

Catriona McKeown

Gina gazed out the viewport. In the distance, the sun was rising, heaving itself up from somewhere under Earth. Peeking over the planet, it created a thin line of bright, blue light. A light so much more intense from up here than she imagined it would look like from … well, down there.

'You're not going to sit there waiting for it to come up again, are you?' Gina's sister, Helen, bustled about the room picking up after last night's party, her golden, high ponytail flinging around as she moved. 'It's the same every day. It never changes.'

'I know, I know.' Gina sighed. In all her sixteen years of life, she had never wanted anything more than to be able to explore her father's Earth, as he had done. She pulled herself away from the window to join Helen in the clean-up. 'I just like to imagine, you know, what it would be like from down there.'

She placed a photo of their father back on the shelf, running her finger over his brown hair. People used to say she looked like her dad, they shared so many traits and features, but not anymore. Now, as she moved closer to adulthood, she looked more like her mother, like Helen did. 'The sky behind him looks so pretty, doesn't it?' Gina said, a quiet longing in her voice. 'The pinks and purples, and then the snow-capped mountain in the background. Don't you ever wonder what snow would have felt like? What this place, Japan, would have looked like in the Spring?'

'You know that was long before the accident. Long before we were born,' Helen said. Her eyes wore a tired wisdom that contrasted the youthfulness of her face. 'That mountain probably doesn't even exist now.'

'But it looks so perfect from up here.' Gina picked up a white plastic plate and placed it on another.

'It does today. Remember last month when that huge swirling cloud covered most of Earth's surface? Who knows what was going on down there?'

'It was just a storm,' Gina muttered.

The girls, laden with plates, cutlery and the odd cloth serviette, walked into the kitchen and placed the leftovers into the sink. Helen turned to her sister. 'Look,' Helen pointed at a large landscape painting over the sink. 'This is what happens when people long for a place different from where they are—Mum couldn't let go of Earth, either. But this is a place that doesn't exist anymore.'

'I like Mum's picture.' Gina reached out for the still image. Her fingers danced over the purple flowers sitting within the flower bed, just outside the fake window. The rolling green hills lulled her into more thoughts of what it would feel like to have grass under her feet. Real grass, not the fake stuff laid outside Ebenezer's Cafe. Real, soft grass. 'I want to go there. I want to go back.'

'Gina.' Helen sounded annoyed. She rested her hands on her sister's shoulders. The hands were heavy. Authoritative. Although she was only three years older, Helen had taken on the mother role in Gina's life when she was only young. 'You know I only kept that there because it reminds you of Mother, and God knows we don't have enough to remember her by. But this Earth,' she pointed to the picture, 'no longer exists. You must remember that. We can't go back. Not now. Not ever.'

'But we don't know that. All we know is—'

'All we know is we're running out of resources and sitting out here, waiting, is getting us nowhere. We have to leave, to find a new planet. Now, enough daydreaming. It's nearly time.' Helen looked deep into Gina's eyes. 'Today's not the day to live in yesteryear. Today is the first day of the rest of our lives.'

***

Gina and Helen walked the corridor together, arm in arm. Gina noted how Helen walked with an air of confidence about her—one thing she alone had inherited from their father. Their father had had a surety of character; he knew when he was doing the right thing, whether he was or not. Helen was like that, too.

They reached the assembly room. Gina squeezed Helen's hand and felt her sister squeeze back as the doors opened. The room was already almost full, with most of the ship's six hundred or so residents. In the middle of the room stood the coffin. A few people around it wept. The dead man's daughter, Patricia, was among them. In her early twenties, she was the oldest female on the ship and would be Helen's greatest rival for change.

Gina waited for Helen to kiss Patricia and offer her condolences, and then followed suit. The service was short; there were none of the pastors or clergy Gina had seen at past funerals, as there were none left on the ship. It had been an oversight to not have someone train under the last pastor. He had died so suddenly.

Patricia offered a prayer for her father's soul to be at rest. Her younger brother sobbed beside her. Having lost her mother at a similar age, Gina knew this would be hard on Dylan. He was still only twelve; not even a teenager yet.

Six pallbearers lifted the coffin and took it from the room. Gina, in unison with the rest of the room, turned to the great window. With Earth as the magnificent backdrop, the sun now shining over its surface, she held her breath for that awful, final moment when the body was expelled. Wrapped in cloth, the body floated out into the void, just as all the others had done before this one.

The coffin was pulled back into the room and ushered through a side door. Coffins were kept for future services—that decision had been made early on in the ship's time above Earth. The adults were dying so quickly and no one knew how to make more coffins. They hadn't planned, within just a few short years, for over half the population to be wiped out. And from what? They still had no idea what the virus was or where it had come from. All they knew was it was selective—preferring those in their thirties and older—and how highly contagious it had been.

From within the crowd, Gina caught Jordan watching her. His face erupted in a smile before contorting into a silly face. Her heart fluttered. He looked taller than he had yesterday; his jaw seemed a little wider, firmer. Or perhaps she was just allowing herself to see the man he was becoming. She shook the thought off. She knew she shouldn't lead him on when … well, they wanted different things. She would have to convince him over to her point of view if anything was to really happen between them.

After the body was expelled, everyone took their seats around the assembly room. Patricia sat at the front, in her father's seat. Helen sat among five others to her right—these were now the elders.

Patricia stood and began the proceedings. 'Thank you, everyone, for your kind words at my father's passing. His passing is all the more distressing knowing he was the last of us remaining who ever walked the surface of the Earth. I feel a great sense of loss, not just personally, but for humanity as a whole.'

Gina's heart skipped as she watched Helen stand up next. She almost groaned aloud at the thought of what Helen was about to say.

'Yes, it is a momentous day, to be sure,' her sister said, arms raised. 'Ours is the new generation. It is our responsibility to now do what those who went before us failed to do and begin the search for a new home.'

A murmuring rumbled throughout the room.

'Helen, really?' Patricia turned to her.

'Today is the first day of the rest of our lives,' Helen said, looking at the faces around her. 'Do we want to wait around here just to die as we run out of resources?'

Another rumble of voices, this time louder.

Brandon, another of the elders, stood. He was the second oldest on the ship and the grandson of the pilot who had launched humanity's chosen few into space. 'We still know too little about space and our universe.' He frowned in Helen's direction. 'Deploying the ship deeper into space when we have no clear location to head in would be like, to coin a phrase of my grandfather's, searching for a haystack to put a needle in.'

'And I suppose,' Patricia said, 'you would have us follow *that* generation's great plan for us? To begin to create the next generation before we have even found a home for us to raise them in?' She put her hands on her hips.

Brandon shrugged. 'It at least could be something we put into action now.'

Gina noticed several people whispering arguments to each other with frowns on their faces. She looked at Helen, wondering if she was noticing too.

'I'm inclined to agree with you, Brandon,' Patricia stated. 'However, we need to take it slow. Our parents were much older when they had us.'

Helen rolled her eyes. 'The last thing we need is the added complication of women giving birth while we're trying to determine the future of humanity. Most of our medical staff are women. Would you have them distracted by their own health concerns while we make such critical decisions?'

People started calling things out from among the crowd. Some for, some against, none of them making any sense.

'But,' Brandon yelled above the noise, 'isn't the continuation of humanity what we need to maintain as our main goal? What is the point of working out where we are going to make our home if we have no children to raise there? What if we continue to die young just as our parents have before we've had the chance to continue the human race?'

The room again erupted in an array of voices.

A hand wrapped around Gina's shoulder. Jordan; no one else would take such liberty with her. She looked up and smiled.

'Let's get out of here,' he whispered, his breath soft on her cheek.

He led her through the crowd and a side door. She glanced back at Helen, who was face to face with Brandon, yelling at him.

As the door shut the noise of the assembly out, Gina sighed with relief. 'Should we have left? What if they decide something important in there?'

Jordan shook his head. 'They're not going to decide anything today. They'll make the decision in a closed room; just the elders. That way Helen and Brandon can fight it out, and Patricia can reason with them, and they can all come to a different decision from the ones presented to us.'

Gina chuckled. 'And what makes you such an expert on this new council we have?'

He shrugged. 'I just know people.'

They made their way to Ebenezer's Cafe and took seats opposite each other in front of the window. Gina slipped off her shoes and ran her feet through the fake grass under their table. 'You know, Helen had people over last night. A dinner party, of sorts.'

'Oh?' Jordan raised his eyebrows. 'And I wasn't invited?'

'It wasn't up to me. It was very political.'

Jordan nodded. 'But you'd have had me there if you'd had more say?'

Gina felt heat rise to her cheeks. 'Of course.'

'Well, that's okay, then.' He held her hand and played with her fingers, then leaned in to kiss her.

She pulled back.

His face flashed confusion and hurt. 'Sorry, I thought—'

'No, it's okay. It's not that. I just …'

'You just?'

She grabbed his hands and held them tight. The last thing Gina wanted to do was hurt him; he was her best friend, and if she was going to share her life with anyone, it would be Jordan. 'We only have so many years left of living on this ship before we run out of resources.' As he raised his face to look at her, she searched his eyes for understanding. 'I'm just not prepared to commit to the kind of relationship you want, knowing any children we have may not live to find a way through this.'

'You mean, if we have kids they might be born just to die on this ship when the resources our parents handed on to us run out.'

'Yes.' Gina needed him to understand—they'd had this conversation too many times already. They were running out of time. 'Without a clear vision, how can we begin the next generation, knowing we might be sentencing them to this?'

'You have a different solution?'

Gina pointed to Earth, enormous in the cafeteria window. 'Every window we look out on this side of the ship reminds us of where we really belong.'

'We don't belong anywhere anymore,' Jordan said, sorrow in his voice.

'Don't we? No one ever talks about going back,' Gina said.

'To Earth?'

'Yeah.' Gina relaxed a little; he seemed softer this time, more willing to listen. 'Have you heard of the Goldilocks theory?'

'Of course, the need for a planet to be perfectly positioned in a Solar System—not too hot, not too cold—to sustain life.'

'What's the chance of us finding another Earth in some other solar system? One that is reachable? And even if we do find one, why should we travel halfway across the universe, when we may not even have to?' She took a breath. 'Maybe, over the past thirty years without humans on there, destroying the place, Earth has been healing itself.'

'As if,' Jordan said, shaking his head.

Gina swallowed her frustration. 'Yeah, as if something like a whole planet, a whole *planet* that at some stage began from pretty much nothing to having everything that it had when my parents lived down there, could heal itself. Whether you believe it was started by a bang or Intelligent Design, either way, it's miraculous. Think about it, then imagine it recovering.'

Jordan nodded. 'But they said it never would. It couldn't.'

Gina was encouraged by his delayed response—he was listening to her, really listening. 'Your grandfather said that. My dad always said it could get better.'

'Your dad believed in Intelligent Design. What if whoever—whatever—was behind it left a long time ago?'

'What if it hasn't?' Gina's foot tapped with excitement. She picked up the plastic-coated menu from the cafe. 'Do you know who Ebenezer was?'

He chuckled. 'Some duck who hoarded stuff and was mean to everyone. I always wondered why they named the cafe after him.'

Gina shook her head. 'Before there was a duck there was a real man, Ebenezer, who believed in a god who created the world. He believed this god helped people, that he intervened in their lives and made things better for them.'

Jordan scoffed. 'Why name the cafe after that sort of thing?'

'Dad told me about this guy, Ebenezer. Maybe someone who helped design this ship also believed in a higher being—and was reminding us to have hope.'

Jordan seemed exasperated. 'Even if that was the case, how

long would it take for Earth to recover? A thousand years?'

'Maybe a hundred?'

'Well,' Jordan said, 'even then, that's more time than we've had.'

'Yeah, it is. But the ship was launched before we were ready, before we knew where we were going, before we had a solid plan. This ship has been sitting up here for over thirty years and we're no closer to finding another liveable planet that we can travel to. What if there isn't one out there? What if down there is all we *do* have?'

He squeezed his lips into a tight smile, almost as though in defeat. Had she convinced him?

He leaned back and ran his hands through his dark hair. 'What do you think we should do, then?'

Gina took his hand and rubbed it. 'I think we should go back.'

He laughed.

'I'm serious,' Gina said. 'Not everyone. Just a few of us to start with, to check it out. See whether there is grass growing, whether the air is clean—'

'*If* the water doesn't kill you. *If* the soil can grow food.'

'We won't have any of that up here soon anyway. We could take a few supplies, just in case.'

'It would be a one-way trip. There's no way to find fuel to get back up here.'

'It would be worth the risk.'

Jordan stood and paced the floor. He was talking to himself like he did when he was thinking through difficult decisions. She could see the anguish on his face.

He sat back down. 'How would you let everyone back here know if it was safe to return?'

Gina pulled a device out of her back pocket. 'I've been working on a communication device like the ones they had on Earth. I found one and it was pretty much in working order. It's not quite strong enough yet, but I reckon I'm close.'

Jordan stood again, holding his hands on his head. 'It's too risky. They won't let you go. I won't let you go. I don't want to lose you, Gina.'

Tears welled in Gina's eyes. 'They might. They might let *us* go.'

Jordan stepped away from the table, his eyes wide. 'You want me to go with you?'

Gina brushed a tear from her face. 'I do.'

Jordan sat down, his eyes filled with wonder. 'I don't get it. How can you sit there so calmly and tell me this is what you want?'

'Because I feel like it's what I'm meant to do,' Gina said. 'What *we're* meant to do. I wouldn't want to go on such a crazy adventure without you by my side.'

'You have a peace about you,' Jordan said, 'that I don't remember ever having experienced before. But that doesn't mean you're right.'

'Being at peace just means I know this is something I have to do.'

He raised his eyebrows. 'You're going regardless? Even if I say no?'

'I don't *want* to go without you,' Gina said, 'but I'll never be content staying here just surviving, Jordan. There's more to life, and I suspect the more is down there, not up here.'

'Okay,' Jordan said. 'I'll talk to Brandon.'

Gina closed her eyes and breathed out, relief flooding over her.

'Now,' he said. 'Tell me more about the mountains your dad talked about.'

***

Helen burst into her sister's room and pulled the curtains back with more force than necessary.

'What is it?' Gina asked, shielding her eyes from the light.

'I've just been speaking to Brandon, that's what.' She paced back and forth in front of the window. 'He told me about your plan. To go back.'

Gina rubbed her eyes. 'Does that mean he's approved it?'

Helen stopped pacing and glared at her. 'It's not his choice, Gina. It's *all* our choice. We all have to agree to it. All the elders.'

Gina sat up. 'And?'

'He has approval from everyone except one.'

Gina's mouth fell open. Who would stop her from being able to go back to Earth, and possibly save the human race?

'I,' Helen said, her breathing short, sharp, 'was the last on his list.'

'Oh.' Gina's heart sank. But surely Helen wouldn't stop her from going?

'Yes *oh*. He should have started with me, knowing he'd need all of us to agree to it. Then it would have stopped back then. Fewer people would have known about it. Fewer people would need to be aware of why you couldn't go.'

'I can't?' Gina swung her legs out of bed, the betrayal of her sister being the one who said no seeping in. 'I thought you were going to tell me it was decided. That we could go.'

'No,' Helen said, her face firm, determined. '*You*, Gina. I'm not going to let *you* go. You're the only family I have left. Mum and Dad are gone; it's just you and me. I'm not opposed to the idea of a small party returning, but why does it have to be you? Let someone else go instead.'

'Who will want to? It's a one-way trip, with no guarantees on the other side. Besides, I know how to fly a pod. I've done it a thousand times before, and I know more than anyone on this ship how to grow plants, how to catch food in the water, how to catch water from the sky.'

'You know those things in theory, not in practice, because of Dad's stories. You might get down there and find you don't know how to do all of that after all!'

'Maybe, but I have a better chance than anyone else.'

'And Jordan?'

'He's my sanity-keeper. And he'll keep me from doing anything really stupid.'

'It's so risky,' Helen said. 'I may never see you again.'

'You might, though.' Gina looked into her eyes, pleading for her to see reason, to see the importance of the mission. After a while, she shuffled over to her bookcase and pulled out a photo album. 'Look.'

She placed the album on Helen's lap. Page after page were photos of all the trips their father had taken around the world. A beautiful world, full of trees and streams and mountains and the clearest of blue skies.

When her sister reached a photo of a white Australian beach, she slammed the album closed. 'I know as well as you do what Dad believed. He was *the only one* who believed it.'

'The only one on this ship,' Gina said. 'There were others. People who weren't chosen.'

'Only those who were mentally stable, smart and strong were chosen. The fact Dad was the only one who believed says more about everyone else than it does about him.'

Gina rubbed her hands down her pyjamas. She may well be humanity's last hope. Why couldn't Helen see that? 'Please, it's worth a try, Helen.'

'I can't lose you.'

'You may not. We could be together again, all of us, back on Earth. You, me, Jordan, Brandon. We could grow crops and plant trees and go fishing and—'

Helen put her head in her hands. 'Everyone else thought it was a good idea. If I say no, I'll be judged for putting my needs before the good of the community.'

'I guess that's why he left you until last,' Gina said. She rubbed her hand over her sister's back. 'I believe in this, Helen. I really do.'

'Does Jordan?' Helen asked, her face full of concern.

'Not too many guys would agree to go on such a crazy journey.

But he has hope we'll succeed in finding a habitable Earth down there.'

Helen chuckled. 'He's been smitten with you for as long as I can remember. You know, we could send others with you. Give you a better chance of survival?'

'There are so few of us left now, we can't risk sending others until we know it's safe. Until we breathe the air and find land to see grass growing.'

Silence fell. Helen rubbed her thumb down Gina's face, just like their mother used to do when she was a little girl.

'So, I can go then?' Gina asked.

Helen squeezed her hand. 'It seems I don't have any other choice.'

Gina kissed her sister on the cheek. 'I've perfected my two-way radio, you know.' She pulled the gadget out of her bedside drawer. 'We won't know for sure until we're on Earth, but I'm confident it will reach you back here.'

Tears glistened in Helen's eyes. 'Okay, here's the deal. Once you're there, you let me know you're safe, and then you get to land. Monitor everything for safe radiation levels. Before you do anything, find shelter; you've seen what those storms can be like down there.'

'I believe in Intelligent Design. I believe we'll be guided. Everything will be okay.'

'I wish I had your faith, little sister,' Helen said. She drew her into a strong embrace. 'If you can find a house to shelter in, one that wasn't destroyed, it will be a miracle but it might be what saves you both.'

'Then that's what we'll aim for.'

'I don't like this, but I trust you.' Helen's voice faltered. 'Just … you know, don't die.'

'I promise you,' Gina said, 'I will do my best not to.'

***

A small party stood at the launch pad, with Gina and Jordan dressed in full space gear. Helen clipped her sister's helmet on. Final supplies were added to the pod.

'It's going to get hot when you enter the atmosphere,' someone said.

Gina looked at a young man who couldn't have been more than sixteen. Did he think she was brave? Was she brave? She didn't feel it.

Jordan gave her a light punch on the arm. 'It's now or never, Gina.'

She blew one last kiss in Helen's direction. They entered the pod and took their seats.

'Looks like a nice day on Earth,' she said, the round ball shining blue back at her.

'Hope we touch down near land,' Jordan said, fiddling with his belt buckles.

'That's the plan. Just off the West Coast of a country called Australia.' Gina flicked a few switches, a fresh wave of excitement washing over her.

'I've always wanted to see the beach,' Jordan said. 'I've heard Australia's beaches were the best in the world.'

'Really?'

'My mum told stories too, you know. About Earth.'

'You've never mentioned them.' Her finger paused over the ignition button.

'They always made her sad,' he said. 'I guess they made me sad too.'

'The stories Dad told us about Earth were always emotionally packed. I loved that though. I loved his passion.'

'I know that passion,' Jordan said, looking intently at her. 'I'm just passionate about something else.'

'Which is?'

'Don't you know?' He looked her up and down.

Gina fluttered her eyelashes, making him laugh.

'Are you ready?'

Jordan gave her a thumbs up.

Gina pushed the button and the pod moved toward the door opening before them. She pushed another button and the pod began to move more rapidly. 'Here we go.'

'You know, we may just survive this,' Jordan said, hope in his voice, as the pod launched from the ship on its trajectory course towards Earth.

Gina grimaced a little as the g-force took hold. 'We may. And it will have been worth it, don't you think?'

Jordan picked up the communication device. 'Definitely.' He pushed the power button. A green light appeared above it.

'So far so good,' Helen's voice rang through the pod.

'Talk to you from the face of Earth!' Gina replied as they began their descent.

***

Jordan must have stirred first, as Gina woke to him tapping on her arm. 'Gina?'

Gina opened her eyes and groaned as she moved in her chair. 'Hey. You okay?'

Jordan waved his hand from side to side to indicate he was. The pod bobbed up and down rhythmically on the ocean's surface. It was warm inside, thanks to the sun's rays. 'How long has it been since we hit the water, do you think?'

Gina looked out the window beside her; the sun reflecting off the water hurt her eyes. 'It became dark not long after we landed and it seems I missed the sunrise this morning.' She stretched and reached up to remove her helmet.

Jordan grabbed her arm. 'Do you think it's safe?'

She tapped a screen in front of them. 'The radiation monitor seems to think so. And besides, I'm hungry.'

They unclipped their helmets. Gina breathed deeply. 'So good,' she said, moving her neck around. 'You forget how heavy those things are.'

Jordan groaned. 'Why didn't we do this last night? I might have slept better.' He reached behind him and pulled out some protein bars. They peeled back the wrappers and took bites at the same time.

'Well,' Jordan said, 'it's not Ebenezer's Cafe, but it's not bad.'

Gina chuckled. 'What, the food or the view?'

'Both,' Jordan said, looking up through the glass roof of the pod. Gina looked too, but there was no sign of the spaceship sitting outside the Earth's atmosphere.

'What do you suppose Earth smells like?' Jordan asked.

Gina raised her eyebrows. 'The ocean is calm. We could open the hatch, take a walk around on the roof.'

'We won't be able to seal the hatch again. Not properly.'

'Come on,' Gina said. 'I'll try again to call my sister. Perhaps we'll be able to get through from up there.'

***

'Dad always said the beach smelt of salt,' Gina said, standing on the roof of the pod. 'But it really does! It's on my face, in my hair, everywhere!'

Jordan laughed. 'Lick your lips. You can taste it!' He put his face up and held his arms outstretched. 'The air is so clean, so fresh. I've never experienced anything like it. You were right; the Earth is healing itself.'

Gina took his hand and squeezed it. 'We've still got a way to go yet. Like, we haven't reached land.'

Jordan pointed to something way off in the distance. 'Hopefully, that's the land we aimed to be near when we hit the water.'

'Perth, wasn't it? A small city,' Gina said.

'It's our best bet. It's the area of Earth the least affected in the last days.'

She turned the communication device on, so the green light lit up. 'Helen? Are you there?'

There was no answer.

'Helen?' Gina said again, 'Helen, are you there?'

Jordan looked up into the sky. 'Ebenezer's Cafe is up there, somewhere. Everyone will be stopping for breakfast soon.'

'Helen will be cleaning up after last night's political debate in our lounge room, no doubt.'

There was a crackle.

'Helen?' Gina yelled this time. 'Helen, are you there?'

'Gina?' It was muffled, but it was her sister.

'Helen!' Gina laughed. 'We're breathing in salt air!'

'Gina! You're okay! Are you on land yet?'

'Yes, yes, we're okay. We're okay! We're heading for land now.'

'We're tracking what looks like … storm … way. You … fast.' Helen's voice was breaking up.

'Helen, what? What did you say?'

Helen crackled a reply, but Gina couldn't work out what she was saying.

She took her spacesuit off and threw it back inside the pod, tucking the communicator into her coat pocket. 'Come on, let's go.'

Gina's heart raced the whole way as they sped on top of the water towards land. As they drew closer, her breath caught in her mouth. 'Look,' she whispered. 'Can you see that?'

Jordan peered over the controller that was directing them closer to their goal. 'Those tall things?'

Gina laughed. 'Yes! Those tall *green* things. They're *trees*, Jordan! I'm sure of it!' *Just like in Dad's photos.* The Earth was lush and green. Things were growing.

A thousand questions ran through her mind. Would the plants be radioactive? Would there be safe dirt to grow crops in, that they could eat the produce of, just like they had in her grandparents' days? Her heart almost burst with hope.

Jordan guided the pod along the edge of the land until there was a break in the cliffs. 'It's a beach,' Jordan said. 'That white stuff, it's sand.'

Gina laughed. 'Sand! Can you believe it?'

They opened the hatch, the nose tucked up onto the sand, allowing them access to the beach without having to touch the water. Gina scanned another instrument across the ground. 'Only low levels of radiation. It's safe.'

She bent down and began to untie her boots. Jordan did the same. Gina removed her socks and placed her bare foot on the sand. She giggled. 'It's hard. Cold.'

Jordan, a little closer to the land, did the same. 'This sand is warmer, softer, I think.'

Gina moved closer to him. She took his hand and laughed. 'Come on,' she said and began to run up the beach, dragging him behind her. 'If this is how sand feels, I've got to feel grass.'

As they reached the top of a small sand dune, Gina squealed as the moist grass tickled in between her toes. Jordan gasped. Before them was an old house, completely intact though overgrown with lawn and vines.

'Shelter,' Gina said.

'It's a miracle,' Jordan whispered. 'It seems we might just survive this, after all.'

Gina smiled. 'And you doubted if Intelligent Design was real.'

FETCHING THE FLAME

Janeen Samuel

It was a long walk to fetch the flame.

They were in forest for the first part. Rain dropped through the trees, and branches thrust wet leaves in Lahana's face and caught in strands of her long hair. She couldn't ward them off because both her hands were carrying the pot, but at least they were out of the wind.

When they came out onto the heath they were among bushes that were just high enough to scrape at their legs, leaving nothing between them and the gale. It hurled the rain at them, driving water under their cloaks, stealing the warmth from their bodies. Lahana felt cold and soaked right to her core. *As cold as the dead fire*, she thought, so it served her right.

For the twentieth time that day she relived the dreadful moment when she'd woken to the first greyness of dawn. She had turned to the fire pit beside her and seen nothing, only darkness. She had reached her hand in, probing deeper, and felt only cold wet ashes.

At first she hadn't lost all hope. There were the perimeter fires around the camp; sometimes one of them would last through till dawn. Or sometimes one of the aunties or uncles, getting up in the night to relieve a full bladder, tossed some wood onto one. But no such luck this time. They were dead too.

If only, she thought, *I had been just a little sterner with myself.* She had woken in the night as she was meant to do because she was the one on duty. Keeping the fire alive was always the task of girls like her—girls who had just changed from children into women. She'd known what she needed to do and it was such a trifling thing—to raise herself on one elbow, reach out to the woodpile, and feed the fire. But she had been snug under the fur, rain falling around her and she'd been having such pleasing dreams. She'd told herself it was early yet, the fire still had plenty of fuel, and if she waited the rain might stop. That was all she remembered. She'd let herself sink back to sleep and hadn't woken until the fire was dead.

The heath stretched upwards before them under a blotchy grey sky. As they climbed, it continued to unroll. She felt as if they would be toiling up it forever and never reach the top. But she knew she had to keep on because the band were depending on her—on her and her mother, Looba, trudging patiently at her back. She thought of her father, uncles and cousins all out hunting with nothing in their bellies. She pictured the aunties and children searching in vain for late berries. She thought of the meal cakes set out confidently last night on the stones, useless until they could be cooked. A fresh wave of guilt washed over her. She could hardly bear it.

She raised her head, feeling the cold of rain in her face, and—at last! She could make out a shape far off on the highest point of the horizon. Also, away to the right on the northern slope leading up to the summit, something was moving.

Two things. She narrowed her eyes against the rain. They were human figures.

Her mother had seen them too. 'Ha. It looks like you weren't the only one to sleep too sound last night.'

It was almost the first time Looba had spoken since they started. She hadn't needed to say anything because the aunties had already said it for her, over and over—how Lahana was a disappointment and disgrace, an ungrateful girl who had failed her duty and brought shame and suffering on her clan. She had been grateful for her mother's silence. She was grateful now for her words. *To sleep too sound*—that didn't seem so very shameful.

She peered at the distant figures, wondering what her fellow sinners looked like, but they were too far away.

They trudged on, side by side now, and Lahana glanced sideways at Looba's swollen belly. She hadn't wanted her mother to come on this long walk, because the baby was due before spring. 'I can go alone,' she had protested, though she had shaken with fear at the thought. *How will I know what to do? I'll never get it right.*

The old aunties wouldn't hear of that. 'It's the duty of the mother to go,' they said. 'If she hasn't trained you right then it's for her to make that good. She's the one who has to carry the gold.'

The gold wasn't much, just a pin with a fancy knob. Lahana could have carried it easily. But no, everything had to be done according to the law.

As a denser mass of rain came over them, horizon and figures disappeared in its greyness. If her mother became ill from the journey, Lahana would be swallowed up forever in guilt as thick and grey as this.

The rain swept on past them and a faint silver sun appeared. The two strangers were closer now. Looba said, 'Ha, I know that cloak pattern. They're from the Green River band.'

Lahana stopped so suddenly that her mother bumped into her. The Green River people were their worst enemies. 'Will we wait till they've gone?'

'Keep on. It makes no difference. You know the law, and the words.'

Lahana moved on but her limbs felt heavy. The Green River band had killed her brother in the last skirmish. He had been older than her; he used to tease her and pull her hair, but she missed him badly.

They reached the summit just before the strangers did. It was wide and flat, outlined by a circle of stones. The summoning platform itself was a round structure made of rocks. It was as high as Lahana's chest and about as long across as a person. *Did people build it?* she wondered. *Or has it always been here?*

As the Green River people approached, Lahana saw that they w a young woman and an old one. The young woman got to the top first and stood panting, glaring at Lahana and her mother without speaking. She was a heavily built girl with a square sullen face.

The old woman arrived behind her and stepped into the circle. She was the first to speak. 'I swear that hill gets steeper every time I come up it. Peace before the flame.'

'Peace before the flame,' said Lahana and her mother.

There was a short pause, followed by a reluctant, 'Peace before the flame.' It was the young woman who had spoken, but not as though she meant it.

The old woman looked at Lahana. 'So! Another girl who spent last night dreaming of romance when she should have been tending the fire.'

'I was not!' protested Lahana. How did the old woman know? Was she a witch? Her face was wrinkled and the parts of her skin that showed under her cloak hung in folds. Though she'd come up the slope quickly enough, she moved bent forward a little from the hips.

'Is she your *mother*?' Lahana couldn't help asking the young woman.

'My mother's dead,' said the girl sulkily.

'I'm her granny,' said the old one. 'She's my youngest's youngest, and no more sense in her than any of the others. Now, Meeran, let's get on with it. I don't want to be shivering on this hilltop any longer than I have to.'

On the circumference of the raised platform there were four flat rocks facing north, south, east and west. The old woman stepped up to the northern one and, taking gold from under her cloak, laid it on the rock.

Lahana gasped. It was a breastplate made entirely of gold—three big, linked pieces. She bit her lip in shame as she watched her mother, face expressionless, lay their own offering on the eastern rock. It was the gold pin meant to be worn in the hair. It looked so small beside the other offering, the knob on its end no bigger than her little fingernail. The stranger girl, Meeran, raised her eyebrows, her lip curling. Lahana hated her.

'Right,' said the old woman, 'into position, you two girls, and let's get started.'

Who does she think she is, ordering us about? Lahana looked at her mother, wondering if she shared her reaction. Looba merely nodded.

Lahana knew what she had to do. She stood one step back from her offering on the platform, the pot held out before her. On the north side, Meeran did the same. Behind Meeran, the old woman began to sing and they all joined in.

The song was called 'Calling the Flame-Lizard'. Lahana had known it ever since she was old enough to sing anything at all. It was one of the songs that mothers and aunties and grannies taught to all the girls. It was the kind without proper words, just sounds that seemed to mean nothing. 'If you're good girls and tend to your duty you'll never have to sing it in earnest,' they'd been told, and Lahana had thought that if she'd never need to sing it why learn it? But the song had embedded itself in her brain nonetheless.

Singing it there on the bare hilltop, with the wind snatching the sounds as soon as they were out of her mouth, felt very different from chanting with all the other women in the warm glow of the fire. Some of the sounds almost seemed to make sense and some of them were different from what the Green River women were singing. *Will that matter?* Lahana wondered. Immediately she faltered, forgetting what came next. The strange words only came if you didn't think about them. She stared at the ragged lines of the western mountains tumbling away into mist and kept her mind blank till the end of the song.

When they stopped, the sound of the wind in her ears seemed

very loud. None of them spoke or stirred. It was only their eyes that moved, scanning the grey sky. Nothing moved there except clouds. The horizon was hidden by rain, but as far away as Lahana could see, from the dark forests of the south to the marshlands of the north and away to the west, no creature was visible. She couldn't see the east, at her back, but Meeran could and it must have been as empty as the rest because after a while she said, even sulkier than before, 'It's not coming.'

'Give it time,' said her grandmother.

'Should we sing it again?' asked Lahana. She would have liked to turn her head to show she was asking her mother and not this bossy old woman, but you were supposed to face your gold. Because in truth you were the offering and the gold was just a price—*Take this instead of the girl.*

'No, no,' said the old woman. 'No need to pester the beast.'

'Just wait,' Looba said.

So they waited. The rain had eased to a drizzle but the wind was as savage as ever. The platform protected them since the wind came from the southwest, but only a little. Lahana wondered how their song or the scent of their gold could possibly reach the flame-lizard in all this wind.

'What if it doesn't come? How long are we supposed to wait?' grumbled Meeran.

'It'll come,' said her grandmother again.

'But if it doesn't?'

'Then we wait till we're likely to die of cold if we stay any longer and then we go home.'

'Without the fire! We can't. Grandpa and the uncles will be so angry.' Meeran's voice was high and shaking, as if she was about to cry.

Her granny made a snorting noise. 'Angry? I'll give 'em angry! If it hadn't been for men being so stupid we'd never have needed to come here in the first place.'

'What's that you say?' asked Looba.

'Don't you folk know that story? In my grandma's grandma's time it was, or maybe *her* grandma's. The men made the fire and the women tended it.'

'*Made* the fire!' said Lahana. 'How could anyone make a fire?'

'I don't know, do I? Or I'd not be standing on top of this perishing hill. You can be sure the men didn't let on to the women how they did it. You know what men are, make a big song and dance and secret business of everything. It was hard work I daresay, and being men they thought it was easier to get the women to tend the fire and never let it go out instead of them making more. They were too busy carrying on with all their men's rubbish and making war. In the end they made such a big war, so many men killed, they woke up one day and realised there was no one left who knew the secret. Not in any of the bands. So that was that.'

'The story I heard,' said Looba, 'it was the flame-lizards who stole the secret.'

The old woman snorted again. 'That'd be the men's story. How can you steal a secret? Someone takes it, you've still got it. They don't want to admit what fools they were. Believe me, I've had three husbands, I know men.'

'Could anyone make fire if they knew how?' asked Lahana.

'Why not?' said the old woman, her eyes still fixed on the gold. 'If a man can do it, I'm sure a woman could.'

Lahana stared at the gold pin in front of her. Fire was golden. Was there fire in gold? Was there a way you could get it out?

'It's coming! It's coming!' yelled Meeran, raising one hand to point at the sky.

'Don't you drop that pot, girl,' snapped her grandmother. They all looked where she had pointed. Something was moving in the western sky. *Just a bird*, Lahana told herself, but it wasn't flying the way a bird would. As it came closer she saw it didn't have wings. A series of sails fanned out around its neck and along its back.

It came gliding on the wind like a fish in water until it was right over them. She could see the webs stretched between its front and back legs, extending all the way to its tail. It circled to the north, and the weak sun shone pink through its webbing. Meeran turned around to watch, even though she was supposed to keep facing the platform. It turned east, circling behind Lahana. There was a whoosh and a thump and it was on the platform.

Lahana nearly jumped back in fright, but she made herself stand still. She watched as the sails smoothed themselves flat against the lizard's sides. It was huge, far bigger than any lizard they hunted. Its tail hung over the end of the platform as it reared up its head. Stretched flat it would be even longer, maybe as long as three people.

The lizard started to turn and Meeran ducked as the tail swept past her. It turned until it was facing Lahana. Its head, above her, was as big as her own. Its mouth was shut but she could picture all its teeth. And the fire? No, she couldn't imagine that.

Holding her pot up to it, she sang the invitation. Her voice sounded high, not like her own, and her hands shook. The words of this chant were strange too, but she knew what they meant. She was inviting the lizard to take her gold and give her its fire in exchange.

The lizard bobbed its head down to where the gold pin lay. Its tongue, blue as a thunder cloud, flicked at it once. Then it raised its head and turned away.

Her offering was rejected.

What now? The gold was instead of herself, that was what the invitation song meant. Must she offer herself? She had seen big lizards tearing at carcasses. She shuddered.

The lizard had already turned towards Meeran. Her face was drawn with fear, though she still managed a sneer in Lahana's direction. She lifted her pot and opened her mouth to sing her own invitation. She'd got out only one word when her grandmother put a hand on her arm.

'Hold it a minute, Meeran.' The girl stopped, looking even more frightened as though she thought she'd got something wrong.

The old woman picked up the golden breastplate from the rock. Above her, the lizard watched her closely. She cocked her head up at it.

'You just wait a minute too, my friend. You know me, don't you? I've been here before with foolish girls. And when I was a foolish girl myself.'

All the time she was talking she fiddled with the breastplate.

'Ah, that's it!' The old woman held up her hands. She had two links in her right hand and a single one in her left. Moving around the platform, she put the single link on Lahana's rock, beside the pin.

'Granny!' Meeran sounded shocked and angry. 'Grandma, give that back!'

'Mind your own business, Meeran,' said her grandma. She turned to Lahana, 'Now, sing your invitation again.'

Dazed, Lahana obeyed her. Over her singing, she could hear Meeran protesting, though the only words she heard were as she finished, '—and they killed my brother.'

Tit for tat, thought Lahana. At that moment the lizard's right foot shot out and hooked the gold—pin in one claw, link in another. It bent its head, its mouth opened, and a long flame shot straight into her upheld pot. She held it steady, not daring to breathe, until she heard the crackle of the fuel in the pot. The mouth snapped shut and the lizard raised its head.

There was a final phrase of thanks to be sung but even before she'd finished it the lizard had swung back to Meeran.

Behind her, her mother breathed a great sigh of relief. 'Come away now. We need to get that home as quick as we can.'

'Just a minute,' said Lahana. She waited, watching until Meeran finished her song and the lizard had taken her offering in its left foot and bent its head to her pot.

Lahana let her mother lead her away. They'd not gone far when they heard a loud scraping and flapping behind them. Turning, they saw that the lizard had launched itself into the air, its sails raised. It skimmed over their heads then wheeled north, sailing over Meeran and her grandmother. The two of them had started down the slope too, heading to their own home.

'Come along,' said Looba, 'don't dawdle.'

'Wait,' said Lahana, 'there's something I forgot to do. Wait!' she called as she raced around the curve of the hill. Up ahead, the old woman stopped, though Meeran went on a few paces before pausing, without turning.

'Thank you,' Lahana said as she panted up to the old woman. 'I …' She had been going to ask what she could give her in return, but that felt wrong. 'Just … thank you.'

'You go on home, girl,' said the old woman, 'and take good care of that fire. If you must dream, dream a way of making fire. And you too, Meeran,' she added, raising her voice, 'because the gold will all be gone one day and then what will you do? Clever girls like you, you must be able to think of something.'

'I will,' said Lahana. 'Thank you. Goodbye.'

Lahana turned and rejoined her mother.

'There was no need for all that business with the gold. She could just have waited until the lizard had gone, then given us some of their fire,' Looba said.

'It wouldn't have been the same,' said Lahana. She couldn't quite explain why, but she knew it was something to do with the way the old woman had shared her gold.

The wind was at their backs as they went downhill. The warmth of the new fire began to creep through the pot and into her hands, into her stomach, where she held it against her, and into her heart. Other girls had lost the fire. It wasn't so bad. The old woman had done it and she'd still got herself three husbands.

As for making fire, there had to be a way. Not out of gold, because there was no more gold, not unless her band could find another band willing to sell to them, and the goods to barter for it.

Was there fire in gold, anyway? Gold didn't burn. Wood burned.

Wood could be orange and red and yellow, like flame. Maybe the fire was already in the wood, hidden somehow. All she needed to do was find a way to let it out.

THE CLOCKMAKER AND THE TIME MACHINE

Jo Hart

Clang! Clang! Clang!

The hammer beat against the iron cog. Metal screeched against metal until it finally came free, falling to the floor with a thud. Helm took a moment to rest, wiping beads of sweat from his grimy brow and leaning his bronzed, muscular arms on his workbench. Though not yet twenty, his face bore the weary look of someone who'd had a hard life, making him appear older than his years.

Despite his young age, he'd gained a quiet reputation in his village due to his skilled hands and mechanical mind. He knew his skills would have been worth more in the city, where the mechanical age was in full boom, rather than in a village where many still relied on the old methods, but the city was not safe, and he made enough money to ensure he and his sisters would not starve.

A small, narrow face beneath a mop of brown hair that resembled a bird's nest peeped around the workshop door. Her hazel eyes and slightly upturned nose were an exact replica of his own. Only Teeara had inherited the blue eyes of their mother.

'What is it, Cen?' Helm asked. His sisters knew they weren't supposed to bother him when he was working.

'Are you coming in for dinner sometime this century?'

'I'm nearly done.' He waved his hand to shoo her away.

'Yeah, right. See you around midnight, in other words.'

'Just put my dinner aside.' He searched the dusty floor for the escaped cog.

'You know Teeara won't be happy,' Cen trilled.

'Well, someone has to work to support you two, and this needs to be finished by morning.'

Helm spotted the cog by the table leg and bent to pick it up. It shuddered and rose from the ground, passing his outstretched hand and landing with a *thunk* on the table. Helm straightened up, looking over at his grinning little sister.

'You're welcome,' she said. Her face disappeared from the doorway.

'Show off,' Helm muttered. He had lost count of the number of times he had wished for her ability when working on his contraptions. To think how much easier it would be repairing all those fiddly little parts.

He shook his head. No one ought to wish for an added ability of any kind. Cen's gift was also her curse. If the authorities were to ever find out what she was …

A shudder rippled through his body. There were rumours about what the authorities did to abnormals—disturbing experiments, even extermination. They assured the public that they only took abnormals to the off-world ships—those huge mechanical structures held up in the sky by giant white balloons—for the safety of the population, and denied killing or experimentation of any kind. But even the thought of Cen alone in some cell on one of those ships was enough motivation to keep her abilities hidden.

One day he would save enough money to take Cen far from the city—further even than the small village on its outskirts where they had stayed hidden for the time being. Sooner or later the scouts would come. Once they finished ridding the city of abnormals, they would start expanding to the outer villages.

For now, the village would have to do, though. The houses were spread out on little plots of land on long, winding, dirt roads, not squashed together along cobblestone streets like the ones in the city, which afforded them privacy from curious eyes. For the most part they kept to themselves, except for when Teeara made the hour-long ride to the colourful and crowded market square for supplies, or when Helm needed to make deliveries to his clients.

For now, Cen was safe.

***

Rapping upon the workshop door woke Helm the next morning.

A customer. Neither of his sisters ever had the courtesy to knock. He heaved himself up from his chair, trying to ignore the gnawing of hunger. Teeara would kill him for leaving his dinner untouched. Helm tried to smooth down his coarse brown hair with his hands and slapped his cheek to wake himself up.

A portly gentleman wearing a frock coat and top hat stood patiently on the other side of the door, holding a gilded mantle clock. He was from the city—men from the village never dressed so well.

'Good morning,' he said. His high education was audible in his speech, pronouncing each word gracefully. 'I am Prestley Weir. Are you the one they call Helm?'

'Yes, I'm Helm. What can I help you with?'

'They tell me you are some sort of mechanical genius.' He peered over Helm's shoulder into the dilapidated workshop, as though trying to see the evidence.

'I'm good at fixing stuff, if that's what you mean.'

He opened the door wider to invite the man inside. He knew in the city it was customary to have a separate sitting area to receive clients, away from the dirt and clutter, but his workshop was an old storage shed that he had converted and he had no room for such a thing.

There was a small movement behind the man—the rustle of a

gown and the flash of a lace sleeve. Only when the man came inside did Helm get a good look at Mr Weir's companion. She wore a full-skirted dress in a soft flouncy fabric, full of ruffles and decorated with bows. Her porcelain skin was offset by the deep crimson of her dress. Her sleek curls of ebony hair bobbed about her shoulders as she moved through the workshop.

How different she was from his sisters, who wore the dull colours and coarse fabrics of country girls, and quite often wore his hand-me-down trousers. Indeed, even in the village, he'd never laid eyes on such beauty encased by such opulence. He assumed her to be the man's daughter; they shared the same eyes and high cheekbones.

'What brings you to our village?' he asked, tearing his eyes away from the girl—no, woman, for she couldn't have been much younger than himself—to focus his attention on the man. 'Surely there are many clockmakers and mechanics in the city.'

'But none who can fix this little beauty,' the man said, laying the clock on the only available space on Helm's cluttered workshop table. 'I was told there was a man out this way who happened to be an expert at fixing anything mechanical. Upon arrival in your quaint little village, I was pointed in your direction.'

Helm frowned. He was not pleased his reputation had reached the ears of those in the city. He preferred the quiet anonymity of country living. He glanced towards the house, hoping Teeara had heard this stranger's approach and hidden Cen from sight.

'What seems to be the problem with your clock?'

'Ah, it's not just a clock, you see. It's a time machine.' He smiled smugly, rocking back on his heels. 'An heirloom passed on from my grandfather. I'm not sure it ever worked in his possession, but I am determined to have it in full working order again.'

Helm's heartbeat sped up and his mind swirled with a mixture of shock, fear and curiosity. 'You do realise time machines are illegal?' He kept his voice low, though it was doubtful there was anyone to overhear them.

'Of course I know they're illegal. Even more reason not to take it to a workshop in the city.'

'I won't rat you out to the authorities,' Helm said, crossing his arms and setting his mouth in a grim line. 'The less I have to do with them the better.'

The man nodded, as though in confirmation of his good judgement.

Helm considered simply telling Mr Weir he couldn't fix it and sending him on his way. He hardly needed to be mixed up with anything illegal. If the authorities found out about the time machine and came to the house to investigate, it would put Cen at risk of being found out. However, he eyed the timepiece with longing. The lure of working on something as rare and interesting as a time machine was not an opportunity that presented itself to him every day. Imagine the possibilities! What if he used it to protect Cen—perhaps he could take her to a time in the distant future where people like her were no longer persecuted, if such a time existed.

'I'm not sure I can even fix such a piece,' he said, 'though I admit I would relish the challenge. It would make a change from clocks and pocket watches.'

'I would pay you handsomely,' Mr Weir said, 'very handsomely.'

Helm bit his lip and crossed his arms as he weighed up his options. The man had come to him rather than one of the tinkerers in the city as he didn't want to draw attention to the time machine, which meant he was taking care not to get caught. That offered some comfort.

At the same time, it also made Helm wary. He knew nothing of this man or his motives. Was it mere curiosity, or perhaps familial pride over a rare heirloom, that motivated him? Somehow Helm did not think so. There was definitely something more to it to warrant attempting something so illegal. The man wrung his hands together in front of him and licked his lips as he awaited Helm's reply. Helm studied his face, searching for any sign of malicious intent, but he only saw desperation.

Helm blew out a puff of air as he came to his decision, hoping he wouldn't regret it. The offer of a handsome payment was too tempting to ignore. Helm could only make so much money in a small town that had not really caught on to the mechanical age. His family was always in desperate need of more income, especially if he wanted to save enough to take Cen somewhere safer. If it could benefit Cen in the long run, wasn't it worth the risk?

'I'll see what I can do.'

The two men shook hands. The young lady had remained silent during the exchange, her eyes downcast, but just before she turned to leave, she looked up and gave Helm a soft smile.

***

Helm threw down his magnifying goggles. It was impossible. What did he know of time machines? As far as cogs and springs went, he knew all there was to know, but he knew nothing of the intricacies of the space-time continuum that allowed someone to travel backwards and forwards through its folds. He doubted many did.

The door to his workshop inched open.

'Cen, I'm working, get lost!' he barked.

A familiar porcelain-white face appeared through the doorway.

'Oh, my apologies, miss,' Helm said, his cheeks turning red. 'I thought you were my sister. Please come in.'

'It is me who should apologise,' the young woman said. 'I should have knocked.'

Though Helm usually did not allow clients inside the workshop while he was working, he welcomed her interruption. He was intrigued by this lady from the city dressed in her finery and was grateful for the opportunity to see her again without her father's presence.

She entered with elegant steps. Helm reached over, helping to remove her black velvet travelling cape, turning to hang it on the coat hook on the back of the door. She wore the same flouncy, cherry-red dress she'd worn earlier that day. He noticed the dress was cinched in at the waist and he wondered how well she could breathe. The lace-cuffed sleeves draped over small, slender hands that had likely never experienced a hard day's work. Her lips were painted in the same cherry red as her dress. She reminded Helm of a doll Teeara had owned in their childhood.

'I haven't finished yet.' He pulled his eyes away from her and back to the clock on the table in front of him. It was safer to focus on the clock than to gaze in awe at her. He might be a lowly small-town tinkerer, but he was still a gentleman. A gentleman should never stare at a lady, no matter how intrigued he was by her, nor how much his heart fluttered at the sight of her.

'I'm afraid you feel my father has given you an impossible task.' She sighed, brushing a gloved finger along the edge of the workbench as she examined the odds and ends strewn across it.

'I must admit, I know nothing of working with time machines. It is nothing like a clock, despite what it looks like on the outside.'

She nodded, picking up a spring and placing it back down again. 'If anyone can do it, you can.'

Helm felt his eyes widen. Had his reputation really preceded him so much that this city girl would place such confidence in his skills?

'Have you ever heard of Professor Geldof Heinkan?' she asked, studying him. Her face remained passive, but her eyes were full of intelligent curiosity.

He felt his heart resume fluttering now that he was meeting her gaze. He could not remember ever feeling this way in the presence of a lady before. Of course, he'd never been in the presence of a lady such as this one. He forced himself to stay present and not get lost in her eyes.

'I've heard of him. He was the one who discovered how to time travel, right?'

She nodded. 'Have you read much of his work?'

'I'm not much of a reader.' Helm dipped his head and his cheeks burned red. The truth was, he'd never learnt to read. Not many of the village kids found much use for books and reading. Reading was for the learned folk of the big cities.

'My father and I have read all his works,' the girl said. 'Maybe I can help.'

Helm looked up again, studying her face. An earnest pleading was etched in her features.

'Your father wants to time travel so badly?'

'More than you could know.'

It was clear she did not intend to say any more on the subject. He picked up his magnifying goggles and put them back on, adjusting the glass pieces to find the magnification he needed. She retrieved a stool from the far side of the room and perched herself by the workbench. Helm tried not to be distracted by her dark, mysterious eyes as he returned his attention to the clock.

'I don't know your name,' he said, without looking up.

'Yanna.'

He tinkered with the clock's innards while Yanna watched on in silence. Occasionally, the rustling of her dress captured his attention, and he smiled at her.

'He's doing it for me,' she said suddenly.

Helm was startled at the sound of her voice and cursed quietly as he dropped a tiny screw.

Together, they moved springs, cogs and tools around the bench as they tried to relocate it. Their fingers brushed as they both spotted it at the same time. Yanna's cheeks flushed as crimson as her dress. Electricity tingled through Helm's hand and warmth spread through his chest.

'So why exactly is your father doing this for you?' he asked, trying not to fumble the screw again. How was it that this girl he barely knew left him feeling so unsteady and lightheaded? It took all his willpower to return his focus to the work at hand.

'In the future there's a cure. My father wants to travel there to heal me.'

'Cure?' He looked up again. She didn't look ill. Her complexion was milky white, but it wasn't sickly pale. Her eyes were bright, her cheeks full of colour, and she walked with grace and sat with a straight back. If she was so deathly ill that her father would consider breaking the law to find a cure, she showed no sign at all.

Yanna looked at her hands and spoke in a whisper. 'Can you keep a secret? You didn't turn my father in to the authorities over the time machine, so I think perhaps you can.'

'I'm not a fan of the authorities, but don't feel you have to tell me anything. Maybe it's better I don't know in case they ever question me.'

She sighed. 'Perhaps you are right.'

She returned to watching quietly, and Helm resumed fiddling with springs and sprockets. He glanced up at Yanna now and then, trying to determine what kind of illness infected her. She was certainly not deaf, and her eyes followed his fingers as they worked, so she couldn't be blind. Did her dress hide some sort of physical disfigurement?

Finally, he put down his screwdriver and lifted his magnifying goggles. 'I know I have no right to ask and it's incredibly rude of me to pry, but it shall drive me to insanity not knowing. I swear I will tell not a soul, even my sisters.'

She smiled and he was willing to bet she was glad to tell him. 'I have an ability.'

Helm's eyes widened. 'You're an abnormal?' He refrained from saying, 'like my sister'. Cen's secret was her own, not his to share.

'I have dreams. I can see the future.'

It was a big risk that she should tell anyone of her ability, no matter how much she thought she could trust them. He felt both shocked and flattered that she chose to share it with him.

'When you say your father is trying to find a cure …?'

'I had a dream that in the future a cure will be discovered to free abnormals of their abilities. We'd be normal like everyone else. The authorities would have no reason to take us away and lock us up or experiment on us.'

Helm's teeth clenched, though he tried not to let any emotion show. 'The authorities couldn't possibly experiment on people. It would be unethical.' Even to his ears it sounded unconvincing.

'I've seen it,' Yanna said, her dark eyes reflecting the flickering candlelight as her voice turned stony. 'In my dreams. They tinker with their brains in the same way you tinker with these clocks.'

'No.' Helm shook his head, trying to shake away the image of his sister, but he couldn't un-see Cen's tiny body strapped to a table as they cut her open.

'You understand now why we're so desperate for you to fix this time machine. If only we could travel to a time where I can be cured of my curse, I would finally be safe.'

'I'll do everything I can.' *For Cen as much as for this girl*, he added in his mind.

'I dreamt you would fix it. That's how we knew to find you.'

At first, he was surprised at her statement, but then relief washed over him. It was her psychic ability, not word of mouth that had led them to his workshop.

'Any idea how I manage to fix it?'

Yanna shrugged. 'I couldn't really tell. It was too intricate; I didn't know what I was looking at.'

'You said you read all of Heinkan's papers. Maybe if you tell me everything you remember about his theories it would help.'

'He talks a lot about gravitational pull, mass and the forces that affect time. From what I could interpret, one can move forwards or backwards through time in certain conditions. It had something to do with the density of gravity or something like that. I didn't understand it. Science is not one of my strong suits.'

Helm studied the inner clockwork of the timepiece in his hands as he absorbed Yanna's words.

Gravity.

Mass.

Time.

Gravity could affect time depending upon mass. If that could be contained within a centric sphere and amplified, could that propel someone within the sphere forwards or backwards through time?

For the first time since Yanna had entered the room, Helm became so absorbed in his task that he forgot about her eyes and simply worked to the meter of her explanations. He searched through crates and on shelves to find what he needed—magnets, springs and weights. If he could create a gravitational force within the clock, it might just work. Now he knew what he was looking for, he understood that the clock already held certain parts that must have been part of the original time machine function.

It was well past midnight when he took a step back. He met Yanna's gaze.

'Is it done?' she asked, her voice a breathy whisper.

'I won't know for sure until it's been tested, but I think so.'

She slipped down from her perch and rushed to Helm, throwing her arms about his neck in a tight embrace. 'Thank you. Thank you. This means the world to me.'

She tilted her chin to look him in the eye. Helm's heart pounded. Her lips were mere inches from his own. His hands slipped around her waist, sliding over the silky red material of her dress.

'My pleasure.'

She stood on tiptoe so his lips could meet hers. They were just as soft as he'd expected. She tasted sweet like honey. Their kiss deepened and he pulled her closer. Her hands grasped at his unkempt hair. If only time could be tamed outside of the time machine because Helm would have made it stand still.

Finally, they broke apart, gasping in deep breaths. Helm leant in to resume their passionate exchange, but Yanna pulled back. Pain crossed her features.

'I have to go. Father will wonder at my prolonged absence.' She lowered her eyes and let out a reluctant sigh.

A warmth had spread through Helm's body during their kiss and already it was fading away.

'Will I see you again? After you're cured, will you come back?' He didn't want to let her go—didn't want to risk never seeing her again.

'Of course,' she answered, but there was sadness in her eyes. Had she already seen their future? Did she know they would never see each other again? He was positive that if the machine worked, it would work in both directions, so there was no doubt she would be able to return.

'Can you promise we'll see each other again once you're cured?'

She gave him a soft, sad smile as she slipped out the door. 'We'll meet again, I promise.' Her voice broke as she closed the door behind her, not quite meeting his eyes as she walked away.

Helm did not return to the house or find comfort in his bed for the few remaining hours of darkness. He sat beside the time machine, brooding over Yanna's promise. He concluded their reunion would not be a happy one. Perhaps she would stay in the future. Perhaps the time machine would trap her there, and when he finally did meet her again, he would be an old man.

When Yanna and her father returned mid-morning, it was all Helm could do not to grab hold of her. Instead, he watched from a distance as Yanna and her father stood in the paddock behind Helm's workshop, took hold of the time machine and wound the key to set its inner gears in motion. A ball of energy grew from the clock and the air around them crackled with magnetic static.

Then they were gone.

Helm stared at the blank space in the middle of the paddock for over an hour before Cen tugged at his arm.

'What are you doing?' she asked, glancing around.

'Nothing.'

'You missed dinner *and* breakfast. Teeara is going to be mad if you miss lunch as well.'

'Yeah, I'm coming.'

The two walked side by side back towards their little house.

'Did those city folk pick up their clock yet?'

'Yeah. They came by earlier.'

'I bet they paid a fortune.'

Helm stopped short, looking down at the envelope in his hand. Prestley Weir had slipped it to him just before they'd left. He opened it and thumbed through the notes. 'It should get us through the winter.'

Cen carelessly made a row of daisies rise from the ground and form a chain. She dropped it down on top of his head and laughed.

Helm smiled back, but when she skipped towards the house his smile became tense and grim. If there was a cure in the future, maybe there was hope for her to live a normal life without having to hide.

He wished he'd asked Yanna how far into the future this cure was. He wished he'd had the presence of mind to use the time machine himself and take Cen with him. What kind of a brother was he? But then would he have risked using an untested time machine on his little sister with no idea of the full risks and consequences?

No. He wouldn't.

He would just have to comfort himself with the knowledge that there would be a cure out there someday, and until that day came, he would continue keeping Cen safe and hidden.

As for Yanna … he would simply dream about the day they would meet again.

OVER AND OUT

Adele Jones

Vivia smacked the steering wheel with her palm as the car sputtered and died. Seconds after making an ungainly park in a vehicle-way emergency stopping space, someone tapped her window. A Global Government Citizen Aid. *Great, I'll be even later to work than I already am.* She lowered the window and resisted the urge to slap the bland civility off the CA's face.

'Howdy, citizen, you've not made it into the emergency stopping space. May I assist in relocating your antique car?'

'Super, my own Texas Ranger on a steed of battery-powered, carbon-neutral polymer. No, sir, I do *not* require "assistance", especially from *you.*'

The CA's obligatory smile dulled. 'You *know* the GG forbids that kind of talk.'

Vivia popped a hand over her mouth and gasped. 'My bad, a-gendered human.'

Pink tinged the CA's cheeks. He was rather dishy for CA. Sculpture surgery likely, and the emerald eyes permanent optical overcoats.

'Citizen, if your car ain't *fully* in the emergency stopping space, the autonomous vehicles, which comprise ninety-five percent of the city's traffic—'

She could nearly hear him say '*not* including yours'.

'—will register this threat, slowing unnecessarily. Can't afford a bottleneck on the multi-storey freeway.'

She looked to the football-field-wide megastructure overshadowing the CBD, now featured across every dense population zone. These strategically placed conduit towers harboured innumerable throughways that could connect a commuter from any incoming direction directly to their desired vehicle-way without stopping. Autonomous vehicles only. Already the 'hazard' of her *unacceptable* park was impacting the usually dizzying flow of exiting traffic—not that commuters noticed, with their focus on air-screens or other devices.

'Maybe if people drove their own cars, they'd realise a few inches won't kill anybody?'

'I'll convey your recommendation to the GG *after* I've helped rectify your error.'

Wow, this guy really is the bomb—of stupidity. Vivia threw open her door, nearly tossing him off his over-glamorised scooter. 'Bite me. I'll walk the three blocks to my office.'

The whirr of his scooter followed. 'Citizen, you must allow me to assist.'

Whipping around, Vivia's wild, dark hair flung about her face. 'You can *assist* by getting ethanol mix from a gas station. I get the whole "renewable energies" thingy but you'd think in a *fifteen*-mile radius someone would have sense enough to …'

Wait. Why are the cars all going faster?

'Citizen—'

'Shut up. Look!' She pointed to the mega-freeway obscuring the morning sun.

Cars careened from their lanes, smashing, crashing, a rain of autonomous vehicles from the road tower above. Vivia flinched as a car flew towards her relic and crushed it to half the thickness. Crimson splattered the windows.

Blood. Her stomach clenched. Nothing high-tech could change that.

The carnage edged closer. Backing away, she realised every street was chaos, not just the superhighway. Pedestrians screamed and ran for cover as a bus slammed to the ground and rolled nose-to-tail towards them. Heartrate ramping, she jumped behind the CA on his scooter and slapped his shoulder, which was unexpectedly muscular. *Is that aftershave?* In what GG world was a CA allowed to be masculine?

'Go, go, go!' When he didn't, she reached around his well-toned torso and forced the throttle to full. Her jeans and T-shirt proved a fortuitous wardrobe choice.

Steering from behind, she ignored the spouted list of guidelines she was breaching as she dodged cars left and right. They had the horsepower of a motorised mobility aid but somehow made it to her office. She dragged the CA off the scooter seconds before a car ploughed it down. Texan ranger-man needed no further convincing and bolted up the steps behind her, into her office above a contactless robotic fast-food joint.

Parting the curtains, she watched the insanity unfold. What in the Quadrants had happened?

***

People emerged from wrecks, human cries at a volume her one-way, bulletproof glass couldn't block. The whole city had been stopped by whatever error—*or was it terror?*—had caused this.

Ignoring the CA, Vivia swung into her office chair and flipped up the air-screen of her virtual desktop. The keyboard projected before her and she hacked into the Deep Space Network, or DSN. Running checks for hardware or server failures, it had to be an issue with the global positioning signals, the relay network or the autonomous vehicles' safe-to-stop GPS-fail software.

The CA leaned over her shoulder. 'DSN access is highly

restricted. And that operating system and hardware don't look standard issue. Someone's made some unapproved upgrades.'

Great, dingo brains has decided to pay attention. But gosh, he smelled good.

Everyone knew CAs were GG spies, but presently she had bigger whales to free. She focussed on the diagnostics on her screen, received via the highly illegal, holographically concealed satellites on the building's rooftop.

'From your accent, I reckon you're from the Southwest Quadrant.'

Vivia spun in her chair. Until now, she'd been ignoring the smouldering coals inside her, but that fanned them into a bushfire.

'I'm Australian? Bingo. Unfortunately, when the GG idiots divided up the world, they Cut. Australia. In. Half. So, depending on state, I could be from the Southwest *or* Southeast Quadrant.'

The CA began to look positively constipated somewhere between GG idiots and cut Australia in half. 'Citizen, you know I'm under constant surveillance?'

She figured now wasn't the best time to tell him all GG monitoring and Personal Identification Chip, or PIC, links were blocked by the firewall and cloaking systems she operated. The only information allowed in and out of her office was what she enabled, encrypted with a self-developed program.

'Maybe they can "survey" this. Eight months ago, while on a *virtual* tour with my PIC checked into Houston, Texas, those genii called in the loan repayments keeping the nations of the world afloat—which nobody could pay. So they closed the figurative borders *immediately*.'

'And based on your PIC location, even though you'd not physically left the country, you became an instant citizen of Division Eight, Northwest GG Quadrant?'

'What do *you* care?' *And my family.* She'd been forcibly deported from Australia as an illegal alien right in front of them. They'd tried to defend her, promised appeals, but not one message since. '*Twenty* years since the last global pandemic and they chose *that* day?'

'Plenty worse places than City Fifty-five. Good weather. Jobs. *Great* Tex-Mex food.'

Vivia scoffed at his use of Houston's GG name, and everyone got the same GG allowance no matter what job they did. Though he had a point with the Tex-Mex.

A notification drew her back to the computer. She scanned the diagnostics. *Interesting.* Cross-referencing the city surveillance feeds, she identified a delay in the DSN signals milliseconds before the cars had gone crazy.

'It's not a signal loss, but a cancellation. Plus a malware loop in the safe-to-stop programming on *all* autonomous vehicles?' That had to be previously uploaded. Scheduled update?

With a few taps, she sent a preliminary report. Internal terrorism, with a level of sophistication not seen in the previous threats she'd traced.

'You're a private investigator?'

Not having heard one siren, she accessed the emergency vehicles server. 'Don't wet your recycled pants. I *was* a digital security engineer, but it turned out I wasn't on the vocation reassignment list. So I got to pick my profession.'

Australians were already noted conservatives, resistant to tracing and cautious about technology. *Deliberately* selecting a profession high on the GG's 'risk of destabilisation' list made her even more questionable. She'd never investigated anything, but given the GG's promise to provide every new business with the necessary start-up resources, it'd been the coolest payback for them hijacking her life.

Entering codes and detailed coordinates, she manually assigned emergency vehicles to a grid of locations about the city, ensuring collision avoidance sensors were enabled.

The CA's scooter … She'd driven it. By rights, the anti-theft mechanism should have read her PIC and stalled it.

Shutting down her system, she stood and confronted him. 'You're not a CA. You're a rebel.'

Muscles flexing below the genderless uniform required of GG officials, he removed his helmet to reveal lazy caramel curls. *No helmet hair there.*

'Vivia, I'm Nathan, and I'll say this once. The GG's not a person, it's a rogue software with a near impenetrable operating system, and you're not playing by its rules. This is a set up.'

Feet prickling, she calculated how quickly she could grab her taser from her desk drawer. Until she knew exactly who this Nathan guy was, right down to his tantalising five o'clock shadow, she wasn't going anywhere. 'How would you know that unless *you're* setting me up?'

'I's fixing to warn you. The GG'll run its incident diagnostics, including surveillance footage. That, with your report'll be all the evidence they need to arrest you for this terror disaster.'

'I alerted them!'

'Using illegal hardware, servers and self-developed software? Only two categories of indictable offences exist in this new regime—thought and speech crimes, and treason. According to it, you've violated both.'

She knew the first category was punishable by house arrest or temporary electrical impairment. The second drew a penalty of permanent impairment and death. 'I can look after myself.'

'In thirty seconds GG control agents'll break into your office and arrest you. I reckon you can go with them and have your brain fried or come with me and take the GG out.'

Through the window, she saw armed control agents approaching the building. *How are they here so fast?* 'If I do this, I'll never see my family again!'

'Brain dead's not an awesome second prize. Twenty seconds.'

Vibrations shook her as the steel front door was blasted away. Her pulse whoomphed in her ears as heavy footfall thundered up the stairs.

'Ten seconds.'

'Fine.'

Nathan aimed his fist at the floor. A beam projected from the GG ring he wore—standard issue for a CA, except this one temporarily disrupted the solid particles of her floor, down through the layers of the earth. *A de-atomiser?*

The room shook as the office door jolted.

'Go!'

They leapt into the hole seconds before the door exploded across the room. The disrupted layers solidified above them. She was now officially on the GG's hit list.

***

The angle of the transiently de-atomised pocket lessened, closing to rock behind them before spitting them into an open space. They tumbled to a stop, dirty but unharmed.

Vivia glanced along a large tunnel and scrambled to her feet. 'De-atomisers? Now tunnels? You'd better start talking.'

'It's an underground inter-earth network undetectable by the GG.'

'Not gonna be secret for long if you pull that de-atomiser stunt in front of them again.' She still couldn't believe the de-atomiser was real.

'Yeah, was a bit close. But hey, no problem for saving your ass,' Nathan said, pushing to his feet and dusting off his flimsy CA uniform, so shredded he may as well be wearing jocks and no shirt.

Toned much? 'It's arse. And what do you want, a medallion?'

Directing her to an old electric—aka untraceable—jeep, they got in and bumped along the tunnel, illuminated by self-energising micro-globes.

'The GG program was originally designed to simulate random stress stimuli for studying individuals or larger populations.'

'Like that turn-of-millennia Big Brother phenomenon on steroids?' How daring to mention history, but then, this was no longer the GG.

'Maybe. It could generate anything from great scenarios like job promotion or collecting the lottery, to disasters like family illness and environmental catastrophes or war. It'd gather data on the responses—individually and collectively—and from this, figure out algorithms for controlling people. By cultivating co-dependence on the system, general apathy and addiction to comfort, while dictating the information provided through restricted media outlets, it could project and enact the perfect conditions for population manipulation. Problem is, eight months ago it got smart.'

A light ahead caught Vivia's attention. 'What happened?'

'Turned on its creators. Framed them for crimes against humanity, gained control of the global banks, called in the international loans, and you can pretty much figure the rest.'

She brushed hair from her face. 'So all those people killed just now?'

'It's a program. It don't care, as long as it maintains control—and fear's a key way to achieve that. Besides, a spectacle like that's one helluva way to remind citizens what can happen when even *one* person goes rogue on the system.'

'While depicting itself as protector of the terrorised masses?'

'Pretty much. But I see why it targeted you. I ain't seen no one infiltrate GG networks like you did just now.'

She snorted. 'Just doing what I had to. How will you beat it?'

He glanced at her. 'Vivia, one of those creators survived—Freyja Mien. She's the one who noticed your talents and defiance to the GG. She reckons you can help us.'

Vivia blocked his words with raised hands. 'No way. I work alone.'

Nathan steered into a cave—more like a cavern—and pulled up on the roadside. It was a thriving underground village. 'Bit late for that.'

***

'Nathan!'

Vivia hopped from the jeep as a fragile beauty with champagne-blonde hair in a perfect pixie cut jogged towards them. Compared to this elf, Vivia's amber eyes and athletically robust build made her an ungainly wombat.

'You convinced her,' the woman said with a gorgeous Irish lilt, her wide blue eyes swallowing Vivia up.

Nathan offered an unconvincing shrug. 'Vivia, meet Freyja Mien.'

'Wonderful. Now, no more eavesdropping, mister!' She held out her palm.

Vivia watched as Nathan reached behind his ear and pulled out a pinhead-sized metal speck. A nano-thread trailed off it, directly from his ... *skull?* She gulped down hints of breakfast as the thread lengthened and pulled free.

'An Intercranial Neurotransmission Device—IND. Not as dramatic as it looks, though its use is highly restricted,' Freyja explained, her nose wrinkling. 'Just a little something I invented.'

'Highly restricted use?' Vivia tried not to sound ignorant.

'Interferes with neurotransmitter signals if worn too long and risks infection, hence stringent time-use limits. The benefit is the wearer can read minds while preventing anyone reading their own.' She pulled a spritz bottle from her pocket, sprayed the wire, then wound it into a tight coil around her finger.

Vivia felt like someone had dropped her in a roasting oven. Her eyes shot to Nathan. 'You could read my mind?' she wheezed, wishing she could repeat the ground-swallowing trick.

'Only when close,' he said. Then with a wink, added, 'I won't say if you don't, dingo brains.'

Freyja laughed and brushed Nathan's semi-bare chest with her hand.

So that's how things are.

She then coupled her arm with Vivia's. 'I'm so pleased you're here.'

Despite a truckload of jealousy, she couldn't deny Freyja was nice.

'Let's get to work, Vivia.'

***

After another long day thrashing out plans with the Think Tank Team—TTT—Vivia's brain was sliding out her ear. Without the fortification of her morning hot chocolate, she'd swiftly degraded to hangry—and had every day since joining the rebels. Grinding her knuckles into her eyes, she refocussed on the image projected before her.

In a matter of weeks, Freyja had pulled together over three dozen international IT specialists covering every angle needed for analysing the GG's hardware, coding and software capabilities.

'This hardware diagram is correct?' she asked, mind processing.

'It's all we have,' Freyja said, shrugging an apology. 'I'm primarily a programmer, not an engineer.'

'A sophisticated quantum computer with a self-regenerating sub-atomic power source?'

'Yes. It can only be switched off by physical destruction, which risks destabilising the cells—'

'Like an atomic bomb,' Vivia concluded. The reality of a world forced to engage small-scale nuclear energy to sustain its dependence on technology and devices.

She felt the eyes of the other TTT members upon her, read the criticism in their faces.

'Are you all certain we can't corrupt or override the system remotely? Won't the GG detect our PICs?' Not that Vivia's was implanted anymore. She'd had it removed by backyard surgery and wore it in a band.

'Not below a ground depth of fifty metres,' Freyja said. 'Blocker bands are worn when above.'

A tall man whose name Vivia couldn't remember swivelled in his chair. Gesturing in her direction, he addressed Freyja. 'We've been over this. The GG's self-defence mechanisms outclass every security system known. It 's practically untraceable and will block unauthorised codes or inconsistent transmissions. We need *physical* access, which Doctor Mien's knowledge will enable.'

Doctor Mien? Suck up!

Vivia was unconvinced. There were gaps in their knowledge and everyone seemed to have forgotten the GG wasn't only a futuristic operating system, it was a warped, super-powered, psychological analyst. Psychology wasn't her area, but her dad's. In her twenty-four years, a little had seeped in.

She stood, reminded of why she worked alone. 'Okay, I'm not in your league, but I've got questions. Like, why don't you have psychologists and military strategists on the team?'

'We've tried that,' Freyja said.

'All together at one time?' she asked.

'From the "I don't do teams" star,' the tall, skinny guy muttered.

Earthiness clogged Vivia's lungs, despite the re-oxygenated air being cleaned by high-efficiency particle air filters. Knowing it was night made her feel buried alive. She missed the expansive sprawl of stars, missed the moon, missed constellation gazing with her sister and astronomer mother, while her dad kept them company on the picnic blanket in their yard.

A hand rested on her shoulder. 'Alan, let's remain civil. It must be hard for Vivia, knowing what they've done to her family.'

What?

'The impairment they received after challenging the GG on your deportation was cruel.'

Vivia's ears rung as if slapped. 'I'm going for a walk,' she said, voice catching like Velcro hooks on carpet.

'I didn't mean to reopen wounds, but the GG's hurt you, Vivia. You *belong* here.' Freyja's voice was gentle.

Unable to speak, Vivia shouldered past Freyja and ignored Alan's 'soft' comment. Rushing into the street, she nearly bowled Nathan over at the building's entry.

'Easy. How you doing?' he asked, steadying her with his hands. 'Vivia?'

Wrestling away, she sprinted down the first tunnel she reached. Tears blinded her vision of the low-lit road. Tripping, she pounded face-first into the dirt and rolled to a stop on her side. Drawing up her knees, she clutched her stomach as sobs ruptured from her until she felt sick.

Her mother's brilliant mind, her father's remarkable understanding of the human condition, her sister's teasing and harebrained ideas. Impaired. Permanently. After being held for public viewing like mindless slugs—reminding all of the cost of disloyalty—they would have been put down like sick dogs.

'Vivia?'

She felt the warmth of Nathan's body as he kneeled beside her.

'Go away.'

He placed a hand on her arm. 'Freyja told me what happened. She didn't mean to upset you.'

Vivia jostled into a sitting position, facing him. 'I didn't know,' she said, the words razor blades in her throat.

Understanding washed his face. 'That's a mean way to find out.'

'But impaired?' The ugly crying started again and she buried her face in her hands. Nathan pulled her to his chest and wrapped his arms tight. Not creepy, but secure. Except they didn't really know each other. *And Freyja.*

She pushed away and wiped her eyes. 'I don't want to cause trouble between you and Freyja.'

He sat straighter. 'Freyja? There's nothing like that between us.'

'Oh.' She frowned, remembering the woman's actions when they'd arrived.

He shrugged. 'I prefer a wombat kinda gal—cute from the outside but can scratch her way through hell if she's determined enough.'

'Dingo brains,' she muttered.

'Reckon it's a step up from bomb of stupidity.'

'Shut up.'

He got to his feet and offered a hand. His casual denims and button-up shirt, with sleeves rolled to his elbows, made him look every bit a cowboy. Still, Vivia hesitated.

'It's just a hand, Vivia. Ya'll so set on this solo thing, you're forgetting we all need help now and again. But next time, could you slow up a bit? Think I might have strained something.'

Reaching up, she placed her hand in his warm, firm grasp.

***

Vivia surveyed the landscape through long-range digital binoculars. With the sky so clear, she could see to the ocean. She sipped remnants of hot chocolate, courtesy of Freyja. She didn't know how Freyja had known, but it was good.

'Two hundred metres inside the perimeter. No evidence of detection,' she told Nathan through the in-ear comms device. They'd been scouting out their target site for a week, day and night, every angle, above and below. Tomorrow was D-day, when they'd physically infiltrate the GG and shut it down. Permanently.

Who would've thought the GG hub was near San Francisco and not an Asian technology centre? The de-atomisers still blew her mind. Depending on the strength of the de-atomising field, it could cause temporary disruption of solid matter to create a space pocket or blast something into non-existence. To access the deep subterranean rebel tunnels they used a front-mounted de-atomiser and a rear-mounted re-atomiser to drive their vehicles through rock, with little trace of their path.

Their IT systems were another matter entirely.

'Alan, you got that holographic shield up yet?' she said, frustrated by the decrepit technology. Freyja insisted it kept them off the GG's radar, but Vivia had successfully operated her office system without GG detection.

'I'll be in aged care before this thing loads,' Alan grumbled. If their holographic camouflage wasn't enabled, even with blocking bands the GG could detect them by satellite or drone surveillance.

The other teams checked in. All were experiencing technical difficulties.

This is ridiculous. They'd set up a short distance from the temporary access tunnel but couldn't advance until the system was up.

Another voice crackled in their ears. 'Radar's detected a squadron of drones closing in.'

'Copy that,' Nathan relayed. 'All teams, retreat.'

Adrenaline surged through Vivia as she ran for the nearby tunnel. Though lugging equipment, she sprinted ahead of the group into the temporary access point. Throwing the gear into the van, she heard a pulsing hum.

Vivia turned. Still exposed, the rest of her team were surrounded by attack drones. 'Nathan—'

High-pitched whizzing signalled an explosion of panicked communication in her ears from other teams.

'Re-atomise the access tunnels now! Cease communications.' Drones could trace any comms frequency.

'Nathan, I need to go back.'

'Cease comms!'

Stuff this. Vivia jumped in the van and ripped it into gear. Reversing out of the tunnel, she spun the van around and drove at the drones. They locked onto her. Steering away from her team, she drew the drones with her.

In the distance, armoured vehicles raced towards them. *GG control agents.* She spotted a rocky mound and drove the van up it so the grill was aimed skyward. The drones came in range and she activated the front-mounted de-atomiser, vaporising them out of the sky. *Die, suckers!*

GG vehicles closing in, she reversed to level ground, changed gears, and floored the accelerator. With a hard right, she bounced underground and activated the re-atomiser on the bumper. Rock closed in behind her.

Hitting the brakes to avoid ploughing down her team, she yelled, 'Get in.'

***

They'd been driving along a deep inter-earth tunnel for an hour. Still the team buzzed.

'You kicked butt, Vivia!' Alan said.

'Drones deleted,' a woman in the back declared, blowing off her fingers like an imaginary gun.

Pulling up at base camp, they tumbled out of the van, laughing and slapping each other on the back. Nathan met them outside the central command tent. An eerie chill crept through Vivia when she realised their vehicle was the only one back. The set of Nathan's jaw froze her like a blizzard.

'Where are the others?' she asked, unbalanced by his solemnity.

'That bit of backroading singlehandedly blew this entire operation.'

What? She marched up to him. 'It's called bush-bashing. And I saved my team.' The group jumped in with support, but Nathan's glare silenced them.

'You also led the GG to our front door. We've had to shut down miles of tunnels, even cities, in the network, and completely abandon the GG site.'

'We'll think of something else.'

'You and what army?'

She blinked as Freyja, shell-white, emerged from the tent. 'They're all captured, Nathan.'

'Like the military strategists and psychologists were in previous attempts?' Vivia asked.

'They'll be impaired, euthanised,' Freyja said.

Vivia swung around to confront the other woman, questions she'd suppressed surging like a geyser. 'That wasn't a detection, that was a trap. How did the GG know?'

Freyja edged nearer Nathan. 'They must have spotted us on an earlier patrol.'

'We always changed our pattern.' She glanced over her shoulder to catch the eye of her team. 'I don't believe we need to physically disable it or use old technology.'

Murmurs rose behind her.

'Enough inferences, Vivia,' Nathan said, tone hinting rebuke.

'I'm a PI. Investigating's my job.' She forced a smile.

'It's alright, Na,' Freyja said, hand creeping into his.

Again with the touchy thing.

Vivia lifted her chin. 'Nathan *knows* I can set up private network obfuscation that evades GG detection. He watched me do it. I also think the GG's manipulation can be played in reverse by hacking in and remotely priming it with scenarios *we* dictate., By knowing how people will respond, we'll have the upper hand and can turn it on itself.'

'Trick the algorithm?' Alan asked.

She nodded.

'Give me *one* example of how that might work,' Freyja said.

'I don't know, but I'm convinced we can figure out something.' Despite Nathan's hostile vibe, she had to say the rest. 'It seems to me this approach systematically eliminates all the people who could *together* defeat the GG.'

Nathan gripped her shoulders as if grounding her. 'You're talking crazy. Freyja knows the system better than anyone.'

'What if she's manipulating everyone, just like the GG *she* created.' Vivia shook so much she could hardly speak.

'What the hell?' Nathan's lips pressed together and he stepped between her and Freyja, who had dainty tears shimmying down her cheeks.

'What's got you so "military"?'

He flinched. ''Cause I was, like my daddy. You're not the only one whose family was impaired.'

Vivia's abdomen jolted as if punched. 'Nathan, I'm sorry.' She reached for his arm, but he pulled away.

'Vivia, Freyja's got a kill-on-sight fugitive alert against her. I *know* that for a fact. I reckon it's time to paint your butt white and run with the antelope—or get out.'

Silence descended like carbon dioxide, killing any hint of support.

'Take me back to Houston.'

***

Nathan seemed tense as he drove Vivia to the Houston access tunnel. Pulling up, he turned in his seat to face her. Her chest ached from maintaining an unemotive front.

'You don't believe me, but Freyja knew I was craving hot chocolate and thinking of my family. Though she claims she's not an engineer, she made the IND. I think she's wearing it all the time.'

'I know more than you think. This is for your own good.'

She snuffled unshed tears. 'Dingo brains.'

'If you ever wanna come back, or need me, use this. It's a tracker. Activate the "find me" function and I'll be there.' He handed her a small device, along with a handheld de-atomiser. 'Good luck stopping the GG alone, wombat. Stay safe.'

***

Vivia knew the instant her PIC was scanned, GG control agents would be after her like leeches to blood. So she'd gone without it. What could she buy anyway?

With the temporary de-atomiser, she'd gained access to her office via the robotics fast-food joint. The damaged door of the building had been replaced, but that didn't mean it wasn't under surveillance. Her office door was still trashed.

Righting the desk, she climbed on it and removed the ceiling light cover. Unscrewing the bulb, she unclipped the fitting and pulled on the wiring. A device the size of a lipstick tube fell out—her fully synchronised back up system. She hopped down, placed it on the desk, and started work.

Cloaking and firewall enabled, plus some serious onion routing, she searched up Freyja. Nathan was right. Show her face to the GG and Dr Mien was toast. Interestingly, she had a navy seal background, involvement in highly controversial research, and several double degrees, including engineering and psychology. *Liar.*

Next, she searched for information on each failed rebel mission, cross-referencing all linked reports, aberrations and GG chatter. *What?*

The captured teams from her mission hadn't been impaired, they'd been released as hostages rescued from the dangerous rebels!

How? The rebels must have some high-level allies. *Did Freyja know?*

Vivia then searched service providers through which the rebels might have set up private networks to see if she could detect a pattern, but their traffic was so well masked it was difficult to recognise a signature. *Wait, what's this?*

It seemed to be a ghost network independent from any GG servers. Identifying robust authentication, firewall and network intrusion detection, she knew this *had* to be it. *Can I get in?* Maybe, but not without detection.

Penetrating the network proved challenging. When it seemed she'd cracked it, she deciphered multilayered encryption only to find a honeypot—an empty decoy database. Freyja was good, but she wasn't *that* good. Though it was well cloaked, she started picking up a pattern, one she recognised from her time with the rebels.

Nathan.

He must be playing Freyja's game on herself, feeding her only what he wanted her to know about the rebel operations, while with each mission learning more about the GG's vulnerabilities and collating it through this highly secure server.

And I stuffed it up.

For all her 'I work alone' attitude, she needed the rebels as much as they needed her.

A voice crackled in her ear. *Alan!* She'd forgot to take out the in-ear device.

'I chose you well, Vivia.'

'Freyja?'

Freyja stood in the gap of the obliterated door. Hands trembling, Vivia shut down and pocketed the backup system. Her fingers brushed the tracker Nathan had given her. Activating the 'find me' function, she waited as the other woman crossed her office and turned, putting her back to the window.

'This is all a game to you, Freyja.' She hoped Alan could hear.

'And what fun helping the rebels beat the *nasty* GG. Such a ludicrously simplistic exercise to rid the world of threats to the pinnacle of my career. By the way, I've just sent an anonymous alert that you've been sighted here.'

Vivia had no more than thirty seconds.

The tracking device vibrated. Nathan was close! But so were the GG. 'What if you're caught?'

Freyja laughed and casually produced a stun gun. 'I won't be, and bringing *you* down is worth the risk to protect my creation—a self-governing population regulator that answers to no one, even its creators … mostly.'

Through the window, Vivia could see GG control agents swarming into the building. 'I don't get it. The GG wants to eliminate you.'

Twenty seconds.

'Are you sure?' She raised the weapon.

'You're controlling it with specific stimuli like I suggested.'

'Worked to remove you, didn't it? Which makes me the most powerful woman in the world. One day soon, when every rebel is dead, I'll re-emerge to take up my rightful position.'

'Not happening, Freyja.'

Ten seconds. The tracking device vibrated harder.

She scoffed. 'Even if I let you live, no rebel will believe you over me. They *trust* me. You trust *no one.*'

'Not quite.' And then she heard Nathan's voice in her ear.

'Directly below you, wombat.'

Grabbing the de-atomiser from her other pocket, Vivia activated it and dropped through the floor. As Freyja and the invading agents fired, the ground solidified above her.

Vivia landed hard into Nathan, bowling him across a temporary tunnel. 'Perfect timing, dingo brains. Sorry to stuff your op.'

Righting himself, he scooped her up and kissed her. 'Sorry for that turnip carry-on at the tent. I knew what she was up to but had to cover. We've learned a heap, but it was hard maintaining a ghost server and filtering the data she received without making her cagey. When she disappeared, I reckoned she'd be on your tail. You're too smart for your own good.'

Heaviness filled Vivia and she leaned into him. 'So smart I wrecked everything.'

A chuckle vibrated his chest. 'Not everything. This network's bigger than you *or* Freyja know, though she won't know nothing once the GG control agents are done with her.'

'What a waste.' She tipped her face to his. 'How were the captured teams released?'

'Freyja believed she was taking us out with her traps but didn't know undercover rebels in the justice department were vetting any charges, reassigning PIC identities and deploying the released teams to the Southern Quadrant rebel headquarters in Australia.'

'Australia, huh?' They walked to the jeep together. 'Hey, cowboy, wanna help me take down a rogue software?'

He smiled. 'Fixing to, wombat.'

THE ROCKSWAY FLIGHT

Russell Hume

'How much longer till we get there?'

Tierney sat impatiently in the corner of the airboat, his round back pressing against its wicker wall. He dangled his forearms over his knees and gave a loud, nasal sigh. Sel rolled her eyes at him as she checked the tension on the overhead ropes. He was, without a doubt, the laziest and most annoying travelling companion she'd ever had to work with.

'About another four hours,' she said tersely. 'It was about four hours when you asked me a minute ago, it will still be four hours when you ask me again in another minute. Now, go check the wind speed and direction, please. And stay away from the cases.'

Tierney snorted again as he rolled sideways, pushing himself to his feet. Sel looked at the looming clouds in the distance and flipped the lenses on her goggles to give greater magnification. The brass frame gave a tiny but satisfying click as the extra glass discs plopped in front of her eyes. The device made her look like some bizarre insect, with two rows of 'eyes' that moved up and down with various deft movements of the fingers. The insect effect was enhanced by the new lenses she'd had fitted, which exaggerated the size of her eyes.

She glanced around at Tierney, who was quietly hovering near one of the cargo crates. He was incorrigible. But his father was the Burgermeister and wanted him to learn the value of doing some real work. Sel had been given the opportunity to provide tutelage.

She could have refused; passed him on to another pilot. But this cargo run was very much about priorities. For Sel, the nearly double pay rate for taking on such an obnoxious apprentice meant that she moved one step closer to affording her own craft, and with it, the freedom of escaping the routine and barely lucrative trade runs as soon as possible. Sometimes sacrificing ease and comfort made sense in the context of a larger priority.

'Tierney!' she shouted. 'Stay away from the cases!'

He threw his head back in exasperation. 'Aagh, Sel. Come on. I'm so—'

'Stop there,' she said. 'If you say "I'm hungry" one more time, I'm throwing you over the side. It'll get me to Rocksway faster without the added weight and I'll have more stock left when I get there. Now. Wind speed.'

He waddled back to the instrument bank, muttering, 'But I haven't had anything for ages.'

Sel turned her attention back to the skies. 'You ate three honey bars not ten minutes ago.'

'That doesn't count,' he said, dropping his shoulders. 'It takes at least five bars and a caramel bread to equal lunch. And if we have four hours to go, we'll have to stop and eat soon anyway.'

She gritted her teeth. *Let's just get through this. Remember, priorities.*

'Tierney, airboats don't stop. Wind speed. Please.'

'You know what I mean. Uh, the needle says … seven.'

Seven. That had picked up faster than expected. Sel dashed to the other side of the airboat, clicking through lens changes, examining the grey mountains through the clouds ahead. The cold air whipped against her cheeks. It was getting gusty. She lifted the goggle apparatus off her head. As beautifully crafted as it was, she needed a better view than the low-mag lenses could offer and reached instead into a jacket pocket for her collapsible spyglass.

'What about direction?' she shouted.

'Huh?' Tierney squinted at her as his ridiculous mop of long, curly hair blew across his face. 'It's north. No, wait … west. It keeps changing.'

'Damn it. That's not good.' She twisted the focus adjustment on the narrow tube while peering through it and breathed slowly. 'Okay Tierney, come and look at this and learn something.'

He grimaced and mock-jogged to the bow of the ship to join her.

'Look there at the clouds near the mountains,' she said, handing him the spyglass. He put it up to his face and squinted his other eye closed.

'This is a rarity. We shouldn't be seeing it this time of year. See the little balls of cloud that burst up every so often at the bottom? The Updrafts of Hyacinth. They're caused by hot winds that come from the north and whip through the cave channels at the base of the mountains,' said Sel.

It wasn't hard to make them out through the spyglass. Every few seconds a random patch of cloud in the distance puffed and rolled upwards, like smoke from a freshly fired cannon. Unlike cannon fire though, each distant updraft was accompanied only by a low rumble. In fact, they seemed rather innocuous.

'Yeah. I see 'em. So?'

'So … big, big problem for airboats. Wildly unpredictable. If we can see any, even this far off, that means another could hit us here. We're already over the exposed cave channels, so we need to change direction to get out of their way right now. We need to make sure everything is locked down, just in case. Quickly, go fasten the cases.'

Priorities. It was remarkable how the natural world could change them so brutally in an instant.

Tierney, however, failed to grasp this new one. He handed the spyglass back to her and whined. 'Can't we do that after lunch?'

She glowered, took a deep breath, and stepped up to him, her nose an inch away from his. 'Do you not understand that one of these could kill us?'

Her voice was quiet and measured and her eyes seared the point home. Shouting was never so intimidating.

He stood there for a moment with his mouth open before bobbing out of her way as she pushed past him to get to the rudder and the instrument rack.

She yelled instructions back to him. 'Move it, Tierney. We've got to lock everything down now. If the cases slide around one of us could get hurt. Or worse. *Fix them!*'

***

Sweating, Tierney looked around for an obvious course of action. A single opened case, the same one he'd raided earlier, caught his attention, and he moved almost instinctively to it. It was at belly height, bigger than him, stacked on top and alongside dozens of others just like it. Binding them tightly together again meant it would take forever to get to their contents later. He couldn't scoop out an armload of honey bars now—there'd be too many to keep hidden. Surely it couldn't hurt to keep just one box looser than the others.

With his pudgy fingers fumbling, he wrapped the rope over and around the timber case, crisscrossing hard knots to leave access through a loose plank at the top.

The wind picked up around him suddenly. The airboat lurched, and the balloon ropes creaked around its edges.

'How's it going up there?' Sel called out.

'Yes, nearly there.' He panicked when he realised the other end of the rope wasn't attached to anything solid. Picking it up, he turned himself in circles, looking for an anchor point. He found one to his left and reached down, winding the rope between the hooks as his feet twisted clumsily in the mass of loose rope behind him.

***

Sel leaned hard on the rudder, turning the ship at a right angle to avoid heading into the epicentre of the updrafts.

In hindsight, it was too late. Or perhaps too early. A groaning gust just off starboard lifted the clouds in turbulent billows that filled her entire field of view. She pushed all her weight into the lever, desperately willing the vehicle to miss the brunt of the swelling pockets of air. In the middle distance was Tierney, standing awestruck and still against the skyscape of rolling cloud, until the radiating wake rocked the entire airship like a toy in a bathtub and he tumbled over.

Sel had barely drawn another breath when a second eruption caught her by surprise. In a howling rush of warm air, the gondola lifted rapidly on its side. She could do nothing but watch as Tierney gasped and fell against its thatched wall.

'Hold on! Hold on to something tight!' she yelled.

The olive-green balloon above them twisted and bounced like a panicked goat trying to free itself from its bonds.

'Hold—!' she screamed again, her voice drowning in the crushing wave of air.

The overhead ropes went slack. Sel's stomach moved up towards her throat as the airship began to fall back towards the earth, tipping even further sideways.

Through the tumult she could see Tierney, his body rotating helplessly sideways across the floor and through a tangle of rope. A second later, the momentum took control of his body and he rolled, almost gracefully, over the side.

Sel gasped and wrapped her arms tightly around the instrument gantry, bracing herself for the impact of the gondola snapping back against the tension of the balloon ropes. It jarred with a sickening thud, tugging violently on the balloon then bouncing in recoil. The boiler hissed and clanged behind her, although the pipe seals remained intact.

Amazingly, all the ropes held, including the one wound around Tierney's left leg, locked in place by the anchor hooks, which had been ripped out from the timber floor by the force. The crate at the other end of the rope was the only one not bound to the deck, and it too had gone over on the same side, around a separate line of the overhead ropes.

The gondola and the balloon continued to twist and bounce in the unstable air, out of sync with each other. Sel took almost a minute to process what had happened. She steadied herself, moved cautiously to the edge of the gondola and peered down. At one end of the rope was the wooden case, still intact and spinning like a toy. And there was Tierney, dangling upside down from the other end by his left boot, about fifty feet below her. His arms, hair and shirt all hung down from him like washing, swaying in the wind.

'Tierney!' she called, tentatively.

He didn't answer. Was he unconscious? Was he dead?

'Tierney!' She suddenly felt numb, holding her breath and searching for any sign of life from him.

Then … 'Sel?'

His timid voice was barely audible through the wind. Sel gasped and felt her face flush with relief. 'Tierney, okay. Hang on, I'll get you up.'

She grabbed onto his rope with two hands, closed her eyes and heaved as hard as she could. But the rope was tight and burned at her skin even through her thick leather gloves.There was no budging it. He was just too heavy.

Digging through the storage locker at the stern, she tossed various engine spare parts, tools and instruments onto the floor around her. All she retrieved that could be of any use were some spare lengths of rope. She thought of tying one end to Tierney's line and the opposite end to one of the other crates to use as a counterweight, but she then dismissed that idea. Without the ability to control it, it would be a risky manoeuvre that would almost certainly result in tragedy.

Instead, she hitched it horizontally around the two hanging lengths that were draped around the overhead cables. It would do nothing to get Tierney back on board, but at least it would make his rope stable and might prevent him from dropping should the binding of the case counterweight give way.

'Tierney? You're just going to have to hold on until we get to Rocksway,' she called. 'I can't pull you up and there's nowhere to land safely until we get past the mountains and forest.'

Tierney's body spun slowly at the end of the hooked rope, knocking him every so often into the dangling crate, now closer to him thanks to Sel's binding.

He let out a feeble grunt in reply.

***

Sel made a quick check of the rest of the airboat. She searched briefly for her goggle cap but had to accept that it had likely been lost in the updraft spill. The balloon itself looked fine, and although one of the overhead ropes at the stern had snapped, all others were intact. Apart from the crate that had gone over the side with Tierney, the rest of the cargo was anchored in place. Half the coal chest had spilled out onto the deck, but the boiler continued to chug away like nothing had happened.

The change in direction had at least brought them into a quieter part of the sky. The wind had settled, and the Silver Forest soon emerged into view as Sel made small adjustments to the rudder to re-correct their course. She turned her attention back to Tierney, mainly to confirm that he was still at the end of the rope. Leaning over the side again, she called down to him, 'Are you still alright down there?'

To her surprise, while upside down, he'd managed to grab onto the opposite end of the rope bearing the weight of the wooden case and had pulled himself up onto it like it was a mid-air lifeboat. He'd unhitched his foot and tied his end of the rope through the loops holding the crate and sat cross-legged on top—a manoeuvre only possible because of Sel's binding above. Gripping both hanging ropes in his left hand to steady himself, he used his right to push something into his mouth. As Sel lifted her spyglass to get a clearer view of his tenuous platform, he glanced up at her, squinting against the whiteness of the clouds above.

'Yeah, I think I'm going to be okay here, for a little while at least.'

She could see that the crate was essentially intact, except for a single missing plank on its upper side in front of him. Tierney reached into it with his free hand and retrieved another honey bar, peeled its paper and string wrapper away with his teeth, and took a generous bite.

'It's only bars in this one,' he called out to her, baked crumbs spitting from his mouth into the open sky as he spoke. 'Some of them were lost when we fell out. But I think there are enough to last me until we get there.'

Sel frowned but said nothing. It was true; they ought to be fine from here. She knew that when they approached the airdock in a few hours' time, the Rocksway stevedores would see their unusual arrangement and hook Tierney's crate safely out of the way as they landed. And at least the rest of the flight to Rocksway should be peaceful. It would give Sel time to reflect on her priorities some more, especially in light of today's near-catastrophe.

She looked down again at her suspended passenger as he swayed in the warm air, packing food into his mouth as calmly as if he were on a family picnic. With the danger now behind them, the clouds gave way to the brightness of the day. And as the sky became clear, so too did the realisation that even Tierney had priorities.

THE TRUE WRITTEN LIFE OF ED SPECOLTA

Penny Jaye

Minnicent is holding my hand. Her eyes are red. Her nose looks sore, like she's blown it too often in cheap paper tissues. There's sparkly pink gloss on her lips and she's biting the bottom one.

I try to speak, but only gurgled noises come. My chest is tight. My arms won't move.

'I love you.' She releases her bottom lip and the words fall out. It's as if she never meant them to be. But I've heard and her eyes widen as she realises. 'I didn't mean to …' she says.

I can't tell if she's apologising for the words, their meaning or something else. She stands. The noise of the chair on the hospital floor screams in my aching head. I shut my eyes to avoid the pain.

When I open them again she's gone. Mum and Dad hover in the corner with someone who might be a doctor. But I don't look at them.

I can see the notebook.

She's left it. On the table beside the bed. A familiar pencil juts from the final few pages.

The monitor beside me beeps.

I can't breathe.

I can't move.

I can't see.

***

'I'll write your biography,' Mince had laughed. She was spread over the end of my bed, ankles in the air, dreads tied in place with one of my old shoelaces.

We were bored, it was the weekend before school went back and I had three too many notebooks in my stack of school supplies. Mince now had one of them, her chewed pencil poised over the blank first page.

'Do I have to live it if you write it?' I asked.

'Ha! Wouldn't that be fun?' Mince grinned. But she shook her head. 'Don't worry, everything I write will be true. But I'll make it interesting! How should I begin?' Then she answered her own question. '"There was once a boy …"'

And she began writing. Just like that. Only I didn't pay that much attention to what she was mumbling because the bones in my face had started aching. I rubbed my jaw and felt the stubble on my chin. Huh? I'd shaved that morning, I knew I had. But now my cheeks felt rough with a three-day graze. My hair dropped into my eyes. I brushed the dark curls out of the way.

Dark curls?

Ignoring Mince, I spun round to catch my reflection in the square of wardrobe mirror not covered by comic book posters. My face—was it?—stared back at me. My cropped blond hair had been replaced by dark curls. The definition of my jaw had changed, the stubble I felt with my hands was an even bluish stain around my chin and sides of my face.

I frowned. The face frowned back. I opened my mouth. The face did the same, showing off perfectly straight teeth without the chip in my front incisor I'd had ever since Mince and I had crashed the billy cart in fourth grade. It had been her fault; I remember that as clear as anything. But it was gone. My tooth was straight and strong and pearly white.

'What are you doing?' Mince interrupted my self-analysis.

I stopped prodding my teeth and swung back to her. That's right, I swung. Gangly, adolescent me. I ducked to check my reflection again and I wasn't gangly anymore.

'Shall I read what I've done so far?' There was a shyness in her tone I'd never known her to use around me before.

I shrugged and rubbed my shoulders. They were aching like my face.

Mince blushed, but she sat up anyway. She started reading. 'Ed Specolta was the type of guy who drew the attention of everyone. His strong jawline, three-day stubble and mass of dark curls framed an irresistible set of deep brown eyes. He was strong, athletic and …'

'Athletic?' I laughed. 'I thought biographies were supposed to be factual.'

'It is,' Mince smiled coyly.

Coyly?

Mince was my best friend. She was funny, realistic, game, smart but never *coy*. Not with me, anyway. Not ever.

Suddenly my jeans felt too short. So did my t-shirt. My *favourite* t-shirt, the one I wore almost every day. I could see Mince sneaking a glance at my abs. Abs? My reflection confirmed it. I had abs.

I narrowed my eyes at Mince. 'What are you writing?'

***

She took the notebook with her. That and her big red eyes. I had accused her of lying. Of playing a cruel joke on me. I told her we couldn't be friends if I couldn't trust her. Threatened I'd tell her parents about Dixon Conroy's bedspread if she didn't quit the game. But she wouldn't budge. She said she didn't know why I was being so mean. That we'd been friends since preschool—that part was true—and why would she lie about the colour my hair had been all those years?

But my hair had been blond. Dirty sink-water blond. Hadn't it?

Then she'd burst into tears like the heartbroken teenage girl she'd always vowed she'd never be. And she'd left. Run past the family photographs on the hall wall that confirmed her story and stumbled down the front steps just as my mother said, 'Now, Ed, why do you keep making all the nice girls cry?'

What?

I'd never had reason to make girls of any type cry. They never treated me any worse than a pet dog.

***

I woke the next day bleary-eyed yet strangely coordinated. I'd barely slept. Three times the mirror had confirmed my altered appearance; once before my shower and twice after. My hair was dark and my body rippled with muscles I swear I didn't have before yesterday. I was exactly as Mince had written me. Except for the earring. She hadn't written that bit, but it was real and stung like hell when I caught it on the end of the towel.

When I asked Dad about the earring over breakfast, he said I'd got it done last holidays. Said if he had his way it wouldn't be there, and why was I asking him about it anyway?

I remember now, *really* remember, talking with Mince about piercings once. She'd said I'd look semi-savage with an earring and I had laughed off the suggestion.

I finished getting ready and took the bus to school like normal, crowded up the front with barely any space to turn. The bus driver nodded to me as I boarded. Two other kids called out from further back, 'Way to go, Ed!'

I smiled. They were all looking at me. Like they knew me. Like they respected me, either that or were afraid of me. Several of the girls grinned in my direction. I had to double-check it was me they were checking out. They were. It felt good. And yet … not really.

The bus pulled up out the front of school and I leapt from the top step and jogged across to the side lockers where I knew Mince would be waiting for me, like always. Only she wasn't alone. Our spot—the bench against the back of the maths block—was crowded.

As I skidded to a stop the entire group turned and rose to meet me. Guys slapped my back and started telling me about stuff I really didn't care about. The girls moved apart so there was space for my bag. Space beside Mince, who blinked at me with a remnant of hurt from yesterday. Then she quietly slipped her pencil into her bag and pushed her notebooks out of sight.

I grabbed her elbow and pulled her aside, away from the others. 'Look, Mince, I'm—'

'What?' Her eyes flicked to the others and then back to me. She was daring me to make up to her in public, like she always did. At least that hadn't changed.

'Look, I'm sorry about yesterday. I'm just really confused. Like *really* …' I let out my breath in a deep sigh.

'You smell like mint,' she murmured.

'Huh?'

I did. It was true. But now that I thought about it, I hadn't even brushed my teeth. I'd been too busy shaving.

Mince giggled. 'I forgive you,' she whispered. Then she did something she'd never done. Not ever. She reached up, brushed the hair that had fallen into my eyes and kissed me.

***

Best friends don't kiss.

At least they didn't the last time I checked. But the group—our group, Mince told me casually—didn't even blink. The bell rang, and everyone split. Mince strode away, books on her hip. I recognised the notebook among them and hurried after her.

One of the year twelves slapped me on the back as I passed the senior lockers. 'Awesome match on the weekend, Ed!'

Mince grinned and slipped into the food tech room. I followed and managed not to stub my toe like I usually did on the raised lip under the door.

'Try to be on time, you two,' Ms Phoebe scolded as we took our seats. But for once she didn't seem terribly annoyed. I tried to concentrate on the lesson, but my head spun. Then Ms Phoebe asked me to come to the front of the class and demonstrate how to whip a meringue. Somehow I knew exactly how to do it. And as I was heaping the perfect, shiny egg white into a pavlova shape on the baking tray, Mince gazed at me like I was from a different, but entirely desirable planet. In fact, half the class looked at me like that and it wasn't just the food tech group either.

In maths, I somehow found myself in the top stream class—Mince's class. Biology had me leading the dissection of a sheep's heart instead of sitting queasily out the back door. In history, my group kept waiting for me to tell them what to do. By the time it was PE and I'd kicked yet another goal—I hate soccer—I decided to fake a knee injury just to get away from everyone slapping me on the back and cheering my name.

It's not uncommon for people to fake knee injuries in soccer. You see it all the time on TV. What I didn't understand was how, as I crouched under the banksia tree behind the canteen making sure I wasn't seen by the rest of my class, my knee really did start hurting.

It was just a mild throb at first, so I shifted my position. But it grew to agony. As if someone had jabbed a pencil under my kneecap and was trying to pry it off like you might do to the lid of a pot of paint.

I bit my lip and tried to straighten my leg, inching closer to the wall. Through the branches, I could see Mince, with a group of girls all seated on and around a picnic table. The girls were laughing and checking their phones, but Mince was ignoring them. She was writing. And as she wrote the pain in my leg grew intense to the point I did cry out. I couldn't help it.

And Mince lifted her head and looked at me. Across the grass, through the branches. Right at me.

As if she knew exactly where I'd be and why I was in pain.

***

Mince stood back as the paramedics helped me onto the ambulance trolley.

I suppose I should have been grateful that she'd known where I was, that she'd been so quick to call for help. But I wasn't sure I was.

I sucked the stick for pain relief the paramedic had given me and stared at her. The stick made my head feel funny, but the pain still roared. Mince looked like she was going to cry. She hugged my backpack as if it was … well, me, I guess. And the thought was suddenly unsettling.

I pulled the stick from my lips. 'Show me the notebook,' I managed to say.

Her eyes widened. She opened her mouth to say something but the paramedics began rolling me away.

'Wait!' I tried to sit up. Pain stabbed my knee. 'Mince?'

The school nurse blocked my view. The paramedics pushed the trolley up the driveway and into the waiting doors of the ambulance. Then the doors shut.

But I thought I'd heard her. I'm sure I heard her. She'd said, 'Everything I write … it's true.'

***

When I woke from the anaesthetic they told me my ski-boarding career was over.

They told me softly. With tears in their eyes. They told me gently, watching my face as if I would care. But I didn't even remember the snow.

'He's in shock,' one of the nurses said to Mum when I wouldn't speak. 'It often happens to bright young men like him. Will take a while to sink in.'

'He was headed to the world championships next month,' Mum said.

The nurse shook her head in pity. 'Such a shame.'

Mum left the room, phone in hand, as if going to make a call. The nurse began humming. She tapped the cylinder connected to the drip and rechecked paperwork at the end of my bed.

'Have you seen Mince?' I asked. My voice sounded strange. Deeper. Husky too.

'Mince?' Nurse glanced at me over the top of her reading glasses.

'My friend. She's got dreds. Freckles. A nose ring.'

The nurse's face brightened. 'Ah yes, Minnicent. She's your girlfriend, right?'

Girlfriend? 'We've been friends since pre-school, but …'

The nurse smiled as if to assuage my fears. 'She's been here every day since the accident. I'll let her know you're awake when I'm finished. She'll be glad you're awake. She's been keeping a record for you.'

'A record?' I frowned. It made the skin on my head hurt. Like I'd had stitches or something. I reached up.

'Oh no, don't fiddle with the bandages. We've got to wait for Dr Tarsaveriam before we fiddle with those.'

I felt my forehead. Any 'dark curls' I might have had had been shaved out of the way. Half my skull was bandaged. 'I hurt my head?'

'Yes,' the nurse watched me carefully. 'Can you remember the accident?'

I hesitated, then lied. 'Oh, yeah. I remember.'

The nurse looked relieved and marked something in the notes on my hospital file.

'But tell me,' I attempted to be casual despite my throbbing head and the fuzziness in one eye. 'You said Mince—I mean Minnicent—is writing a record? What kind of record?'

'As far as I know, it's just a record of everything that's happened to you. You know, the accident and everything since then which, to be honest, isn't as much as she seems to write.' The nurse shook her head and smiled. 'Young love, hey? I've got to go check on a couple of other patients now. But if you need anything, just press the call button, okay?'

***

I could hear them.

Mum. The doctor. Minnicent—she was crying. And Dad.

The room felt hushed. My body ached, my chest was enclosed in pain. I couldn't move. My lungs filled with air and then lowered without my willing them to.

'Once we take away the ventilator, it won't take long,' the doctor said softly. 'Whenever you are ready, let me know.'

My lungs filled again.

And again.

And I waited.

***

Something was being dragged from my throat. I could feel it burning. My head was cradled on someone's lap.

Was it raining? I could feel the raindrops. Minnicent was laughing …

No one called her Minnicent except her grandmother. Her grandmother died.

Last year.

I visited the hospital with Mince once. Saw the tubes down Grandma's throat. The bandages around her head. The way her eyelids trembled when Mince cried.

I only went once. Mince went every day.

And the week they switched off the machines—the week her grandmother died—I didn't see Mince at all.

It rained that day too.

***

It doesn't hurt anymore. It feels like I'm on a lilo, floating. Like the world is somewhere and heaven somewhere else and I'm sort of hovering.

Mum is holding my hand. She's been crying. Minnicent is

behind her. And Dad—I can't see him. But I know he's here. I can hear him.

'Will you finish his story?' Dad's voice is strained in a way I've never heard it before.

Minnicent sobs.

Mum looks at her.

'I don't think I can,' she says.

Dad comes forward. I can see him now. He looks old. He's grown a beard. It's golden. He holds a worn notebook in his hands. It's tatty and the corners are curled up. He opens it and I can see there's only one page left.

Dad offers the book to Minnicent. 'Please?'

She shakes her head. Tears stream down her face. I see now that she's cut her dreadlocks off. Her hair is short, spikey and soft. 'I can't! Everything I've written is true and it hurts. Hurts so much.'

The lilo I'm on bobs as if it has a leak. As if hovering is almost finished.

I feel Mum's grip tighten around my hand.

And then I hear him say it, 'Write the truth as it is, not as you might have made it. And then let him *live.*'

***

Minnicent lies on her stomach across the end of my hospital bed and kicks her ankles in the air. 'They're going to let you out today!' She smiles and taps my shin under the blanket. 'You'd better change into something decent. No more daggy hospital gear for Ed Specolta.'

I grin at her and then motion to the outfit Mum has laid out on the visitor's chair, all ready to go—blue denim jeans, a button-up shirt and zippered jacket. It's all two sizes bigger than I used to wear, but Mum assures me it will fit. It seems Minnicent and I are the only ones who can remember the way things were, before the notebook, before she started writing. But Minnicent doesn't say anything about that. She just watches me scratch the spikey regrowth on my head.

Watches me rub my scar with hesitant familiarity.

'What?' I ask when she doesn't look away.

She just shakes her head. 'You're really lucky to be alive.'

'Yeah. I guess.' I drop my hand to my lap and stare at the weave in the blanket. 'The doctor said I'll have a pretty brilliant scar to tell the story.'

We stay like that for a while, without talking. I can't tell her how weird it feels not to know the whole story of what's happened. Somewhere between the snow-board accident and seven months in a coma I've lost track of the details. I know, if I wanted to, I could read all about it. I have the notebook now. Minnicent gave it to me after I woke up from surgery. She said she never wanted to see it again. And I haven't argued. I just read the last page, to make sure there was no more space for anything else, then slid it out of sight. I guess I'll return to snow-boarding, like everyone expects. But I think I'll pass on the soccer. It just doesn't feel like me, even in this new version.

Minnicent nudges my leg and breaks the uncomfortable silence. She has a cheeky sparkle in her eye. 'Do you want help getting changed?'

She runs a hand through her soft straight hair and scrunches her freckled nose up in hope. Then she waits for my answer. She is actually really pretty. Funny how I never noticed it before. 'You know you are the best friend I could ever have, right?' I say.

She groans and rolls over in mock despair. 'I'm guessing that's a no?'

'Yeah.' I laugh and climb out of bed to collect the clothes Mum has left. 'It's my life. I need to write it the way it happens.'

'But …' Minnicent looks suddenly shy. Her wide, wild, honest brown eyes are full of questions.

'Don't worry.' I say. I wink at her, then pull my pyjama shirt over my head and toss it at her on my way to the bathroom. 'I'll make sure my life is something you'd like to read.'

ROMANO'S

Jack Garrety

I was seven when I first went to the haunted violin shop in West End. I didn't know Romano's was haunted. Not then. Twenty years on, I can't even say for sure that it was. Perhaps that assumption was just another 'gap filler' between seeing a chunk of the world and being able to understand it.

I remember it was raining that first day and Mother (she was always Mother, never Mum) bustled me along, pretending to share her inadequate white umbrella, shuffling in that half-run-quick-walk way she did when she was in a hurry, 'ladies running', she called it.

I didn't mind getting wet. I still don't, but it made Mother's carefully coiffed and curled hair flatten, sharpening her small elfin face and making tear tracks down her powdered cheeks. Mother's recipe for life was to treat its tough bits like rain puddles—walk around them if possible, if not, wear very high heels and move briskly through, head high, pretending they weren't there.

The door to Romano's had a little brass bell at the top so whenever it opened the quiet tinkle caused everyone, customers as well as staff, to stop talking and turn to stare. We must have made a curious pair; me, stick-thin, unruly red curls wound into tightly plaited pigtails cowering behind Mother, who glared them all down before shaking off the white umbrella and standing it in a corner. If it had been a dog she would have said, 'stay'. I wanted to wait with it—disappear into its quiet, utilitarian purpose where it was simply accepted for what it was. However, as always, Mother had other plans. She grabbed me by the upper arm and steered me to the glass-topped counter at the rear of the shop.

'Mr Romano, please,' she said when one of the eager young people asked if they could help.

Straight to the top. I cringed away from her hold. Her fingers were strong from years at the piano and she gripped harder, eyeing me with that brow-pinched 'Stand up straight, Emily!' look.

'Yes?'

His voice was rumbling and deep, underscored with a rich European heritage. He had long swept-back greying hair, maestro-style, but wisps of it had escaped, falling haphazardly about his face so he was constantly flicking it back, patting it into place with long, artist's fingers. He was the first man I'd ever seen who wore clear nail lacquer. The nails were immaculate.

'I'd like to arrange violin lessons for my daughter, Emily.' Mother indicated me with a downward motion of her head. Slowly, he turned huge black headlight eyes on me. I remember being scared. He was so big and said nothing, just stared. He took my hand in both his and turned it, pulling and wiggling each of my fingers. Finally, with something that could have been satisfaction, he harrumphed and released it, dusting his hands together.

'Tuesdays. Four o'clock. We give her trial for three weeks. You will need violin. Come.'

He waved his hand and walked off, clearly expecting us to follow. He led us through a passage into another area. Romano's had three shop fronts, all joined together. This one was darker than the one we'd left. It smelled of old dust and what I now recognise as a cross between rosin, sweat (it was hot in there) and strict discipline. The air was thick with it.

Mr Romano trailed his fingers along a row of hanging violins. There were two tiers of them all along one wall. He paused at one in the lower collection and took it down. It was smaller than the rest. His deep black eyes took on a dreamy look as he ran his fingers lightly across its surface, cocking his leonine head to listen acutely as he plucked at a couple of the strings, then twiddled with some small knobs at the base, plus one or two of the pegs at the top. Then he handed it to me with a flourish. I remember taking hold of it at the top as if it was Puss's leftover smelly fish. I looked to Mother for direction, but she was already under his spell. I half-expected her to swoon if he played anything. There weren't many people I'd seen who could do that. He went up a grudging notch on my wow meter.

'No. Like this.' He positioned the instrument on my shoulder, gently bringing my chin onto the moulded black plastic, then pressed down more firmly. He eased my hands from the violin and stepped away.

'Hold!' he commanded. I pushed my chin down harder into the plastic mould, praying the violin would not slip sideways, imagining the expensive instrument smashing into polished pieces on the floor.

'Is good. Perfect for her.' Mr Romano nodded again, taking the violin back, the hint of satisfaction glimmering brighter, though still below the surface. I felt incredibly pleased with myself, as if I'd passed some test.

They left me there then. Presumably to 'settle the terms', as Mother liked to call it when we bought things. We may have looked like money, but when Daddy died, he'd left more debts than assets so Mother was constantly trying to make arrangements to pay things off. Invariably, she'd overcommit and as Peter, my elder brother, used to say, the mad payment shuffle would begin. I didn't know exactly what that meant then, but I'll always remember the embarrassment when people with stern voices arrived wanting to see Mother.

***

I saw the ghost during my second lesson.

I was in the same hot room, or salon, as it was called. All Romano's lessons were given there. I was with Katie, my new teacher. Mr Romano had lost patience with me during my first lesson and huffed off. He must have realised I wasn't going to be a prodigy.

Katie was one of the young people I'd seen in the shop on the first day. Like the others who worked there, she was a student at the Conservatorium. I worshipped her because Mr Romano intimidated me, and despite her kind, soft voice, Katie always stood up for me. She could see my potential. I don't think I could have continued if not for Katie.

'I just have to speak to Mr Romano for a minute, Emily, honey. Just practise those couple of bars for a sec and I'll be back, all right?' she said.

I nodded, sawing the unwieldy bow, chasing elusive notes but I sounded like that tomcat on the fence at home, howling mournfully at Puss.

'Does your tongue play an important part in this piece?'

I stopped abruptly and spun around. A young man with short brown hair and a wide smile leant against the wall, his arms folded. I remember his blue eyes twinkled with a kind of inner light.

'What?' It sounded rude, but then he'd started it. I was self-conscious about my tongue because it would sneak out the corner of my mouth whenever I concentrated too hard.

The man wore a scuffed leather apron that went from his chest to his knees. I couldn't read the faded gold letters spread across a large open pocket at the bottom. When he came close, I recognised the smell of wood shavings and hard work—the same as the men doing renovations at school.

'Are you a carpenter?'

He chuckled, his face beaming with mischief. 'Almost. I'm Benny. I make violins but rather than a carpenter we are called luthiers.' He waved his arm at the rows behind him.

'Did you make all those?'

He shrugged in the same way Mr Romano did, opening his hands and moving his eyebrows like hairy caterpillars.

'Try holding your left hand a little higher, like this.' He held up his hand and I tried to copy it. I felt my tongue slide out again as I hesitantly began to play.

'That's much better, Em,' Katie said, bustling back.

'Oh, this man showed me how …'

He'd gone.

***

Benny came regularly after that, but never when anyone else was around. After the first couple of times, I quickly learned not to mention him, as Katie put it all down to my imagination.

As I improved, Mr Romano began to take part of my lesson, showing me a new technique or demonstrating a more difficult phrase. I was never sure whether he did this to show me or to show off.

One day I summoned up my courage and asked him about Benny. 'Where does Benny work?'

Mr Romano was beside me, sway-playing to himself with his eyes closed. I repeated the question and he stopped abruptly. 'What?'

'Benny. The man who makes the violins. Whereabouts does he work?'

Mr Romano's face drained of colour. 'I don't know what you mean. I am feeling tired now. We will finish early today.'

'But—'

'Enough!' Mr Romano stormed from the room.

***

Benny avoided any question that didn't relate to violins or technique.

'Where do you live?' I asked.

'Not far. I have a little room next to my workshop, like Guipetto in *Pinnochio*. Have you read it?'

'Can I see it?'

'What? *Pinnochio*?' he answered innocently.

'Noooo, your workshop. No one ever sees you here except me. Are you sure you're real? I think you're a ghost.'

'A ghost?' he scoffed, slapping his chest. 'Do I look dead?'

'Why is Mr Romano scared of you?'

Benny's face became thoughtful, before saying quietly, 'He's not scared of me. It's just that some people miss their chance, little Em. They see the bus coming and hold off catching it, thinking another one will be along afterwards. It doesn't always happen. Mr Romano is a good teacher who would have once been a great performer. Now, what was I telling you about? Ah, the 'G'. See how this makes it a much cleaner sound all round? Now play with me.'

I loved it when we played together. No matter how bad I was on my own, together we sounded like water falling over rocks, the music flowing and blending between us. He even came with me sometimes when I had an important concert. It was easier when he was there.

I read books about ghosts, just in case. Mother would have had a fit, but I sneaked them home inside others and read them under the bed covers with a torch from the kitchen drawer. I had to stop, though, because they made me scared. Benny didn't scare me.

Benny was so passionate—about violins, playing and life. Could he be dead? I passed all my exams with his help, though Mr Romano took all the credit, preening himself in front of Mother.

I'd insisted early on that if she wanted me to learn violin then she must pay for my lessons before anything else. She'd seemed surprised, but agreed, as if sensing something changing between us. I think she was pleased as she could continue to pretend, to Mr Romano at least, that we were rich, though she would still insist on getting terms for my new violins.

I was sixteen the last time I saw Benny at Mr Romano's. I was practising on my own. Katie had left for England the previous year. I only came now out of habit. I felt comfortable practising in that room.

'Emily.'

I stopped playing. He had never called me by my full name, always Em. 'What is it?'

He looked down at his scuffed shoes. 'I won't be able to see you for a little while.'

'Why not? Where are you going?'

He shook his head, 'Not me. You. Please don't ask questions, Emily. He will be coming back soon. When he does, ask him for that violin hanging there, do you see it? Ask him to give it to you.'

I followed his pointing finger to the instrument hanging on the wall. It looked battered and unloved. Amidst all the shiny new stock it was definitely the runt of the litter.

'But I don't have enough money—'

'Ask him. Promise me. Tell him … tell him that Benny says it's time.'

'I don't understand. Where are you going?'

'Not far. Em, remember what I said about catching the bus? Well, yours is coming and ours—mine—is leaving, all right? However, if ever you need me, I mean really need me, use this violin. I will do my best to come to you.'

Then he walked out and Mr Romano came straight in. Just like that. No goodbyes, no explanation.

Mr Romano looked tired these days and was always grumpy. 'What is it, Emily?'

I hadn't mentioned Benny since that first time. I gulped it out anyway, 'Benny said to give me that violin there.' I pointed to the ugly duckling.

He seemed to stagger a little, touching his chest with one of those long-fingered hands. 'What did you say?'

'Benny. I don't know what it means. He just said that it was time and that you should give me that old battered violin there.'

'It was time?' He sounded both scared and sort of relieved.

I nodded. Mr Romano reached out his hand and took down the instrument as if he'd never seen a violin before. He cradled it in both hands and, after a moment's hesitation, held it out to me. I took it. There were deep score marks across the old polished wood. Seeing it up close it looked like a piece of flotsam from some musical shipwreck.

'You better go now. I'll be closing early today,' he said quietly, patting me almost fondly on the head. Shrugging, I started packing up. As I was leaving he called me back. 'You have great talent, Emily. Make sure you catch your bus.'

Romano's burnt down that night. No one knew why—an electrical fault, the papers said. Poor Mr Romano was caught up in it and died among the violins that he loved.

***

Someone rapped twice on the dressing room door. It opened immediately. Matty. 'Ten minutes, Em.'

I smiled tightly and nodded.

Matty hovered in the doorway, his kind face creasing. 'So, are you all right?'

I nodded again, with more enthusiasm. The door closed like a fade-out in a movie.

Tonight would be my first real concert since my breakdown. Everyone was worried and no one would admit it. Except me. I stood and stretched.

I felt like I needed something, yet knew that I did not. It had been stress and anxiety unmanaged that had ultimately brought me undone, leaving me bare, alone and horribly exposed. It's strange how it's called a 'breakdown' as if we are faulty cars left on the road somewhere, our internal wiring exposed, waiting for road-side assist. 'Nerves', Mother called it dismissively. AA had been more help than her over the past twelve months. Where a few too many drinks had been my sledgehammer solution to anxiety for the past twenty years, I was gradually learning to replace it with responsibility and the acceptance of my actions.

Frankfurt was still in the wings, though. The pre-concert feeling of slow-motion panic, the expectant and concerned looks as I just stood there, front of stage, bow poised above the strings before a capacity crowd in the opera house. Behind me, orchestra sounds trailed off unevenly like leaves falling from a tree as one by one they stopped playing, realising that something was wrong.

I had to be led off. My arms still held the violin and bow. Poised. Ready.

That was twelve months ago and a lot of counselling.

My agent was calling this Brisbane concert my soft re-entry. The sub-text was that if I froze here I may as well pack up my violin case and retire to Bourke. No one would take a chance on me after that.

The dress rehearsal with the full orchestra had gone fine—everyone said so. When I spoke to Dr Hodges yesterday afternoon 'we' were all very confident—Dr Hodges always referred to him and me as us. Maybe he was right. Maybe that was my problem; I'd always been alone. Doc didn't quite get it but smiled in that way they must teach at psych college, as if they knew but had the grace not to admit to it, too loudly anyway. I didn't care as long as tonight worked.

In the distance, the orchestra was tuning in to itself. Matty would be going out soon. I took a deep breath, then another. My hand hovered over my violin. It gleamed back at me from its case. On a whim, I snapped the case shut and slid the other one out from where I'd left it under the table.

A string of psychologists had managed to almost convince me that Benny had been a projection of my performance anxiety. Yet, if there was any time that I needed help, this was it and I was prepared to use any talisman, even this piece of junk. Maybe. I hadn't even looked at the violin since I'd been given it yet for some reason I'd asked Mother to bring it in that afternoon. She'd martyred herself, of course, and I'd chastised myself afterwards for both causing her and me unnecessary stress.

Now it was time and I was considering using it. I lifted it out of the case and plucked one of the strings. It sang back true. In tune—how could that be? I tried a quick run with the bow. Perfect. In fact, more than perfect. It sounded like gold. I looked at it more closely, turning it over in my hands. There was a small area of bare wood on the back as if someone had pared away the varnish with a sharp knife.

Another knock at the door. 'Five minutes, Miss McDonald.'

'Oh. Thank you.'

I went out to wait in the wings, realising too late that I still had the old violin in my hand. It didn't matter. It felt and sounded so good.

I hated this part. Before it started.

The first violin excused himself as he squeezed past. There was scattered applause as he cued the tune-ins and took his position. Matty winked as he sidled past. Cheeky bugger. Cute, though. With those black curls and single gold earring, he looked like a rakish buccaneer. We seemed to have a thing sparking between us. Maybe it could turn into something more. For the first time, I was at least willing to consider that possibility. Having him beside me on the podium certainly made me feel better. His strength was palpable. Yesterday at the rehearsal I'd drawn on it. I hoped that I wouldn't need it tonight. This was my show, flop or not.

More applause, Matty took his bow.

I didn't want to look to see if Mother was there. She either would be, or not be. Peter said he would bring her but Mother had always been unreliable.

I had myself to worry about. Everyone kept telling me I was

brave and that everything would be all right. Why do they say that? How would they know what it's like to stand there in front of thousands of people, exposed and alone?

Yet I was more scared not to try because paradoxically, I loved performing. Dr Hodges called it sabotaging oneself.

The stage manager looked anxious. It was time.

I nodded at him, took a ragged breath and stepped out. More applause. I walked to the front of the stage, took a bow and tried to smile, looking down to the fourth row.

There they were. Mother was dressed as if she were on the way to an audience with the queen. She had a strange expression on her face, as if she needed to go to the toilet. No support there, as usual. Peter sat on her left, the side of his deaf ear. He gave me a shy smile.

I allowed my eyes to sweep the room, forcing myself to meet those other eyes, watching and waiting.

Matty rapped his baton, the orchestra came in gradually, picking up the score like an animal waking, stretching one languorous limb at a time.

I waited.

Bow poised.

Ready.

The swell from the orchestra surrounded me, flowing over and through me then out to the audience. I glanced up at Matty—his brow was furrowed, concentrating fully, containing and cajoling the multi-legged behemoth before him, like a mahout with a stick. He flashed me a glance, checking I was ready and managed a quick grin.

I looked ready, but he didn't know I could feel nothing. The paralysis was creeping over me. I wriggled my fingers desperately. They felt stiff and creaky as if they needed oil. It seemed cold on the edge of the stage.

I felt the music building around me, heard my first entry gate coming within it.

Panic flooded me.

I couldn't do it. It was as if my heart was pumping instant freeze throughout my body. I felt tears of frustration pool behind my eyes. I couldn't even cry. Matty flashed me a glance, mildly concerned. I'd missed the first. It was minor; no one would notice, the next one, though, was a leap into nothing. Solo. After carrying us all to the edge the orchestra would stop dead and I would have to carry on alone—fly or sink.

Five bars to go. Four. Three.

I shut my eyes and prayed, went back to when I was ten and the holy was less holy and called on everyone, even Benny.

I saw him when I opened my eyes.

He was sitting in the front row, smiling up at me, blue eyes twinkling, nodding, one leg crossed over the other, upraised foot dancing in time with the beat. I heard him speak as if he were standing beside me. 'Doesn't your tongue play an important part in this piece, Emily?'

I felt warmth and wetness flood my parched mouth. Then he stood, tucking up his old apron as he bent stiffly to retrieve something from under his seat. As he pulled it free I could tell, even from this distance, that it was a magnificent instrument. He fitted it snugly beneath his chin, his eyes locking with mine, and climbed the stairs to the stage, one step at a time. As he came closer he seemed to age a little at a time, his hair growing longer, his demeanour more mature.

I felt the music penetrating the numbness, first with a pinprick of sensation near my heart that rapidly flowed out, filling me with a fire. I felt the need to dispel the energy, to let the music play me the way it used to, to waltz madly through the sacred fire with Benny and emerge cleansed and whole once more. When the gap in the score came, we leapt into the solo void together, slipping and sliding through the frenetic first piece until there was no differentiation between one instrument and the other.

I didn't care whether anyone else could see Benny, could hear him playing, standing beside me, eyes fixed to mine; I could, and whatever was happening it was working, our violins singing to the same vibration.

When it ended, my dress and hair were a tangled, sweaty mess. My tongue felt sore and incredibly dry. I realised it had been poking out the corner of my mouth, clamped in place between my teeth for the entire performance.

Incredibly, the audience was on its feet. Mother was openly crying, while my implacable elder brother was stamping his feet and shouting 'Bravo!' over and over again.

What had happened?

Matty beamed, the whole orchestra rapping their bows and instruments.

I bowed again. Relief, joy, creative euphoria flooded through me.

I'd done it. No, we had done it. Where was Benny?

As quick as he had appeared, he'd disappeared.

Something rolled around on the floor just in front of me. I looked closer. A single curl of wood-shaving was rocking on its curved back in the shifting air. I bent down and gently picked it up, cradling it in my cupped palm like a tiny delicate bird. It felt warm, as if it had just curled off the plane of a fine instrument still in the making. I opened the shaving out gently, it looked the same size as the bare patch on the back of my violin. I looked closely. Burnt into the varnish of the wood shaving was a name—'Benjamin Romano'.

THE SEEKING OF JAVAN

A Monologue

Rosanne Hawke

Javan 140, Final Testament, 2239.7.19

As with all things Inside, even interrogation is conducted alone. I wonder who will be listening. A teacher? One of the scientists? The Leader? In the hope my testament will be kept in the archives for a person like me to find one day, I will disclose my hidden life, even though whoever is listening today must already know.

So I sit calmly in this small bay, waiting for the signal. Would I have done it if I knew I'd be discovered? Absolutely. I feel, yes actually *feel* alive. I have never felt like that.

Petra and I used to wonder if there was more to this pale blue life of nothingness. Did I think that back then? Or have I clothed my memories with what I've recently discovered? Petra was different when no one else was. She told me she *felt*, and although I didn't understand what she meant, she couldn't keep quiet, couldn't stop asking. Then she disappeared.

The green light is flashing. I must start within five seconds … or what? What would happen if I didn't? My behaviour has been well-trained, so I begin.

***

My name is Javan, birth number one hundred and forty. My crime is seeking. I have transgressed the rule. It began when I illegally found my birthmother—she lives Inside. She had also discovered her own birthmother, Iris, so I have a grand-birthmother, who is still living. It was astonishing. Yes, I have transgressed in other ways—I *felt* astonished.

Like everyone Inside, I was designed and trained not to feel emotional impulses. Our teachers said it was these which caused all the world's problems in the first place. We birthlings were forbidden to feel, though I came close to breaking this rule with Petra. I was not to believe, for belief is also an impulse that caused all the warring before the water rose.

My grand-birthmother, Iris, remembered information we were not taught. It was a risk but I visited her sleeping bay. 'You need to know things, Javan.' She glanced at the door, then gave me a burst of information. 'Inside isn't real life.'

I frowned.

'People are supposed to live with a family.'

It wasn't a word I knew. She held my hand and I stiffened. No one had done that before.

'Javan, you were selected from a precise egg and life serum to have certain DNA and attributes to complement the Inside Community. It was known what your personality would be and what work you would do before your birth.'

I nodded. This sounded more familiar. All of us birthlings learned and worked in single bays during the day, meeting to eat together, but we slept in our own bays at night. We weren't allowed to be close or talk about our thoughts like Iris did.

Iris spoke of us as 'girls', but we were never told that was what we were. We all dressed in the same pale blue—there was no thought of diversity or difference. 'We were told our life is good,' I said.

Iris shook her head. 'Family is good. A family is a group living together—a group founded on love.' She said love was good too. I didn't believe her, of course. My training has been thorough and there had been no mention of this love before. I suspected it to be one of the forbidden impulses.

Between my online work and eating periods, I managed to meet with Iris, until one day she told me something shocking. I had never felt this impulse before either. 'Javan, people live in groups Outside.' It was impossible. Inside is a huge, controlled environment. Outside's atmosphere is corrupted with carbon dioxide.

'Outside is just empty space.' That is what we were told.

But she was adamant.

I wondered if she had the elderly sickness already, though she didn't look old like images I've seen on my screen. Perhaps she was remembering the time Before. My group is the fifth generation Inside. Before has been forgotten by almost everyone I know.

Iris's words sounded like an old-time folktale, like those we had in our lessons when we were young, but the thoughts wouldn't leave me. My breeding and training were planned for the purpose of research—to help the community and compile information for learning.

But I had limits—I was forbidden to enter the archives on Inside's computer system. Information was stored there when the world infrastructure collapsed. Information that I may never have known.

It didn't take me long to crack the firewall into areas where I was not permitted to seek. But seek I did.

I transgressed and could not stop. It became a force in me which I now realise is a forbidden impulse, but I didn't ask for guidance from an elder.

In my defence, I can say I didn't understand.

In the archives, I found hidden books. Some sounded ancient—stories, maybe—and I realised that the stories and information I'd read as a child must have been written by a person Inside. Is that what I would have been able to do also? Write stories for the young? Some of the books looked special; I had no word for 'sacred' then. Why wasn't this literature part of our training? We could have understood what it was like Before and reorder our lives and government. But even this I see is a transgression—to suggest Inside could have done better.

I clicked on a moving enactment called *Little Women.* It wasn't unlike my life except that the structure where the girls lived was smaller and they shared it with their birthmother. Instantly, I understood what Iris meant. The girls connected—they touched and put their arms about each other as I'd felt like doing with Petra. It didn't look wrong and they seemed happy. Their birthmother called them a family. The story must be a representation of Before. I couldn't understand why we weren't told this and I needed to discover the truth.

I didn't know how to go Outside. We were made to understand it was unfeasible, that we were fortunate—this was the life we were given when everyone else perished.

We have a courtyard with a frosted glass dome; the closest thing we have to being Outside, although we've never seen the passing of the sun or moon through its roof. I visited and touched the small trees and plants that had been saved from extinction. Members of the community worked at propagating and planting. Our food came from the courtyard, though it was scientifically processed into nutrient-rich packs for us each day. I looked behind some shrubs and saw a door to the lower levels I hadn't noticed before. Was it ever opened? I watched and waited. I took my screen there to work until finally, my seeking was rewarded.

One early morning, long before the signal to wake, a person in odd-coloured clothes walked through that door. From my screen I knew he was a man but since none lived here he couldn't be from Inside. Did he come from Outside? How? Wasn't everything Outside decimated or polluted?

A scientist arrived and escorted him to another level. I stayed hidden and an hour later he returned alone and left through the same door. As far as I knew there were no residential quarters below us. He must be from Outside. If I were to follow such a visitor, I'd need to be quick since the central locking would seal the door at a specified time.

Finally, I had proof. Iris was telling the truth about people living Outside. By this time, I knew I was errant, but still I could not stop seeking. I can see now why impulses are dangerous. I wanted to discover more.

Desire, I realised too late, was one of the deadliest impulses. But isn't this what I was designed and born for? To find knowledge? To help the community?

A different visitor arrived next time. More research brought the answer to why they visited. Iris's comments about how I was designed triggered my research. The men must be delivering the life serum to fertilise the birthmothers' eggs.

It took sixty days to be sure of the nights when a visitor would arrive and how long before the door would lock—just thirty seconds. We had no guards since rule enforcement wasn't necessary. I didn't even think about whether or not I'd need breathing apparatus to venture Outside; the visitors never wore a mask. I only packed water, some food packs I'd saved and a jacket.

One night when everyone was in their sleeping bays, I waited with my backpack behind the shrubbery. When a visitor entered and later returned through the door, I counted to twenty before following him.

I was in a low-lit corridor which curved and led underground until it rose again. I kept my steps light and hoped he wouldn't hear me.

He approached another door and I hung back. The door opened for him. Would it for me? If it didn't, I'd be trapped until the next visitor came. As soon as he was through, I raced to the door to stop it locking. Would I be Outside or in another institution?

The door opened. What relief. When I peered out, I experienced the impulse of shock again—I could breathe! So we had been misled about that. A fleeting thought crossed my mind—what if these impulses destroyed me and those around me, as we had been warned? Still, I dismissed it, anxious to explore. The man had vanished, but a moving light shone in the sky far above me. My screen wouldn't work Outside, so I left it behind.

I had no map and knew not where to go. I hoped I could get far enough away by dawn so I wouldn't be seen from the conservatory on the roof. We had no windows, so I took a risk that there would be enough cover. I didn't even give thought to how I would return other than wait for another visitor.

The ground was flat enough to walk swiftly. I only stopped to drink and eat one of my packs. At sunrise, I turned and could see nothing of Inside. Not a building in sight.

I stood in a desert that consisted of small stones and tufts of coarse grass. I turned in a circle, staring. Golden flashes from the sun as it rose above the horizon spread pink and purple streaks across the sky. My screen had not prepared me for such beauty. A few windswept trees with many thin trunks dotted the landscape. Trees were not extinct after all. That made me smile. My hair moved on its own—from my learning, I knew it must be wind and I lifted my face towards it.

I needn't have worried about where to find people, as shortly a person, probably not much older than me, appeared in front of me. He had brown hair to his shoulders and even some under his nose. He wore strange clothes, darker than that of our pale blue. I scanned the knowledge I possessed. His over garment appeared to be wool, though I had only seen such a thing on my screen.

We stared at each other. I had no concept of people hurting others, yet still I felt a twinge of an uncomfortable impulse. Had I been misguided? Should I have stayed Inside?

I spoke first. 'Could you take me to a family group? I'd like to see one.'

He regarded me strangely. Perhaps he didn't understand my words. Then he grinned. 'Sure,' he said.

My body was exhausted, but I followed. After another fifteen minutes, I almost dropped to the ground. We exercised every day Inside but I wasn't used to doing it all night as well.

The person must have noticed my weakness. 'Not long now, just over this rise,' he said.

Then I saw the tents. Heard noises I'd never encountered before. 'What's that sound?'

He frowned at me. 'The dogs?'

Confusion made my head spin. Domesticated animals were extinct like the others. Was my screen also untrue? I kept quiet. Perhaps he didn't know where I was from. Would I be welcome? There was so much I hadn't thought of or planned for. It wasn't like me.

Children ran about, screeching in a game. We were never allowed to make such noise. People sat beside the tents, cooking in pots on iron frames over fires. I breathed in the aroma of the smoke. The food smelled inviting. Our food had no smell other than the wax packaging it came in.

The young man indicated a stool for me to sit on and, in relief, I finished my water while I watched the people interacting.

An older person the age of Iris sat near me. 'You are from the Inside Community.'

It wasn't a question, yet I nodded.

'They will know you are gone.'

'I will return,' I said, 'I just wanted to see Outside. A family …' My voice trailed away. It sounded stupid. I had acted unwisely.

The person touched my arm. 'What will they do to you?'

I stared at her hand on me. It reminded me of Iris. 'I don't know.' Another impulse filled my chest. Was it fear?

Her touch mesmerised me. 'You can stay here with us—be part of us—until you make up your mind.'

Acting in a way I was never allowed to before, I turned to her in a rush. 'Will you teach me?'

She frowned and took her hand away from my arm. 'Teach what?'

It was errant of me to ask. 'All you know. About what happened. How you adapted to this environment. I was told no one survived.' Iris filled my thoughts again and I couldn't stop asking. 'Do you feel? Do you believe? Is love true?'

The person wrapped her arms around me. It was my first hug and I didn't know what to do, so I sat like a doll in her embrace. Yet inside, I felt like a pre-warming butterfly that had just emerged from its casing.

'We will answer your questions. We have seen others like you.'

There were many families who were happy to satisfy my thirst for knowledge, love and belief.

One group lived in an ancient stone structure with underground bays. They knew of Iris. This was my true family and I wept. They welcomed me as though I had been born in their place before the Warming.

Unwittingly, I had left a trail. My screen could tell the secrets I had sought before I left to Inside workers as skilled in knowledge collection as I am. By two turns of the moon, they found me.

***

The light flashes red at me and I stifle a cough. My throat is dry from all the talking. The first session is finished. I breathe in and expel it in a rush. Will they need more evidence to see how errant and lost I am in their eyes? How I don't have blind loyalty to Inside anymore? That I feel betrayed by them? That I want to live Outside with my family?

Soon a worker will come to escort me to my sleeping bay. Now, it is kept locked until my fate is decided. I must not contaminate the others.

The Inside Community thought they'd designed me to be compliant, intelligent and useful, but they hadn't suppressed my true humanness, my spirit. I hold my hands in my lap and patiently wait, as I have been trained. But where it is not seen, I am transformed. Deep inside me, my tiny new wings are unfolding.

FAULTY CONNECTION

Jennifer Horn

CONNECTION LOW.

CONNECTION LOW.

The sickly-red letters appeared in front of him, obscuring the virtual background and burning the inside of his eyelids.

'No!' he roared with frustration and tugged off the headgear. It dropped to the floor and he gave it a cruel kick. A few shards split off, knocking against the wall.

Tye threw himself onto the bed, sulking. Why did the game keep doing that? The power was fine; he'd checked it. The connection seemed to be getting to the rest of the house. What was its problem?

'How's the game going, honey?' Mum bustled in and quipped, navigating the debris of Tye's room from under her virtu-glasses as she made a beeline for the dirty plates by his bedside. *She's probably playing Guess This Past Landmass again,* Tye thought. *What a stupid game.* He could just make out the little blips of the background music from her headpiece. Looked like no one else was having connection trouble.

'Fine, Mum. Just fine,' Tye spat out.

She swept up the crockery, head blindly tilted to the unseen screen in concentration. 'That's good. Your dinner platform's ready, by the way. Sushi-den tonight, I thought.' Then she gave a start. 'Oh, Madagascar! Old landmass off Africa—it's Madagascar!'

The door shut in her wake and she was off, singing out for his sister across the corridor.

Tye let out a huff. He'd put so much time into Raider450, a fast-paced, popular online scavenger course, and the connection had decided to die only a day away from the competition. He thought about the virtu-paintball party he'd passed up with his friends and the home-gym milestones he was missing because of it. He'd even dodged his turns to mind Gran. Not that she'd notice the change.

He picked up the headpiece. One of the broken elements was hanging off like a ripped tendon. Great. That was the bit that connected to the small disc pressed to his temple. The replacements for it didn't come through the 3D printer. They were MediTeck territory. He'd have to go *Outside.*

Tye swept his hand through his rumpled hair and shuffled down the corridor. The whining of his sister, Esther, scraped through the air, mixed with the punctuated *bip bip* of Gran's wheelchair as Mum parked her at the platform table.

His DomePod was in the corner of the living room where he'd left it on his birthday the week before. It sat there, flat-packed and vacuum-sealed, winking at him with its tiny red light like it was nudging him to drive it now he was of age. His was an upgraded edition—improved solar power and resistance and higher-quality air-conditioning to purify the toxic, shared air that, when it was Outside, would seep through its vents … according to the manual. It was such a recent update that their 3D printer had sounded like a washing machine tumbling dirty shoes when it had printed it.

So over-rated, he thought. Clunky, faux-glass, claustrophobic domes that you were meant to trudge about in whenever you went Outside. Why would anyone want to cloister themselves in those things and bother with all the Outside's precaution fuss when they could go wherever they wanted through the Disc Service? One press to your temple and you could be virtually anywhere. So what if he hadn't seen his best mates in the Outside for years? They had sat in virtual classrooms together, played volleyball in convincing summer conditions and skied in winter ones, and, in the last few years, plotted and completed jungle missions on Raider450. He knew their faces and icons and voices; that was enough.

Mum hadn't used her DomePod since she'd had to accompany Gran to hospital, and between caring for them both as well as her virtu-marketing job, she wasn't likely to go outside for a broken headpiece in time for the competition.

Tye turned from the DomePod to see the platform table cleared and his family seated around it.

'Here you go, Mum,' his mother said as she carefully pressed the synthetic disc onto Gran's temple. Gran cringed at the cold touch of it, but Mum had her other arm ready to keep her scooped upright in the wheelchair. It was a seat now, but it was also Gran's bed, bath, and inevitably, her casket.

'OK,' Mum breathed, attending to her own disc. Esther was already logged into the restaurant, jiggling in her seat as she swiped here and there, most likely creating her custom taro sundae in advance.

'I'll just get us all the salmon sashimi pack—that's nice and quick.' Mum flourished her hands about and soon the platform table was humming with printing instructions. She reached over to squeeze both Gran's and Esther's hands and directed a tired smile at her son. It missed.

Tye sat, and before the food appeared in front of his naked eyes in all its unenhanced beige-ness, he wedged the little disc out of its groove in the table surface and put it against his temple. It was cold, as always, but no longer sparked a shiver through him.

His living room transformed with a snap into the familiar interior of the sushi restaurant.

The gentle kick of soy sauce and ginger found his senses first, then the programmed sound of gently trickling water. Dark wood pressed in cosily around them, backgrounding his family, who hadn't bothered to change to avatars. But the illusion was glitchy—the sushi décor kept flickering in and out with his real living room. He felt the creeping dread before the large red letters appeared again.

CONNECTION LOW.

He prodded the disc against his temple again, cursing under his breath, urging it to work.

'Oh, and Tye,' he heard his mum say as she tapped her chopsticks on the fully printed plate. 'I really need you to do your gran's pills tonight. I've got to finish off some work and your sister's got to practise her virtu-oboe.'

'Yeah,' Esther put in cheerfully, mouth already full of rice. 'It's not fair for me to have to do them while you get to play that game so many nights in a row.'

CONNECTION LOW.

CONNECTION LOW.

Tye slammed the table. 'Can't you just lay off!' he exploded. 'I just wanna get into the next stage of Raider, and I can't do it with this stupid disc deciding not to work.'

A mythological winter could have passed over and frozen them to their seats, and they would not have been any more suspended in motion. Tye felt the pairs of wide eyes on him. He wrenched the disc from his temple and the restaurant snapped away, dropping him back into the stark living room. Mum and Esther gazed blindly in his direction as he glitched out of their virtual vision.

'Tye,' his mum said leaning in. 'We'll have a look at it. The disc's not everything, you know.'

He went to push away from the table but caught his gran's eye. She gazed at him with her glassy, watery eyes, that vague smile glued to her face, her thin hair ghostly next to Mum's shiny black, and hung down uncoiled from her bun. The speckles of darker skin across Gran's cheeks were stretched by her expression. Did she even see him through those cataracts and all that cerebral fog? He wasn't sure she could see the virtual worlds they had her logged into every day, reliving her past decades where apparently the air was able to touch her cheek and real instruments were strummed soothingly by people sitting shoulder to shoulder.

He pushed the chair away from under him and tramped to his room, tugging at the strings of his hoodie. With the door shut and the lights off, he glared down at the luminous river of domes crawling through the streets below. So many people risking the Outside. What choice did he have?

When he looked down at his hoodie strings again, they had been frayed to the core.

***

Tye woke with stark sunlight slicing into his bedroom. Little dust particles waltzed in its rays. He sat up and sent them flurrying. The little sun icon on the corner of his window announced an average of forty degrees Celsius. Apparently, it was oppressively hot, not that anyone would know. The DomePods' photosynthesis was so effective that their inside temperature could be matched exactly to anyone's house. He glanced out of the thick-paned window, the tops of people's domes looking like soapy bathwater as they ebbed down the streets in heavy traffic.

The living room was empty. Murmurs of Mum and Esther's voices behind their daytime doors told Tye that they had eaten already and had started their respective work and school for the day.

He sat at the grey platform table, impatiently pushing the little disc to his temple.

CONNECTION L—

It ripped off with a pop and clinked across the table as he threw it and sighed in exasperation.

There was a function on the platform table for emergencies like his, to blindly re-print a previously-ordered meal. Soon he was faced with a plate of what was meant to be fruit salad and yoghurt. It probably looked fine in its virtual version, but what he saw was a gloopy grey, as if the colour had all been washed out. His neurons had no disc to tell him how it was meant to smell either. He hated having to eat without the disc.

The headpiece was where he had left it, still strewn across his bedroom floor. He picked it up and carried it out to the little disc he used for the platform table. He put all the parts into a pile on the floor next to the DomePod. It was a compact thing the size of a cake tin, with an inner circular plate atop, its tiny red light still winking. He hesitated before pressing the plate, and stepped back.

Tye had once seen a bioengineered flower open up in fast motion, its petals unfolding and a crown exploding out the top. His DomePod mirrored this—the soft faux-glass bloated to a high dome shape and stopped. He stepped forward and was hit with the smell of sharp metal. There was the slightest buzzing, almost like a purr, coming from it.

He looked it over. There were vents like gills cascading down either side of it, with a darker but still transparent section of solar panels at the very top. The dome looked as though it could have been popped like a bubble, and it reflected the living room light smartly. It *was* pretty sleek.

Remembering his virtual training, he stood level in front of the dome and held his hand to the faint handprint in the centre. The dome parted down the middle, held back by unseen hinges. He gathered the headpiece and disc from the floor and climbed into the DomePod with them, making them fit into a little shelved chute below his windscreen. The whole contraption above his knees was one big, curved windscreen.

His breathing reverberated around the dome as he scanned over the controls that seemed to hang opaquely against the inside. Entertainment, air type … ah, navigation. It was like using the platform table, really. The MediTeck centres were easy to find. There was one within four hundred metres of home. He selected it and the navigation urged him to start by leaving the building.

Tye turned to the door. No hands. Great—back to the start. He reached out to flick the dome's surface in annoyance and found that his fingers kept going. The surface was morphing to his hand like a glove. What an upgrade! His hand came down on the door handle, grasping it and pulling it, all within the protective wrap of the surface-turned-glove.

He pulled the main door closed behind him and drew his hand back into the dome. The surface looked as still as glass again.

Tye had not been in the outside corridor for years. It seemed smaller than he remembered, its garish, green-tinged lights paced sparingly along the ceiling. He vaguely remembered heading left for the elevator and found it a few doorways down. His hands morphed through the dome again to swipe the buttons, and it took him down in a box of mirrored sides, where he could see countless clones of himself in soapy capsules as the mirrors reflected each other.

The door clunked open and a harsh light speared him from all angles, pulling at his eyes and clothes, reaching right through him. His hands flew up to block the brightness and through squinted eyes, he swiped the shade settings. Why did anyone do this for fun?

The DomePod directed him along the pavement. Up ahead were two other DomePods coming the opposite way. He froze, feeling anxiety clench his muscles. How did you react to other humans outside the virtu-world? How did you behave *Outside*? This was totally different from being seen in the virtu-worlds. This was like he'd walked onto a stage with a huge audience waiting for him.

He didn't acknowledge them. He looked down at the pavement as the two DomePods passed, pretending to be working out controls. Perhaps they were looking at him, perhaps not. All he knew was that he felt surprisingly sick with the confusion of it.

The four hundred metres between his home and the MediTeck outlet held three more of these encounters—strangers in DomePods, and the conundrum of whether to look up at them or not. He pushed down the shudders from a sudden wave of panic and made sure to look busy each time.

The MediTeck outlet was a tiered asymmetrical building and the doorway told him exactly which lines to follow through the partitioned maze, depending on what customers were there for. Through the partitions, he could hear the shuffling of others making their way through. He could hear discussions, but they seemed like they were a long way away. The walls veered him further and further in, like a labyrinthine tunnel, until at once it ended, spitting him out to face a line of booths with large numbers on them. The one with '3' pinged him.

He walked up to the middle-aged woman standing there, her wool-like hair tied in a bun and the dome around her slightly scratched. Before she could look up, he gathered the mangled headpiece and little disc from the chute at the front of his dome and held them out before him, his gaze solemn.

'Well, what have we got here?' she asked jovially. She beamed at him.

'Um, my tech link's broken,' Tye said, keeping his eyes on the small pile of broken tech.

She extended her arms through her dome enthusiastically and took the debris from him. 'Replacement, then? OK, let's see …' A fringe of cords hung from a panel behind her. She plugged one into the disc and the intact parts of his headgear. It sat in her hand, channelling information with a hum until it finally fell quiet.

'Hmm,' she mused, sitting back a bit and looking at him. He felt her gaze like a spotlight so he concentrated on the floor at his feet. 'It seems you're suffering from low connection.'

Tye felt a flush of frustration. He glared at the floor. 'Yeah, that's what I said was happening. My tech's not connecting.' Why had he bothered to come to the MediTecks if they were just going to tell him what he already knew?

She shook her head, studying him with kind eyes. 'No, it's not the tech. It's coming from you.'

Tye straightened up and shot an offended glance at her chin. 'What do you mean?'

'I mean,' she said, 'your neurons are low on social connection and it's signalling that emptiness to your personal tech. You'd be surprised how much we see this. Have you maybe dropped your daily iEndorphins? Or started living alone?'

The floor was one of those virtual-patterned ones. Little fish swam beneath him and creating ripples that travelled across the room. 'No.'

'Well, is there someone that you can talk to—hug, maybe? Eye contact is good, too.' He could feel her trying to catch his eye. He focused harder on the fish's scale patterns—they looked like a low-res design after-thought. Like the ones in the Raider450 tournament that would be starting now.

'Can I just get a new part please?'

Her eyes dropped. 'Sure.' She busied her hands swiping the air in front of her, handing back the headpiece, which was now curiously reshaped, almost as if it were a lizard having regrown a tail.

'Here, this will at least restore the virtu-world loading process.' She passed the disc over. 'But have a think about what I said.'

***

Tye shed the DomePod onto the living room floor as quickly as he could and retrieved the pile of tech from inside it. As if sensing his absence, it crumpled back into its flat-pack form with a whirr.

Light spilled out of his bedroom doorway. It was strange—he thought he'd left the door closed. With the headgear and disc in his hands, he almost ran straight into Gran, who was sitting in her wheelchair in the middle of his room. Slowly, she raised her head in his direction and chewed her mouth around a bit.

Tye cast an accusing look across the corridor at his sister's closed door. 'Lazy,' he mumbled.

He stepped around the wheelchair, careful to dodge Gran's sock-covered feet sticking out. 'OK Gran, you can stay and watch me win this,' he told her. 'It's bound to work now.'

He drew up his seat beside her and pulled on the headgear. The first level was a Rapid-Eye-Movement target-aim. He gripped his knees in readiness to blink furiously at the enemies.

His bedroom disappeared in a snap, replaced with the dizzying heights of the extinct organisms they called trees. They were often in his virtu-games, stoic and ancient. He could see the squiggly patterns in the bark by his cheek. Spying sudden movement through the canopy, he lurched upwards to get a better view and came up against Gran's armrest.

'Sorry Gran, so close now … Aah, come *on*!' The letters had blinked up again.

CONNECTION LOW.

His heart sank. That was it.

Something moved against his hand—it felt warm and contorted, the skin stretched like old elastic. The fragile hand felt for his own and grasped it. Steadily, his head swimming from the vertigo of the virtual scene unfolding again in front of him, he gripped it back. It stirred weakly against his palm.

The familiar font appeared boldly in front of him, briefly covering the whole canopy. It was not in red this time, but a plain white.

CONNECTION RESTORING.

CONNECTION RESTORING.

LIGHT CLUB

Jennie Del Mastro

My joints creaked and ached, and it was tempting to lie back down and rest for a while. But as the shaking became more violent, I knew I had to move.

I strode out into the darkness, not bothering with a lantern. There wasn't far to go. Areas of ground that we'd cleared of redweed yesterday were flourishing today. But it never made its way onto the brighter part of the plain. Bassa said it hated to grow in any light created by its own burning.

As I pulled up handfuls of the dry, brittle redweed, I looked at the stars speckled and dusted across the sky. The red segment of sun grew to a circle, and I watched as it moved slowly up behind a cluster of tall, narrow shadows, the silhouette of the old city. But the darkness didn't lighten and the stars remained.

I shuttled between the blue firelight and the blushing darkness as quietly as possible, delivering armloads of redweed. Gradually, I became steadier. I could hear the gears whir more smoothly through the hole in my shoulder. Sometimes I looked down at my chest, but everything there stayed as dull as usual.

On my seventy-third trip, I saw Bassa was awake. Two more loads and then I would stop. That would be enough for two days of food or fires for the whole plain. No one could expect more.

By the time I was finished, others were heading out to work, and the games club was gathering. I brought Bassa a bunch of redweed. She bounced up and down to get rid of the shakes and the stiffness. 'Thanks, Linton. Want some breakfast?'

I took the half she offered back to me and tried not to stare through the window in her chest. From the corner of my eye, I could see there was only darkness, except for blue shimmers where the fires reflected off the glass.

A game had started nearby. Long ago, the club had staged fights, with betting on the winners. But too much damage had been done, and the Three had banned that game. Some of us were still nursing one hundred year old injuries—the jagged hole in my shoulder, for example, which left my gears open to the elements. I avoided dust and dirt, and the Three regularly blasted my workings with air and squirted them with oil.

Bassa and I sat down near the circle, far enough that we weren't involved, but close enough that we weren't excluded from the club altogether. She gave me the same secretive, dreamy smile she always did. *The club thinks we belong, but we know better.* At least, I thought that was what the smile meant. There was a large dent in the side of her head; a legacy of the old games. It hadn't damaged anything critical, but sometimes she was vague, and then as sharp as a splinter.

I shifted closer to her. 'I had a dream last night.'

'Really? What was it about? No one's dreamed something interesting in ages. Do you want to interrupt the game?'

'No. Just wait. I've had the same dream a few times.'

'And you haven't told me till now?'

Her wistfulness made my insides flutter. I wanted to tell her, but something held me back. 'It's a strange one.'

'It couldn't be stranger than Oila's dream about redweed turning blue or the old city full of people again or the sun smashing on the ground.'

'I don't know …'

'Tell me. Please?'

'I was walking away from the plain, out into the hills, in the dark. You were with me. I had a lantern with redweed burning in it. And then it went out.'

'Like it always does,' she said, 'and then we turn and go back home.'

'I didn't this time. I didn't need to, because of you.'

Her eyelids narrowed. 'Me?'

'When I looked at you, I saw …' I shifted my position. 'I hope you don't mind me mentioning it. I saw through your chest.'

'Don't be embarrassed. Everyone can see through everyone's chest.' She laughed and touched the glass at her front. Then she leant over and touched mine too. I forgot all about the dream. She had her eyes down again, leaving the next move to me.

I touched my glass, then touched hers.

'Linton,' she murmured, a small smile bending the metal mesh of her cheek. 'Oh, but you were telling me about your dream.'

I continued. 'When the lantern went out, we kept walking and we weren't scared because there was light.'

'A fire?'

'Yes, but not the sort you mean.'

Had I gone too far to stop? She waited patiently, and the game the club was playing went on—the clanging slaps, the pointless words and laughter about nothing.

'I looked at you,' I said, 'and inside your chest, the candle was burning.'

She put her hands to her face. 'What do you mean?'

'It burned with a different-coloured fire, not blue like the redweed. When I touched you, I felt something.'

'It was just a dream,' she said.

'A dream?' asked a voice. It was Chugga. He'd turned from the game, but kept his distance, cradling the cracked glass in his chest.

'A dream? Tell us!' The circle dissolved and reformed around us. Pleading faces were everywhere. 'Tell us, please!'

I considered resisting, but I dreaded the unpleasantness that would follow.

'Please?'

'I was walking away from the plain …'

They hung off every word I spoke.

'But what colour was the fire if it wasn't blue?' someone asked.

'I don't know.'

'Red? Like the sun?'

'No.'

'Brown, like us? Black, like the sky? Silver, like the stars?'

'No.'

There was silence until one person laughed. Soon everyone was laughing. Bassa hung her head.

'Fire is always blue! And how could her candle burn?' The club moved away, gathering in a new circle to gossip and laugh, and retell the story of Linton's crazy dream about Bassa.

'It was beautiful,' I said. Though 'beautiful' barely described the fire or the feeling from the dream. Soft, comforting, I couldn't quite put it into words. 'I think it's real.'

'Shut up, Linton,' said Bassa, and she walked away, leaving me speechless.

I had never heard those words cross her lips before. I tried to decipher her feelings. Embarrassment? Maybe. Fear of being left out? She didn't care about that. She'd sat with me on the edge of the club for years.

Half-consciously, I watched the Three sweep dead insects into piles and swish them out into the darkness. They put down their brooms and made their way towards me.

'You've dreamed of a burning candle,' one said.

'What do you think?' asked another.

'I think it's real,' I said.

They nodded in unison. At first glance, the Three seemed like everyone else, but their faces were expressionless and had no extraneous detail. They always worked together and always agreed.

'You can't stay here,' said the third.

The thought of questioning them passed across my mind for an instant. But nobody ever had. 'I'll go, then. Can I take a lantern, and Bassa?'

'If she wants to go. Yes, you can take a lantern.'

I imagined walking into the darkness, carrying a light I knew would die, with no option of turning around and coming home. If I wasn't alone, maybe I could bear it.

The gossip was over and the game was back. Bassa was sitting in the circle, her head still hanging, apparently humble and grateful for being allowed in the club. They passed words and slaps around.

'Today,' said one, slapping the next one's hand with a loud clang, to signify the turn moving on.

'I …' Clang.

'Went …' Clang.

'To …' Clang.

'Sleep …' Clang.

'On …' Clang.

'Redweed.' Clang.

Everyone laughed, but only because everyone else did.

'Yesterday …' Clang.

'Someone …' Clang.

'Ate …' Clang.

'The …' Clang.

'Sun.' Clang.

More laughter.

Bassa was the one who had said 'the'. It was an obvious, safe contribution. She laughed along with the rest, although nothing was remotely funny. I failed to catch her eye.

When the club separated for a meal, I found her near the

redweed pile. 'I'm going into the dark.'

'Are you?'

'The Three said I had to.' I moved closer. 'They also said I could take you.'

'No.' She took a step away from me, and darted a glance at the members of the club nearby. So she did care about the gossip.

'I'm sorry I embarrassed you. But you made a promise.' I pointed from her chest to mine. 'And the dream showed you coming with me. We could try walking out there with a lantern. Then when it goes out, your candle might light. Please?'

'No.' She put out a hand to keep me away. Her gaze didn't rise above my chest. 'It's just a crazy dream.'

'Why are you in the club? You don't belong there.'

'You don't get to decide that.'

'Bassa, please let's just talk!'

She ignored me and went back to the circle.

The Three surrounded me, lit my lantern and pushed me out. I didn't resist. I went into the darkness.

I walked up into the hills, the ancient city on my right and the dull sun barely visible overhead. My numb thoughts came to life again, and I kicked at the redweed and rocks, and crushed the insects gathered around the lantern. I knew no one was watching my spot of light dwindle in the distance. When I started down the far side of the first hill, the blue plain disappeared, only to reappear smaller with each new hill I crested. Then it was gone.

The redweed collapsed into glowing ash and the light vanished. Moment by moment, the city buildings stood out more clearly. With the light, my fear had stayed at bay, but now it gripped me.

A skittering sound went by, like a thousand light footsteps or like giant insects. I held my breath and stood still until the sounds passed and faded. Nothing else happened. The fear began to ebb. Soon it was manageable—an uneasy, sick feeling, instead of paralysing terror. I placed down the useless lantern as quietly as possible, not wanting to draw the monsters back.

'Why did you bring it in the first place if you knew you'd end up in darkness anyway?'

I jumped and gasped.

'And why didn't you get more redweed and keep it going, you idiot?'

'Who are you?' I asked, 'How long have you been there?'

'Ages,' said the voice.

'Ages,' I said. 'Is that your name?'

'Looks like it,' said the voice with a laugh.

'It was easier to walk out into the darkness with a light,' I explained. 'And it would go out when I sleep, so there's no point in keeping it going.'

We walked together for a while. Ages seemed to have nowhere particular to go.

'Are you lost?' I asked him. 'Are you from the plain? I can't remember your voice.'

'I haven't been there for a long time,' said Ages. 'Can't stand that place. Are they still playing that stupid sentence game?'

'Yeah.'

'I hate that game. I wish they still had fighting.'

'We'd all be in pieces by now.'

'It'd be cool, though.'

Ages told me a story about a secret group whose members would fight each other. It sounded familiar to me. There were only so many stories and they all did the rounds every few years.

'What happened in the end?'

'Don't know,' said Ages. 'We should go back to the plain and restart the fighting.'

'No.'

I told him about my dream. Ages didn't laugh or seem surprised by it. That led me on a disquieting train of thought. What if Ages had dreamed the same thing and had come out here to find a way to light his candle and now, years later, he was still wandering, lost in the dark?

I tried to change the subject, but Ages returned to it. 'You can't open your chest, but maybe you can light the candle by eating something. Something that's not redweed.'

By the sound, I knew he had stooped to pick up a handful and throw it in the air. The particles fell over me and some rattled into my shoulder. 'Please don't do that.'

When the sun set, we found a protected spot for sleeping. The skittering sound came and went again. I felt faint vibrations through the ground. The lightness of it wasn't reassuring. Giant insects *would* have a light tread, their prickly claws scuttling along … I tried to put them out of my mind and munched a few handfuls of redweed. It was good to have company.

Ages was eating too. 'Cockroach doesn't work.'

'What?'

'I'm still dark.'

'You just ate a cockroach?' I shuddered. Cockroaches couldn't make a beautiful fire like the one in my dream. He didn't understand. I shook off the creepy insect feeling again and thought of the candlelight as I drifted into sleep.

Chugga is pretending to think, as though he might not choose one of the common starting words. Almost everyone has their eyes on him, but she *is watching* me.

Or is she? Maybe her vague stare goes past me. Maybe it's just the hole in her head. What's her name? Batters. Batsra. Bassa, that's it.

'This …' says Chugga. Clang.

'Morning …' Clang.

'I …' Clang.

'Went …' Clang.

'To …' Clang.

I search quickly for a word. 'The', obviously. Or the decisive 'sleep'. Or 'games', allowing the next person to end with 'club'. I went to games club. I went to …

'Bassa,' I say.

Now her eyes are definitely on me. Everyone giggles and the game goes on.

'I ...' Clang.

'Woke ...' Clang.

'Up ...' Clang.

'And ...' Clang.

'Saw ...' Clang.

'My ...' Clang.

My turn. Hand. Feet. Redweed.

'Bassa.'

The laughter bursts out loudly this time. I know she'll be laughing too. I can't bear to look.

My turn is coming around again.

'The ...' Clang.

'Sun ...' Clang.

'Is ...' Clang.

RED. DARK. ROUND. *But I can't stop myself.*

'Bassa.'

Hysterical laughter.

'This game is stupid,' I say, and run out into the darkness. The utter loneliness quickly calms me down and sends me slinking back into the blue light. But at mealtime, nobody speaks to me. The circle forms again and I dither around the outside of it, ignored, wondering how to earn back my place.

Bassa finds me. 'Do you want to play? If you say sorry, they'll let you in.'

'Sorry about ...?'

She touches my hand. 'Just about calling the game stupid. Nothing else.'

I blink. 'I don't want to play unless you do.'

She doesn't, either.

I woke to the sound of crunching. 'Are you still eating insects?'

I felt sick. The early morning shakes seemed worse than usual. I got up and jogged on the spot, then felt around for some redweed and chewed it.

'I ate ten cockroaches just in case,' said Ages, 'and also eight moths. As you can see, none of them worked.'

Ages went on eating. The soily, grinding sound suggested he was eating rocks now. The idea unnerved me and I was on my feet, running. The mad whizzing of gears sounded through the hole in my shoulder. I ran as fast as I could, blindly, joints clanking, bolts threatening to come apart. Then I changed direction and with a burst of speed ran straight for the city, then stopped, standing as still as I could. Everything inside me hurt. I feared I had done some damage.

I listened. There was no sound of pursuit. I was alone.

'Rocks don't work,' said Ages.

I bit back a shriek.

'That wasn't very nice,' said Ages. 'I can help you. I know why the Three wanted you to go. *Not* so you can find what you dreamed of.'

'Then why?'

'They didn't want you to end your life there. Everyone who's had that dream has either gone off looking for the light or opened their chest to light the candle at a redweed fire. And you know what happens if you open your chest.'

'What?'

'You don't know anything! If you open your chest, you die. See, this is what I mean. They didn't send you to discover the light. You don't know anything about light. You don't know how anything works. They just didn't want to deal with your dead body. So why don't we go back and stir up their nice, neat little world for them?'

'No wonder Chugga is so careful with his injury,' I said, ignoring Ages' suggestion. I remembered waking one morning to a clanking sound and seeing the Three coming back out of the darkness. The memory was vague, but now I could imagine they'd just tidied away a body. Had someone been missing? I couldn't remember anyone else clearly, except Bassa.

'It's painful,' said Ages, 'and difficult. A few weeks before I left, I saw this guy open his chest. They carried him out into the darkness afterwards.'

'How did he do it?'

'He died, you idiot! Why do you want to know how he killed himself?'

'Why didn't you do anything? You could have stopped him.'

'Why bother? There's something wrong with that place. We have to go back. It's time to break up that stupid, complacent club and start a new one. And mess with the Three.'

'You haven't dreamed about the light,' I said.

'How do you know?'

'You wouldn't feel like that about people if you had.'

'Maybe I have dreamed about it.' His voice came closer until it was right in my ear. 'Maybe I have … maybe I have … maybe I have.'

I let out a whimper and ran again. I don't know why he scared me so much. The fear came from deep down and I couldn't control it. This time I ran for longer, changing direction multiple times.

Something brushed past me and I recoiled, but it didn't grab me. It stood in one spot, rustling lightly. I moved away and bumped into more. It was taller than my head; redweed, I suspected, but I wasn't staying to find out. I pushed through it, protecting my shoulder with my hand. My legs became tangled and I freed them hastily, then moved to run but fell, still tangled, hitting my forehead on the ground with a loud clang. Unimaginable brightness burst inside my head, dancing and lingering in my vision. Vibrations quivered in the earth.

'The monsters are coming,' called Ages. 'Pry open your chest and die, you'll never find the light.'

'But I have,' I murmured, staring. The brightness in my eyes wasn't fading. Lights bobbed and grew, separating and re-joining, finally coming together in a beautiful blinding mass. I blinked and sat up. It was a candle, burning behind glass in someone's chest, just like I'd seen in my dream, and it was coming towards me.

'Bassa?'

Ages laughed, but the sound faded like he'd been smothered.

The woman wasn't Bassa. She was smaller, and she moved smoothly and silently. Her skin was well-polished and gleamed in her candlelight. She began to break away the tall growths of redweed that trapped me. 'Sorry I couldn't find you sooner. You were running all over the place.'

'I was scared.'

'I know.'

'What's the thing I can feel coming from your hands?' Her smile and her voice were full of the same indescribable quality, the feeling from my dream. Soft, comforting … what was it?

She looked at me thoughtfully. 'Warmth, maybe? I'm definitely warm.'

'And what colour is your fire?'

'It's not my fire,' she said. 'But the colour is a bit of white, some yellow; I think you could call it gold.' She pulled me free and caught me in her arms before I fell. The … *warmth* … radiated out of her chest.

'What's the opposite of warm?'

'Cold.'

I wriggled out of her grip, feeling awkward and clunky and dull and rough. 'Where did you get your candle lit?' I asked hurriedly. 'I want mine to burn too.'

She laughed. 'Makes my job easier. But be prepared. I have to open your chest and mine to spread the light from my candle to yours. It's painful.'

'I'll die,' I said.

'Only for a moment.'

She brought out a blunt blade and fitted it into the edge of the glass in my front. I braced myself. There was a pop, and a square rim of metal was in her hands.

'That wasn't bad,' I said, and then I saw the compassion in her face. I looked down. The glass panel was still in me. On one side it had a hinge; the other three sides were lined by rows of tiny round fasteners.

We were just getting started.

She flicked her cover off. Then she inserted the blade into one of my fasteners, turning it a quarter turn. With a body-shaking clunk, it came free and fell to the ground. My teeth chattered with the pain.

'Twenty-nine to go,' she said. 'Now …'

'Stop. Please, stop.'

I rushed away, pausing outside the furthest reach of her light. She stepped towards me and I moved away again. I didn't want to be near that blade.

'Pathetic!' said Ages. 'Go back and punch her in the face!'

I turned my back on the sound of his voice and looked towards the woman's light. She was standing motionless, waiting.

Now the skittering was coming up behind me. I flinched and went rigid. Insects. Monsters. Or had it been Ages all along? I pictured him dancing, tapping away in the dark. He could be a giant insect for all I had seen. Then movement caught my eye. One, two, three things were running past my feet, *skittering* along. More came every moment.

One ran up my leg and climbed to my shoulder, where it balanced on the edge of the hole. I stood very still, hardly breathing, disgusted at first, then curious. Its tiny, clawed hands detached a scrap of redweed caught just inside my shoulder. It watched me with bright eyes before it nibbled on the scrap. I could see its nose and ears twitching. Through my metal skin, I felt the scratching of tiny feet, a quick delicate pulse, and *warmth.* I'd never seen anything so soft and alive.

Once the last vestige of redweed was gone, it scurried down to join the others. All of them headed towards the woman. She laughed and squatted down to stroke them as they gathered around her.

There was a scramble behind me and a crunching sound. 'Those don't work either.'

'No! You monster!' I turned and punched into the darkness, right, left, right, hitting nothing.

'Come on!' yelled Ages, 'Come on! Fight! Fight!'

So I ran again, desperately avoiding the little creatures alongside me. In a moment, I was almost on top of the woman.

'I don't want to be like him. I don't want cold. I want warmth, even if it hurts! Please do it right now!'

She smiled. 'I'm sorry I rushed you before. I should remember what it's like.' She glanced at the hole left by the first fastener. 'Now I'll do one of mine.'

And she did, wincing. One of mine, one of hers, and so on, around our glass doors. Hers came out smoothly, mine squeaked and groaned. The pain grew worse as we went on. By the third row of fasteners, I was seeing her through a haze. I hoped she wasn't feeling as bad as I was. I needed her to function.

Ten, nine, eight … four, three … one.

We were both breathing raggedly. She swung my door open on its hinges, then hers, and took out her candle. The quivering golden light came towards me and faded into darkness.

I woke to find my breathing normal. The warmth had spread out into my fingertips and toes. Behind my closed door, the candle flame gleamed. The little creatures were no longer in sight.

The woman sat in front of me, her head hanging and her door swung open. The candle in her chest burned very low, flickering as though it was on the verge of going out. I leant over and slammed the glass closed, watching as the flame sprang up steadily again.

She opened her eyes and took a breath. 'Thank you, Linton.'

For the first time, I noticed her name stamped on her chest, like mine, above her glass. 'No, thank *you,* Bly.'

A low clinking filled the silence as she replaced each of my fasteners. It took longer than removing them, but it was much less painful. I realised that this was what she did. She wandered the darkness, finding people to light their candles.

'What if people don't help you back?' I asked. 'You'd die.'

'So far, they have helped. I think once their candle's burning, they can't help caring.' As she replaced her fasteners, she glanced up at me. 'There are lots of us doing this. I wouldn't mind your company if you wanted to join me … us.'

'I don't know what we'll do yet,' I said awkwardly.

'We?'

'Not Ages. I don't ever want to see him again.'

'You probably won't,' she said. 'Don't you know what he is?'

'A monster.' I didn't even want to think about him.

'In a way.' Bly popped my cover back into place. 'You're from the plain where the Three work, aren't you? You came from that way.' She pointed, and I noted the direction.

We sat in silence for a moment, and I felt her eyes on me. 'If you change your mind, you'll be very welcome. And we could fix that, too.' She touched my damaged shoulder.

Questions crowded my mind, and I knew Bly would have answers. She offered the chance of being repaired, not just maintained; and helping people, not just existing.

But first, there was Bassa.

I stood up, pressing my cover to make sure it was secure. 'Is there anything else I should know?'

'You'll need a new candle at some stage. Come find us then. And don't lie down.'

As I left, I glanced over my shoulder and saw her light change to a faint glow as she turned in the opposite direction.

I walked steadily and patiently. Sometimes there was a soft breath of air on the back of my neck, and I worried that it was Ages.

It made me want to run, but I kept walking, and soon the feeling disappeared.

It took me two days to reach the plain, so I had to sleep in the dark alone. I made a pile of rocks to lean against and ate strands of redweed as I watched the sun set. Its glow was even fainter now that I carried my own light with me. The tiny creatures arrived to share my supper, then skittered away. They were nice to pat and were certainly not insects. I wished I'd asked Bly what they were called. I closed my eyes and imagined Bassa's back behind mine, each of us propping up the other.

When I woke, my body felt different. *Warm.* I wasn't shaking, and I could move my joints straightaway without stiffness and pain, as if sleep had rejuvenated me.

The sun was already overhead. I set off at a fast walk over the hills, soon seeing the blue dome of light emerge from the dark. It spread out to fill half my vision, then the whole of it. The sounds of the clanging slaps and chanting rose, and as I came closer, I could even hear the swish of the brooms.

I paused outside the edge. Everything inside was going on as usual. Nothing had changed, and nobody seemed to have noticed the spot of golden fire floating towards them, hovering very near, just beyond their light.

The ground around the plain had been stripped almost bare, but I found a small handful of redweed and chewed on it as I watched Bassa. She was playing, of course. What else was there to do? She was laughing and looked relaxed. Part of the club.

I thought of Bly and her friends who would welcome me. But the game was ending. I stepped into the light of the cold, blue fires.

The Three's heads went up immediately and the brooms fell from their hands. I smiled as I caught the eye of others—Chugga, Dior, Oila; I remembered all their names now. Nobody responded. Had they forgotten me? Had I been gone longer than I'd thought?

Then I realised. They thought I'd been snubbing their game for days. They didn't even realise I'd been far away, out of their plain. To them, I was either in the club or out, and if I was out, I was nothing. That didn't bother me, but if they refused to look, they would never see the light.

Bassa hadn't moved. I walked over and sat down near her, as if waiting for the next game. She shifted uncomfortably, but said nothing. She kept her head down and her eyes lowered.

I took a moment to watch her—the serious corner of her mouth and the blue glints around the edge of the dent in her head. Then I moved across and sat knee to knee with her.

Her eyelids flicked up, then down. 'You did it. That's nice.'

'You can't imagine,' I said. 'It looks a bit faint here in the firelight, but you should see it in the dark.'

'Did it hurt?'

'You can't imagine,' I murmured again.

'You're different,' she said. 'You don't clank.'

'I'm not that different.' I touched my glass door, then hers.

She started to pull away, then stopped and grasped my hand, holding it against herself.

'What *is* that?' She wove her fingers through mine, rubbing against them, as though trying to absorb all the feeling she could. With an awestruck smile, she looked into my eyes. 'It's so beautiful.'

I could hardly get the words to the tip of my tongue. The fire inside me had woken all my senses and her touch sent me reeling. I held her hand tightly, struggling to speak. 'Bassa, it's *warmth.*'

THE CHOICE

Anne Hamilton

I heard a dragon singing, singing a lay by the sea. A dark, sweet song, full of high fluted cadence, full of calling. It summoned me as I waited by the lattice, listening to the rise and fall of its lament, listening to the grey sea.

Aislin said, 'Come to the circle.'

'I hear a sound,' I said.

Edin said, 'Come to the fireside.'

'I hear my name,' I said.

Isla said, 'Come to the table.'

'It's only a dragon singing.' But I did not go. I did not go to the circle. I did not go to the fireside. I did not go to the table. For I knew it was more than a dragon. I knew that voice as I knew my own.

Owain said, 'It won't come here.'

'Give away your listening,' said Usain. 'Sit by the fire.'

But there was no fire for me. Only strange copper-green embers. I had been cold for months—all the last summer long.

'I'll just tell it to go away,' I said. I left the lattice and stepped out the blood-hallowed door onto the dreaming cliffs, into the wakening night.

'Don't go far,' said Edin.

Usain said, 'It can hear you from the top of the cliff. Don't go further.'

'Walk in the moonlight,' said Aislin.

But there was no moonlight. No moon in all the lace-grey sky. No glimmering stars. Only the smudged light, dove-grey on ash-grey, folding and unfolding. Dancing, aurora-flickering, a nimbus veil obscuring the harsher night.

'Don't go far,' said Isla.

'Don't go far,' echoed Owain.

But no one came after me. No one then. No one now. Only one came ever, but not for me. Years later, Edin heard a dragon sing for him and came safely to the isle where the blue fire runs.

But on that night, with the dragon song calling deep—deep to deep in my soul—I went down the steep cliff, and my feet were swift and steady though I had never been that way before.

Down.

Down to the forbidden sea.

And still the dragon sang, calling my name in my voice. An ancient lay that I well-remembered, yet well-remembered that I had never heard before. Flutes and dreams and high sky-skirling, all calling me recklessly down to the shore.

Low tide it was, with the ash-grey shells lying scattered on the black edges of small tidal pools. The sands were wide, bleached-grey and slate-grey. Wide with cascades of dark and silent water falling fast to the sea.

The dragon song filled me with sadness and longing, plucking at old, discarded dreams. Yes, wistful and noble was that song, high and mournful was that lay.

I walked across the corrugated sand. A mist of thorns—cloud-soft and needle-sharp, high as a fortress hedge—rose behind me. I walked on and the mist followed.

I stopped. The mist slowed, undulated, waited. It scalloped

around me and raised itself in leisurely folds, wide and tall. Arrow-sharp prickles volleyed from its highest crest, skimming across my bare skin. Too late, I understood the threat. The mist was sentient. A dark shepherd, it was herding me down to the sea.

I knew I was alone now—alone except for a mist as high as a hill and sharp as a thicket. Alone except for a dragon, singing of enchanting doom. The dragon waited and the mist followed.

I walked on. I came at last to the edge of the sea, but there was no dragon there, no sign there had ever been one. There was only a man, not unlike myself, dressed in grey and leaning on a black stave. From the tip of the stave, summer-green flames winged at the air.

It was the stave singing the dragon song.

The man lifted his face. And it was my image that he lifted. No twin. No shadowling. No doppelgänger or follower. He lifted my face because he and I were one.

He said nothing, merely raised the black stave. And so the mist of thorns, high as a mountain, sharp as a field of daggers, shrank before it. And the wild, flickering, summer-blighted flames tongued at the air, singing ensorcellment, weaving enthrallment, threading enchantment in every note.

'Come to the circle.'

'Come to the fireside.'

'Come to the table.'

But it was not my hearth and home that the flames sang of—not the house where Aislin and Edin, Isla and Owain and Usain waited.

'Come to the Dark Isles … come … come … come to the Dark Isles.'

All the tongues were my voice.

The man turned away, walked along the shore, and lifted his stave—always, always, always against the sea. The mist of thorns rose, high as the moon, sharp as damascene swords. I followed the man and the stave that sang the dragon song.

He came to a long sable ship lapped by cold, grey wavelets, drawn high upon the dark strand. Light as a feather, he stepped aboard and set the stave beneath the pale curved mast. And then he turned and reached forth a hand to me.

But I—I clasped hand to hand behind my back.

'Go away,' I said.

He smiled and shook his head. He turned away and turned again. Turned to face me.

'Go away,' I repeated.

Again he smiled and shook his head. He turned away and turned again. Turned to face me.

'Go away and never return.'

His eyes narrowed, but the taunting smile remained. He turned away and turned again. Turned to face me.

What words could I offer to make him understand? To make him leave? 'I reject the summoning.' My heart trembled as I spoke. My voice was steel and strong with a firmness I did not feel. 'I revoke the invitation. I renounce the covenant. I call sea and sky as my witnesses. Go. Away. And. Never. Return.'

There was a shriek of pain then—the black stave writhed in an agony of sound, though not so deep an agony as the cry of loss in my soul.

I knew what I had done. There was no place for me now. The false summer-green flames died as the stave shuddered and cold black fire licked along its length. The voice that spoke from the stave was no longer mine, 'We will go for now, feeble one. But not forever. Power may not tempt you, but mortality will.'

I shook my head.

The stave laughed, shrill with scorn. 'Perhaps not your mortality, feeble one. But that of those you will come to love.' The mockery ceased. 'Our ship will wait for you again on the far shore of the isle where the blue fire runs.'

Then the man who bore my face faded to a wraith, my features wrenching in age and pain as they dissolved in the lambent air. The long, sable ship drew back from the strand and swung into the shallows of its own accord. A dark sail unfurled itself, flicked a skirling wind from deck to mast-top, and then the ship was gone.

I turned.

And turned again.

The mist of thorns was nearly upon me and had grown as high as the distant stars, as dangerous as poison. I dared not return through it. But I knew no other path.

I had not been afraid facing the man with my face whose stave sang the dragon song. But now I was.

I heard a sound.

Behind me.

My heart juddered as another song called to me.

Another song. I tried to close my ears, but it seeped through my skin and, tingling, frisked into my blood and found the doors into my bones. It too was a song from beyond the sea. Free and keen, burning it was. Exquisite burning. My bones were on fire.

Silver in a crucible. I turned to hear it more closely. For all my training, I recognised nothing about it. Not the tune. Not the words. Not the harmony. Not the cadence. No song like it was in our records. Not in any library of the kingdom, not on the green Summer Isle, nor the golden Dales of Spring, nor the Winter Steppes. Yet no song like it could ever come out of the Dark Isles. And what other lands were there but the Three-Quartered Kingdom and the Dark Isles in all the world?

None that I knew.

But the song …

A new song.

Full of calling. Silver in a crucible. Once. Twice. Thrice refined?

The dragon song was but a pale reflection of the new song. A shadow of it. Thrice-deep it was. No, thrice-deep and more. Deepest to deep. Sevenfold refined. Enchanting, but not enchanted.

Enthralling, but not enthralled. Ensorcelling, but not ensorcelled.

What kind of calling was this?

It was setting fire to my memory, burning, burning. Ashes, ashes, all fall down. And then I knew—the dragon song was gone, all knowledge of it, all remembrance, all that might trigger my heart into answering its lure once more.

Disorientated with freedom, I stepped and swayed, unthinking, unknowing. I stepped a solitary stride into the forbidden sea. I felt the wash of warm wave and, hasty, hasty, I turned to the shore. I leapt for the line of shells on the bleached-grey, slate-grey sand. But unknowing again and unthinking again, I turned as I leapt and circled back around to the sea. Shallow grey water lapped, warm and gentle, against my feet as I landed. And a flat stone, opal-flecked, rose to push up my foremost foot. Just to the top of the waves.

I stopped. Stood. Glanced at the mist. It had stopped.

I listened. And softly hummed a bar of the new song. The mist retreated.

I hummed louder. The mist shrank.

I had a choice. The disorientation of freedom hazed my mind.

I could return. I could go back to the circle, to the fireside, to the table. I could go back to Aislin and Edin, Isla, Owain and Usain. I could go back to them, singing the new song. But I knew the companions of my heart could not hear it. For I knew them as well as I knew myself. They would not forsake the illusion, lest the new song prove elusive and they be left with nothing.

The companions of my heart, the ones who'd sworn to defend each other forever, had not come after me. They had not risked the loss of circle and fireside and table. If not for me, if not for their soul-sworn vows, why for a song they could not hear?

I looked down. The smooth, flat stone beneath my feet was hard and solid. I ventured another foot forward. Yet another stone, indigo and shot through with dazzling gold, rose to meet me like a stretch of pavement. The grey shallow water lapped, warmer still and ever gentler, at my ankles, then fell away from the stone. I took another step. And another. And another.

I had made my choice. Soon the shallows were behind me and the turquoise sea played with the pearly light of the midnight sun. Deep green waves rose like towers to meet me. Then, as they crested, they bowed down low, as if in honour. Gently, peaceably, they passed me by with a silvery blue wake. Stones rose, one by one, before me, and sank straightaway behind me. I knew not where I was or where I was going.

But the song … the new song … was ever clearer. Silver-bright, mirror-bright.

The Summer Isle behind me was a thin emerald line. I could see nothing ahead but the woad-blue horizon.

It was far too late to turn back.

If ever I could have returned, I could no longer. And then, descending from the clouds, I saw the first of the blue flames. The fire rushed like petals on the wind. And my heart, at last, remembered a thousand, thousand dreams of home.

LUMINESCENT LOVE

Stephanie Martin

Louise was staring out at the beautiful view of the reflective, icy expanse of Enceladus—the unwelcoming moon she and Bryce had made home eight years ago when they were just fifteen. In the distance, you could often see the brilliant, blue eruptions of the cryovolcanoes at the south pole, and Saturn loomed, never clear due to the ring.

Bryce threw the heavy wrench into his toolbox. The clanking of metal on metal filled the air, startling Louise. He reached over the table in front of him, picked up a red scrap towel and wiped his brows. He looked down at Louise and grinned. 'Time to take this old girl for a spin, I reckon.'

Louise nodded, fiddling a spare screw between her fingers. She watched as Bryce put on his helmet, highlighting a round, stubble-filled face and covering the dark brown hair that was long enough that it stuck out of the helmet. She smiled up at him. 'Careful getting out of the ring. You know the cryovolcanoes have been pretty volatile lately and Jasper reckons it's making the ring even more unstable. Probably why all these darn ships land on our doorstep all battered and bruised.'

'I'd say it's because a decent pilot is rarer than a Lumo Moth these days.' Bryce laughed as he settled into the pilot's seat. 'Besides, Jasper hasn't flown since we got here, Lou. That's why he needs us. He's a heck of a space mechanic, but he's not up for these maintenance runs anymore. I think I know that ring better than he does these days.'

Lou shook her head affectionately as he peeled away and took off. She watched the spaceship slowly disappear. They'd been working on that one ship for almost two weeks, and every afternoon Bryce took it for a maintenance run. Each time he came back unhappy with its performance, which seemed a bit strange to her. Louise wasn't sure why he hadn't been able to turn this one over yet, but then again its owner, their friend Murdock, expected nothing but perfection.

Murdock ran supplies between Earth and the outer settlements twice a year, had been doing so for thirty years, since he himself left home as a teenager. He'd been their chauffeur when they'd left Earth, and Lou had been sure to send letters addressed to her father back with him every time he came through. She never received anything in return, never expected to, but each time it hurt a little more. Bryce had always been there to hold her hand when she needed it, to help soothe the pain, but it never truly went away.

While Bryce was gone, Lou decided to visit Murdock to see if he'd brought a letter. She knew there wouldn't be one, and as she walked to his bunker she grew more and more frustrated with herself for needing to ask.

She stood in front of the door, hands hanging by her side, her eyes glued to the floor. She tried to convince herself to walk away, but she'd come this far. With a sigh, she raised her hand and knocked.

When Murdock opened the door, Lou smiled. The lines of his tanned face deepened as he smiled warmly down at her. He had his long brown hair tied back and his gold earring shone in his right ear. The jangle of his gold bracelets knocking together made her laugh as he swept her into a hug.

'Lou, my girl, how are you? How's my ship going?' He pulled

out of the embrace and held her at arm's length.

'Bryce is still working on it and I'm okay.'

'Just okay? Well, that's just not good enough. You best come in and have a cookie and hot chocolate. I don't think I'll ever get used to the cold out here.'

Murdock ushered Lou inside, his gold bangles clinking together once more. His bunker never changed—it was colourful, extravagant and messy. He moved a rainbow knit sweater, an equally colourful scarf and some books off the chair and gestured for her to sit.

'That boy of yours is taking a while. He hasn't lost his touch, has he?'

Lou looked over at him and frowned. 'I'm not even sure what's wrong with it anymore. He takes it for a run every day, but he still isn't happy with it.'

Murdock nodded. 'Well, there's a reason I come here for my repairs. That boy is the best space mechanic in the outer settlements. Jasper was one hell of a teacher. And of course I come to see you, little Lou. You're not so little any more though. How long have you two been here?'

Lou smiled at Murdock. She felt a wave of pride sweep through her for Bryce. He'd been broken when she'd met him, and he'd thrown everything he had into this place and learning the trade Jasper was willing to teach. Louise had felt like she kind of floated, unsure what her role would be out here. 'We've been here eight years. Although I went off to Titan for a few months.'

'Ah yes, I remember that little rebellious act. I turned up here and Bryce was moping around the workshop like the universe was collapsing. Couldn't stop ranting about how big the workshop felt when it was only him and Jasper.'

'I didn't mean to upset him.' Louise sighed and picked a book up off the coffee table. She looked over towards some letters on the bench. 'Anything for me this run?'

Murdock took the book off her, placed a steaming cup in her

hands and knelt in front of her. 'There isn't, but you know that. Let it go, Lou. That man will never be happy, no matter what you do. Your family, your life, it's here.'

Louise could feel her eyes starting to water. Murdock had never been so blunt with her. 'If I can find a Lumo Moth, he'll let me go back. He'll welcome me back. He'll be proud.'

The sad look in Murdock's eyes made her angry, but he took the cup from her as soon as he had placed it in her hands and put it on the table.

He took her hands and spoke gently, 'Lou, those moths have been driven to near extinction and your father played a massive role in that. And for what? Life on Earth shouldn't be prolonged. That planet can't sustain the population as it is. Do you really want to go back there? You've made a life for yourself here. Would you leave Bryce and Jasper and everyone you've met here?'

Lou could feel the heat rising in her chest, her palms growing sweaty with anger. Who was he to talk to her like that? But as she looked into his kind, patient eyes, the anger dissolved away. He was like a father to her, as was Jasper, more than her own had ever been. He'd always been too busy with his money-making schemes and climbing the political ladder to love her. He'd made it to the top by almost entirely exterminating a rare and apparently beautiful species, and neglecting his daughter.

She knew Murdock was right. This was her home now. She had people she loved here, and more importantly, people who loved her back.

***

Louise left Murdock's bunker with a swing in her step. On her way home, she decided to swing by the Change Room to satisfy her sweet tooth. The café was the place to be any time of the day, any day of the week. It was warm, friendly, there was good music, good food, good drinks and a gondola that took you up to an upper-class restaurant for those fancy nights out.

She remembered the one time she'd visited the restaurant SkyView. Bryce had taken her out on her eighteenth birthday, insisting the ridiculous cost didn't matter, that it was worth it. She hadn't been able to stop smiling the entire night and once had to go to the bathroom and just stand at the sink for a moment to compose herself. Bryce had been incredibly sweet, and later that night, after they'd taken the gondola back down and were hanging out in the Change Room, they'd shared their first kiss in a back booth.

Now as she walked in, she smiled at the memory.

'Hi, Carly,' she called to the petite girl behind the counter with short dark curls around a pale, freckled face. Carly gave her a quick wave and a grin and resumed her conversation with the guy in front of her. Lou hadn't seen him before but took up a seat beside him and waited.

'We take any change, no matter how small, in any currency, that's why it's called the Change Room,' Carly said with a trained bounce to her voice. Louise wondered how many times she said that on a daily basis.

The man nodded and resumed eating his meal at the counter. Carly turned to Louise. 'What can I do for you, Lou?'

'Can I get two eclairs please?'

'Special occasion?'

'No, just feeling like a sweet treat.'

'Well, Bryce is always telling me yours are better, so you must be working to improve our recipe, hey? Maybe planning on starting a rival store?' Carly winked.

Lou laughed and shook her head. 'Don't be silly.'

She handed over the change and walked home, eclairs in hand and Bryce on her mind.

***

As Bryce pulled away from Enceladus and started navigating the ring, his smile dropped away. He wasn't lying to Lou, at least, not exactly.

It was the same argument he'd had with himself every afternoon for two weeks. It still ate away at him, made his insides churn and his heart ache. She'd never forgive him if she found out about this, but he'd never forgive himself if he didn't keep this secret.

He sighed as he began his descent onto the small moon, floating towards the green and grey ripples that appeared to be its surface. The moon sat just outside of Saturn; a moon that looked like any other; a moon that no one really cared for. He flew through the ripples and was able to see the familiar world below, one he had been visiting for the past two weeks.

Bryce remembered his first visit, when he'd lost control of this spaceship. He'd wrestled with the ship until it had crash-landed on this little moon in the middle of nowhere. He'd thought he was going to die when the ship passed straight through those green and grey ripples, revealing the wondrous world below.

Thoughts of Lou left his mind as his eyes adjusted to the view. Every afternoon for the past two weeks, he had his breath taken away by the beauty of the moon. The bioluminescent blue of the moths lit the darkness, leaving trails of green, pink and purple, radiating out to light up a lush forest and illuminating the stunning array of night-blooming flowers. The Lumo Moths were just as magnificent as he had been told.

As Bryce touched down in the place he'd accidentally cleared during his ugly landing two weeks before, he again marvelled at the size of the queen of the night, moonflower and evening primrose surrounding him. The flowers themselves were twice the size of his head, with stalks longer than his legs.

His heart thundered and his stomach flip-flopped with excitement and anticipation as he climbed out of the spaceship, and, as his feet touched the ground, he was in awe of the sparks of light that shot out and rippled across the ground like a wave, eventually dispersing into a sea of vines in the forest beyond, barely discernible at the edge of his vision. The forest rose into the inky blackness where the canopy spread thickly across the entire moon, masking this magical paradise from the outside world.

As his footsteps shot enchanting light in all directions, a moth flapped towards him, slow and graceful. She was beautiful. She landed in the clearing and waited for Bryce to come to her. She lowered her head so he was looking her in the eye, and he reached up and touched her soft cheek. One of her feathery antennae tickled his face in return. He moved around to her left side to inspect her wing and one of her legs. He was careful not to touch her wing, but he ran his hand over her injured leg.

'You've healed up nicely, girl. I can't keep coming every day to check on you. I finished fixing this ship a week ago and Lou and Jasper are going to start getting suspicious if I don't turn her over. I'll come back whenever I get the chance, OK? And I promise there'll be no more crashing or clipping you or any of your brethren. Lucky you were quick enough to move out of the way. Mostly.'

As he spoke, he could have sworn she was listening. Her head tilted to the side occasionally, reminding him of the puppy he'd had back on Earth as a kid. He sighed. 'Oh, how my mother would have loved to see this place. She lived and died for your species, you know.'

Bryce sat on a nearby vine, vibrant colour shooting outwards and upwards, in contrast to the anguish he felt deep in his stomach and chest. He ran his hand over his stubble and hung his head. He felt the feathery antennae touch his cheek again and looked up, but his eyes weren't focused on the moth before him, he was lost in memory.

They came in flashes.

He was eight, crouched next to his mother in their garden, her sunlit face smiling down at him as they watched the ants marching their way through the flower bed.

'All life is precious, Bryce. It's not right for one species to kill another for any reason, but especially not to prolong life beyond what is natural.'

He was eleven and felt the full force of pain and loss as he stood at his grandmother's grave. 'Those moths could have saved her.' His fists were curled tightly, his nails biting the palms of his hands, and he was shaking, from anger or devastation he wasn't sure.

His mother crouched down in front of him, kind and gentle as always. 'Your gran had a long and happy life. She wanted to rest. She was content with her time here, and she never would have traded another life for her own.'

He was twelve, and his mother pulled him into a hug and kissed him on the forehead. 'I have to go now, Tiger. Be good, be brave, be kind. I love you.'

Bryce was trying to be tough, but tears stung at his eyes. 'I don't want you to go, Mum. When will you be back?'

He was thirteen, and he was sitting on a bench in the botanic gardens, the place his mother used to take him all the time. Their special place. He hadn't seen her in almost a year. Apparently, the mission was going well, but he was still angry. Why couldn't she have just stayed on Earth and continued to educate people there? Why did she have to try and reach out to the settlements? He hated those Lumo Moths! He wished they didn't exist or at least had never been discovered.

Deep down, he knew a living thing should not be sacrificed to unnaturally prolong the life of another, but he hadn't recognised that then. All he'd known was that those moths had taken her away from him.

A few months before his fourteenth birthday, his aunt held him in a tight embrace. He could feel her tears soaking his t-shirt.

It was his uncle who spoke first. 'I'm sorry, Bryce. They say your mother's ship was targeted when re-entering the atmosphere.'

He was fifteen, and he was walking onto a spaceship for the first time. Part of him was disgusted, part of him was thrilled. He was still filled with rage and bitterness over what happened to his mother. He'd been despondent and distant since learning of her death. He'd grown apart from his family and friends and had given up most of his hobbies. He felt like life was just happening around him and he had no purpose.

So, the first chance he'd got, he'd left Earth behind with no hopes or dreams for the future. But the thrill he felt upon entering a spaceship for the first time made him feel like he was in control, for the first time in a long time. He didn't know it yet, but this was a new beginning.

He'd been on the spaceship for five days and hadn't made any friends. Everyone else he'd come across had been too cheerful, helpful or inquisitive. And then he'd met Lou. He'd been drawn to her the day he'd laid eyes on her. It was her short, honey-blonde hair and her hazel eyes that had first drawn him in. She'd seemed a little wild and intimidating one moment, yet soft and sweet the next.

Louise was also fifteen and leaving Earth as a means to escape her family drama. Since then, they'd shared an unexplainable connection. It was the kind that made it seem as though the universe revolved around them. There were too many things that had thrown them together time and time again for it not to. She was his best friend.

That was the memory that brought him back to the present, and he blinked up at the beautiful Lumo Moth calmly looking down at him. The familiar feelings of sadness and dread that he'd felt when he'd left Earth were still sitting in his chest.

Louise had been a guiding light in the darkness, a ray of sunshine in every cloudy day. She'd helped him piece himself back together and he'd learnt to smile again. He'd let go of his anger and rage, though it had flared momentarily the first time he'd seen the moths as he'd plummeted down into this clearing. But once he'd looked around and taken in their breathtaking world, he'd finally understood his mother's fascination with and dedication to these beautiful creatures. She'd given her life to protect them, and when he'd truly understood it all, he'd vowed to do the same. Though not, he thought, at the cost of the love and friendship that had brought him back from the brink of darkness.

He stood up and cupped the moth's furry cheeks in his hand. 'How about I bring you another visitor tomorrow?'

The moth stared back at him with large, glistening eyes. He walked back to the spaceship and it followed. He always felt sad to leave, but this time felt worse. He didn't know how Lou would react to seeing this place, but she had to know. With one last look at the moth and the brilliant world he'd discovered, he climbed back into the spaceship and left. He'd be able to convince Lou to see the world through his eyes.

They had such a good relationship. They often joked about a fantasy life or holiday somewhere, but he felt like nothing was better than what they had, and he was pretty sure she felt the same. Would this secret that he'd kept from her be their breaking point? He had to trust that they were stronger than that. But he knew their past and their family ties would make that difficult.

***

Louise was making pasta for dinner when Bryce walked in the door. 'Hey, how did it go?'

He placed a soft kiss on her head. 'Smells good, sweetheart.' He walked over to the pot and picked up a piece of pasta with a fork before placing it on the chopping board to cool. 'It was good. Come with me tomorrow. There's something I want to show you.'

She smiled up at him as he wrapped his arms around her and brushed her lips across his. No one else got to see this gentle, tender side to him and she felt so lucky that he shared that part of himself with her. 'Of course. Everything OK?'

Louise tilted her head slightly as she saw unease in his eyes. 'Yeah, I think so. You'll understand tomorrow.'

A small frown was the only indication she gave that his words bothered her. But then she grinned. 'I got us eclairs for dessert, but

Carly says you can't keep telling her mine are better. She's getting jealous.'

Bryce smiled and traced the lines that ran from her nose to her lips with his finger. The gentle, sensuous brush made her tingle and must have shown in her eyes because he laughed.

She loved that cheeky laugh of his. It was one of the things that always managed to get her out of the terrible moods that thinking about her family inevitably led to. That, and his ability to talk about any random thing at the drop of a hat.

***

The following morning Bryce told Jasper they were taking the day off as soon as they got back with Murdock's ship. Jasper's raised eyebrows were his only show of surprise, and Louise imagined they matched her own. They almost never took days off, unless you counted early on when they'd had three-hour lunch breaks to spend more time together, which seemed silly since they worked together most days anyway.

They were silent as they left Enceladus, and Lou knew he was nervous. She had no idea why. Many possible reasons flitted through her brain. But as they approached the small moon and passed through its canopy, what she beheld was beyond anything she could have imagined. The emotions that warred within her as they descended and landed in the clearing gave her an immediate headache. Wonder, excitement, redemption, dismay, betrayal.

She barely remembered getting out of the ship and she just stared numbly as the colour bloomed beneath her feet and shot off into the distance. She couldn't comprehend what she was seeing and didn't know how to feel about it at all. Bryce was silent, watching her carefully but not touching her.

She walked a full circle around the spaceship very slowly. She watched the moths as they danced by above and around her. There were so many thoughts swirling in her head. Thoughts of her father and how he'd do anything to see this, thoughts of how she might finally gain his attention and respect. Thoughts of Bryce's history, what she knew of his mother and the sacrifice she'd made. Thoughts of the life she and Bryce had made together.

When she got back to him, their eyes locked. She remembered the first day she'd seen those eyes. Truly seen him. She'd gotten lost in them, with their mesmerising golden and brown flecks and the endless and ever-changing blue that sometimes took on hints of green. She'd known he was good and true. She'd known him to be someone she loved.

Now, as she once again sunk deeper and deeper into those eyes, it was like she was re-living every great moment they'd had together. She realised he was the only one who truly understood her. The only one she was completely comfortable around. He was her best friend. They talked about everything, the good and the bad.

Except this, apparently. Tears stung her eyes and her throat ached from the lump that had lodged there. He hadn't told her about this. That was the thing that hurt the most.

'You were supposed to be the one I could truly trust.'

Louise could tell from the devastated look on Bryce's face that the hurt and betrayal she was feeling broke his heart. He stepped towards her and cupped her face in his hands.

'Lou, I love you an unbelievable amount. I love you to the stars and back. I love you to Earth and back one million times over. You mean the world to me.' Louise felt the warmth flood her cheeks. Bryce paused before he said, 'Do you plan to go back? And if you do, why? Is it for them?

'Stop living in the past, Lou. Look at the present and the future, at what you have here, at what we have here. We could continue building a love-filled life together. It doesn't even have to be here. I'd go anywhere with you. But I can't give up this secret. Please don't ask me to. I know it goes against everything your father taught, but destroying this place, these creatures, it goes against everything *I* was taught. We might be too different for us to work, but I'm asking you to keep this secret. Please, Lou.'

Louise could feel him watching her, scrutinising her every facial expression, every move she made, trying to gauge exactly what she was thinking. She watched as the moth came up behind Bryce and seemed to communicate with him. She didn't know what to make of it. It was much bigger than she'd expected.

Floating in front of her was the one thing her father wanted most in the world. Not just her father—almost everyone in the universe. And flying around her were hundreds more. It was too much to take in.

'Bryce, take me home,' she choked out.

She watched his shoulders slump and he turned inward. She recognised that look but hadn't seen it on him in years. She watched as he turned back to the moth and patted its cheek. Again, it reached out and seemed to touch him on the face, almost reassuring him. She couldn't process her feelings; it was almost like she'd felt so much so intensely that her body was now incapable of feeling anything.

***

As Bryce navigated the ring on the ride home feelings of hopelessness threatened to swallow him again. Neither of them said anything, and when he pulled into the garage Lou got out and walked off silently. He knew she needed space, and time to think things over, but not knowing what was going through her mind was killing him. He felt almost physically ill. His heart kept constricting in painful bursts, and his breathing was ragged and erratic. Bryce trudged home to what he knew would be a restless, painful day of agonising over the unknown and pacing so the walls wouldn't close in around him. He hated feeling this way, and it had been a long time since he had.

To keep himself busy Bryce tinkered in his own garage, half-cleaning, half-examining the bits and pieces that made up his many, ever-changing, often-forgotten hobbies. Whatever Louise decided he knew it was unlikely he'd ever see that small moon again.

He didn't want to give up that wondrous world that had brought him peace and closure about his mother. His hands paused on an old rubix cube as he pictured that moth sanctuary, his moth friend, those vibrant colours. He'd fallen in love with that place over the last two weeks.

But as he pictured Louise's eyes, and her face, the way it lit up with joy when she truly smiled, he knew he'd do it. As much as it'd hurt, he'd do it. For her and for them.

***

Once back on Enceladus, Louise made her way to the little bridge around the corner from the Change Room. She liked to sit there and watch the streams of water trickle by. There was a path beneath the bridge and graffiti covered the wall she leant against.

Her mind swirled. So many thoughts and emotions. She held her head in her hands to try and digest them all. She'd longed for her father's attention her entire life and bringing him to these moths would finally get her the approval she needed. Her conversation with Murdock flowed through her mind.

Her father aside, she knew that just one of those moths could make her rich. She could go anywhere, do anything. She could go back to Earth if she wanted or try one of the closer settlements. Try all the settlements. She could be a space nomad, travelling and experiencing any life she chose. Though, in every scenario she pictured, Bryce's face was ultimately all she saw.

As she sat there, determined to be angry at him, she re-lived the memories of the life they'd made together. Their tentative friendship as broken teenagers, talking deep into the night about childhood memories, hopes, dreams and fears. Sharing their first kiss in the Change Room, their ride in the gondola up to SkyView. All the times they'd kissed in this very spot. They'd grown and helped each other in their darkest moments. They completed each other and were there for each other. She sighed. She loved him with all her heart, there was no question.

She stood, wanting to be with him. The rush of blood had her stumbling a little, and she looked at the wall to focus, seeing the graffiti there for the first time. Spray-painted in silver letters was the word 'love'. Taking that as a sign, she ran home.

She burst through the door and flung herself into his arms. 'I choose you, Bryce. I'll keep your secret. But we can't ever go back there. Promise me you won't? If you want to protect them, you can't keep going there.'

Louise watched Bryce stare at her, saw his eyes widen as he took in her words. Initially, he looked stunned and she knew it was likely not just by her choice, but by her resolve to protect the moths when he knew what they meant to her. What they could do for her.

Then, she saw the moment the reality of her words sunk in. While there was a hint of sadness in his eyes she watched as he almost sagged in relief. Then he pulled her into another hug, swung her around and kissed her. 'I promise. You are so amazing. Lou, I really do want to spend the rest of my life with you.'

DESIGNER GHOST

Emily Larkin

Now that I'm thirteen, I'll get my very own ghost.

I can't stop fidgeting in the backseat of Mum's Arrow 3000 on the way to Ghost Designs. I'm nervous, I guess, even though my brother Beckett says the procedure is no big deal, and he should know since he did his work placement at Ghost Designs over the summer.

Beckett and his Etiquette terrier ghost took Mum's passenger seat, even though it's *my* special day. If you ask me, his ghost is doing a rubbish job. Maybe it's malfunctioning and needs to be replaced.

I look out the dark-tinted windows at the jacaranda trees, sweeping the street in purple, and think about how it's not fair that Beckett gets to ride up front, just like it's not fair that he gets to do *everything* first. He's only fourteen—sorry, *fifteen*—months older than me. From the corner of my eye, I see the terrier sit on his lap and paw his chest gently. The dog's body is holographic so, of course, it has no weight and can't really touch him, but it's trying to get his attention.

Beckett flicks his floppy brown hair out of his eyes, and turns to face me. His mouth twists into a smirk. 'You look scared, kiddo.'

I scowl. 'I'm not a kid.'

'Whatever. You sure you can manage one of these?' Beckett pats the terrier, who leans into a touch neither of them can feel. 'You know, Nikki, I heard that ghosts are like roller-coasters at a theme park. You've gotta be a certain height and I just don't know if you're there …'

'Cut that out,' Mum says as she pulls up outside Ghost Designs. The cockatoo ghost on her shoulder chatters in her ear as she puts the Arrow in park. I look out the window again, and the building ahead glitters silver like a giant piece of foil. 'Beckett, remember why you're here?'

'Because you think I'll set the house on fire if I'm left alone?'

'That too. But mostly to *support your sister*. So listen to that dog and be supportive, okay?'

He grumbles something and Mum faces me. 'You ready, sweetie?'

I swallow a lump in my throat and nod.

We clamber out of the Arrow—Beckett running ahead, his dog trotting to keep up—and reach the building. The front doors slide open and then shut with a hiss once we've entered.

The lobby is dotted with large pot plants: palms, and lilies with leaves like green hearts. Framed photos, of people smiling with their translucent blue ghosts beside them, line the walls. I recognise the ghosts as a goat, koala and goanna, and really hope I don't get a goanna.

Mum walks briskly towards the elevator, her cockatoo balanced on her shoulder, and I follow. My hair insists on bursting out of my ponytail, so I tighten the loop holding it in place. The terrier trails after my brother obediently and I remember how it tried to get his attention in the car. I think it was trying to prompt him to check on me; help me manage my nerves. Maybe the thing's not malfunctioning, after all—just doing its best with a charge who doesn't want to listen.

I've got to admit, it made me laugh when Beckett came home

with an *Etiquette* ghost.

Mum swipes her wristband against a wall-scanner beside the elevator. Beckett and I copy her and we all step in. My stomach plummets as we're launched skywards. I never get used to it.

The doors open at floor 303, and a man wearing navy business clothes ushers us into a new room. He motions for us to sit on a grey couch facing a ripple-screen. Mum and Beckett sit on either side of me and Beckett yawns loudly. His terrier taps at his knee.

'Welcome, welcome,' the man says, taking a swivel seat opposite me and in front of the screen. 'I see you've brought family, Nikki—that's good. I'm Darshan, head designer here at Ghost Designs. I had a look at your file, and I see that you will be receiving your first ghost today. Now, with our superior designs, this is likely to be the only ghost you'll need in your life but, in the rare case of a malfunction, we will be happy to replace it.'

A tremble goes through my spine at the word 'ghost', although I've used it countless times. A translucent blue cat slinks around the man's legs: his ghost. I hardly believe I'm about to receive my own.

'As you probably know, each ghost is chosen to suit its charge. That means you will be appointed a ghost to help compensate for a deficiency you have. Our programming assesses your school results to determine your aptitudes and areas of weakness.'

I'm surprised that the man addresses me instead of my mum, and nod. 'My friend Caitlin just got a Grammar cat.'

He smiles. 'Excellent. May I see your wristband?'

I hold out my arm and he scans the band with a handheld device that makes the screen behind him light up. 'Almost there, Nikki. Now, are there any animals you're afraid of?'

I almost say 'bees' but am slapped by memories of a few years ago. On our walk home from school, Beckett would thrust dandelions under my nose, or poke their stems into my ear, yelling, 'Sting, sting, sting!'. Then he'd laugh when I screamed.

Has he always been annoying? I think he's forgotten about my old bee phobia—I had, before this moment—but I can imagine how insufferable he'll be if I bring it up again.

Darshan is waiting, so I shake my head. But I must have taken too long because he softens his voice and says, 'Most people are afraid of something. Spiders, maybe, or sharks. It's just easiest for us if we know we should avoid certain designs.'

'Spiders,' Mum says. 'I thought that having a ghost spider was illegal! They caused quite a stir in a few offices, I heard.'

Designer-man laughs. 'Yes, I heard that too. Ghost Designs has never created a spider ghost—we weren't responsible for any of that—but I thought I'd give Nikki an example.'

I lift my head. 'I'm not scared of animals.'

'Okay. Very well, then.' He turns to the ripple-screen, which looks like liquid metal, taps it, and makes a long, swivel-stroke down its surface. At his touch, dozens of my school reports flash up, overlapping. The images fizzle and blue light streams from the screen, pooling into a crouching frog, who blinks, then twists into a heron, before shrinking into a four-legged figure with a small head and snout, large petal ears, and a thick tail.

'Here you are,' Designer-man says. 'A Maths possum.'

The possum raises its head and looks at me, or through me. Although it's a translucent, shimmering blue, it looks strangely realistic and is kind of adorable.

But my cheeks burn as Beckett caws with laughter. 'Called it! You still can't do times tables, can you, Nikko-Thicko?'

'Shut up!' I round on him as his terrier anxiously bobs up on its hind legs. 'I can too!'

'Can too!' he imitates me.

'I'm just not a Maths genius, okay? Everyone needs help with something.'

'That's right,' Mum says, and the designer glances down and nods. I can't believe I've taken Beckett's bait by yelling at him in public. Designer-man will think we're totally dysfunctional and *rude*, and maybe swap my Maths possum for an Etiquette ghost.

'Ah …' Designer-man holds a black chip over the possum and it dissolves into the ghost's blue form. Then he holds out his hand-held device again; I let my wrist be scanned. 'Well, that's all taken care of. The Maths possum is yours.' He attempts a smile. 'All our ghosts are programmed to learn so that they can adapt to your lifestyle and individual needs. A ghost is a constant companion. You won't need to do anything for this possum to follow you everywhere. I'm sure you will find it useful.'

***

Caitlin messages me later that night via mirror-screen when I'm shut away in my room with the ghost possum. My bedroom walls are a bright princess pink that I outgrew years ago, but I don't have the heart to tell Mum. On my eighth birthday, I went off to school and when I came home, Mum and Dad were splattered in paint and grinning. When they showed me my new room, I squealed in delight. Pink was my favourite colour. Mum let Dad pull her in for a hug, her cheeks flushing with happiness to match my walls.

The next year, I decided I liked blue better, and school moved online so now I'm home basically all the time. We use mirror-screens to sign onto classes and to chat with friends.

Caitlin's a dramatic person, which means she's a great audience. Holding up my mirror-screen, I turn on the video function and tell her about going to Ghost Designs. On my screen, I see her indignant face and the ghost cat curled on her lap. Even though its fur is translucent, it looks patchy.

'Beckett,' she says, 'is the worst.'

'I know, right?'

'I'm sorry that happened, Nik. Anyway, your possum is totes cute.' At this, the cat nudges her arm with a paw, and she sighs. Looking at the cat, she says, 'I meant *totally*. Do you have to correct me, like, all the time?'

'The word "like" is not needed in your last sentence,' the cat says, and Caitlin just shakes her head.

'He really knows how to get under my skin,' I say. 'But I think this time I was upset because what Beckett said is kind of true. I'm *terrible* at maths.'

Caitlin hesitates, torn between her duty to defend me and to be honest. 'It's … well, everyone needs a ghost, Nik. Imagine what it was like when all people had was the internet to look stuff up! It musta taken *for*-ever to get anything done.'

I smile a little and look at the possum by my feet. 'Yeah, guess so.'

'And the internet wasn't, like, that personable.'

'The word "like" is not needed—'

Caitlin shushes her cat, and says, 'I know Mr Norrel says that clicks and search histories were recorded, but it didn't learn *you* like a ghost does.'

'So you like your ghost, then?'

She leans forward, and I can see the freckles on her nose. 'Lo-ove it. I mean, she taps me every three seconds when I say something that's not, like, all accurately or something, but she's super-cute. I'm going to name her "Cuddles".'

I bite my lip. 'That's not allowed.'

'Who cares? No one has to know. But *you* know I always wanted a cat, Nik, and they're too expensive!'

When Dad was a kid his rich uncle had a dog, but that was practically unheard of. Dad says that the government upped the price on pets so that their lives would be valued more.

Caitlin draws her cat closer and says, 'This is the next best thing.'

I know what it's like to want an animal. I used to read and reread books about dogs—like if I learnt enough it would come close to knowing what it meant to look after one. Maybe Caitlin's right about the ghosts. We talk and laugh and by the time we end the call, I feel like it's been a pretty good birthday.

***

Over the next few weeks, Caitlin and I talk on our mirror-screens but don't see each other in person. The last time I went over her house was a while ago, and it was a shock to see she'd gotten taller than me. Since high school started, we don't have as much time for the things I loved most: smashing macadamia shells open with a hammer; making watermelon sandwiches and mango ice-cream; writing comedy skits that we'd someday turn into films. Water-bomb fights in the park.

Still, just talking to Caitlin is a relief. Classes have gotten intense in the lead-up to exams and I know the Maths possum is meant to help me. Its taps on my arm usually mean that I've made a mistake and I'm getting used to its chirping voice.

The possum ghost insists on revising multiplication tables with me, and I play alternative music loudly in my room when we do this so that Beckett doesn't have ammunition to mock me. It's awful, I know, but I get stuck on my eight times tables. I was sick a lot as a kid—some months felt like one long chest infection after another—and I feel like I missed something foundational in lessons that everyone else has built on. Whenever we get to two times eight, it's like my brain glitches and I blurt out, 'fifteen' instead of sixteen.

I remember telling Caitlin not to name her ghost—it's not protocol and I don't know anyone else who does—but when we're alone, I call mine 'Possum'. It just makes everything easier. And Possum is a good teacher, I think, because it never gets bored or impatient and it learns my routines. It curls up in a ball on my bed, imitating sleep, when I lie down at night. It unfurls and follows me down to the breakfast table in the morning, sitting beside my bowl even though it doesn't need food. At first, I find it creepy when it waits outside the toilet or shower for me, but, after a couple of weeks, I get used to this too.

One day after I sign out of classes, I decide to walk to the park.

Possum nudges my foot as I look for a second sock to pull on. I always lose socks.

'There is revision to do.'

'Not today, Possum,' I say. 'I'm sick of being inside. Time to play.'

'You are not a child. Nikki, you may get further behind if you do not study—'

'Nope,' I say. 'Not today. I'm not a child and you're not a possum! But look.' I point out my bedroom window at a square of blue streaked with clouds. 'There's all that space to explore.'

Possum follows me down the street—it has no choice—and sinks into a reverie as we near the park. After I've had a good look to make sure Beckett isn't around, I run to the swings and grab the cool metal chains. The rise and fall in my stomach makes me giddy as I kick the sky. Possum watches, head tilted.

I'm barely a teenager, but I haven't felt like a kid in ages. When did my life twist into endless classes and homework? Right now, my heart swells at the glorious little things—tree branches reaching like hands across the sky, longing to be held; the purple shine on the back of a pigeon's neck; the crunch of leaves under my feet as I slide off the swings and run.

I find a sturdy mango tree and scuffle up its trunk, settling on a thick branch. The air smells like sunshine and fruit, even though the tree's not in season. Possum hesitates at the tree's base, peering up.

'C'mon,' I shout. 'Are you a possum or not?'

'I am not,' Possum says, and it sounds a little sad. 'You said as much before. I am an advanced form of technology nicknamed a "ghost".'

'Just … just climb, okay?' I say. 'Can you do that?'

Possum looks at me, then plants a paw on the tree's trunk. I remember with a jolt that it has no physicality, but then somehow it climbs. Possum's shimmering form travels the tree, moving one paw after the other, tail beginning to swish as it clambers onto my branch, and a laugh bursts from me. 'You did it!'

Possum's eyes close slightly in what might be a smile.

There's a rustling overhead; a furry rope droops from a branch above, and I stifle a cry. Possum opens its eyes to take in a cat-size furry possum, living and breathing in greys and blacks, its eyes bright with fear. The animal scampers out of sight, and a bewildered expression flickers on my Possum's face before it disappears.

***

'He-ey,' Caitlin says on the mirror-screen that night. 'Guess whom just got a hundred per cent for the English exam?'

'What?' I straighten. 'Caitlin, that's amazing! I mean, well done.'

'I know,' she says, cuddling her ghost cat. 'This cat is a frickin' genius. She was all like, tap, tap, tap, and then I fixed the thingies, and boo-yah!'

The cat's ear flicks at this, and my words turn sour. I try to smile, but I've always beaten Caitlin at English. I mean, we never talked about it like a competition, but I thought it was accepted that she was good at being a social, fun person, and I was good at following Mr Norrel's instructions and actually reading the books we were meant to analyse. Caitlin makes grammatical errors all the time. How can she take credit for her cat?

'I know we had to wait a while to get our ghosts, but it's *so* good to see them results coming in,' she says.

The cat snuggles in closer and I make an excuse to end the call.

***

By now, I can get through my seven times tables without faltering. But late one night, when I'm revising with Possum in my room, something strange happens.

'One times eight?'

'Eight,' I say.

'Two times eight?'

'Fifteen.'

'Three times eight?'

'Wait … sixteen.'

'That is incorrect. The answer is twenty-four.'

'No. Possum, I got the answer before wrong. Two times eight.'

I stare at Possum, who says, 'Three times eight is twenty-four.'

'I know that,' I say, stomach sinking. 'Possum, what is two times eight?'

It blinks. 'Fifteen.'

***

My Possum's malfunctioning, but I can't give it back. It nestles on my lap if I watch a movie after studying, and I can almost feel its weight, its warmth. When no one but me is looking, it bops Beckett's ghost terrier on the nose and makes me laugh. If Beckett annoys me, it tries to bite his hands.

We go to the park after I sign out of classes every day. I take a swing and kick the sky, and climb trees and Possum …

Possum learns to be wild.

I think my ghost is male. I can't say why I think this, I just do. The more Possum climbs and leaps and scurries and looks at me with smiling eyes, the harder it is for me to think of my ghost as 'it', or mechanical, or lifeless. So now I call Possum 'he', the same way Caitlin calls her cat 'she'.

I think Possum is fascinated by the furred possum he's fashioned after. He often climbs the mango tree, keeping watch. To begin with, the other possum stays out of sight, probably sleeping during the day, but then begins to venture out more and more. If it appears, Possum gets as close as he can and copies its movements.

Once, he nudges its tail with his holographic snout.

Sometimes, when we're studying at night with the music turned up loud, I repeat my experiment by asking Possum what two times eight is. And I think I finally work it out …

He's not malfunctioning, he's learning. Just like Designer-man said he would. But Possum has learnt my mistake, which is why he gets the answer wrong.

***

When my final report comes in, my stomach's a jumble of guilt and relief. My maths grade is much, much higher than I expected. I was jealous of Caitlin for succeeding because of her cat, but really I'm no different. And what we're doing isn't breaking the rules—teachers know that everyone in our year level has a ghost by now.

Then why does it feel like cheating?

Mum and Dad keep talking about my grades over dinner. Dad's wombat sits at his feet, glancing up at me every so often, while Mum's cockatoo perches on her shoulder. Mum says she's proud. Dad waves a potato, speared on his fork, at me and says, 'So maybe veterinary science isn't out of the question, hey Nik?'

I almost choke on a mouthful of green beans. Helping animals was my dream for a long time, but I'd given up on it after learning that you needed advanced maths skills. I mumble a reply to Dad, thinking about what a catastrophe it'd be if I trusted Possum to calculate how much medication a sick animal needed and he made a mistake. Because Possum had helped me learn algebra, but I'd helped him *un*learn times tables.

'Guess that ghost's working out, huh?' Beckett says, and I think he means it as a compliment. Maybe Beckett's terrier *is* making a difference because, after dinner, Mum brings out a banana cake for dessert and he offers me the bigger slice. I say 'no thanks' and go to my room with Possum and a headache.

***

The next morning begins with a sharp, persistent knock at the front door. None of us rise early on weekends, and I keep hoping that the sound is coming from a neighbour's house. By the time I climb out of bed and go down the hall, my whole family's gathered before the door with their ghosts, looking a mixture of drowsy and baffled in their pyjamas.

Dad opens the door and Designer-man Darshan strides in. 'My apologies for the intrusion, but it was very important to come as soon as I was notified of the error.'

'I'm sorry?' Mum says.

'Nikki's ghost is malfunctioning,' he says. 'This is extremely rare, I assure you. Once I've removed it, I can catalogue what went wrong and send you a replacement as soon as tomorrow.'

Possum shrinks back, his tail flattening to the floor and I stand in front of him. 'No,' I say. 'No, he works fine.'

Designer-man gives me a piercing look, and I know that he registered my use of a pronoun. 'Give me your wrist-band so I can unpair you and remove the ghost.'

I glance at Possum. His eyes are as wide and terrified as the furred possum's when a dog barks. Mum and Beckett shake their heads at Designer-man and Dad scratches his chin.

'Excuse me,' he says, 'I don't want to second-guess you, mate, but my girl just did very well in her maths exam. From where I stand, that ghost is doing wonders.'

Designer-man shakes his head impatiently and draws his hand-held device from a pocket, sending a transparent report marked by graphs floating into space. 'This is what we expected,' he says, jabbing his finger at a peak in the graph. 'While Nikki's results have improved, she could do better. Eighty-six percent is *not* acceptable for one of our ghosts.' Without another word, he strides through the report to me and seizes my wrist. I tug away but he swipes the handheld against my wrist-band.

I turn and Possum has vanished. The air turns freezing cold; shivers race through me. 'No,' I shout, 'no, you have to give him back! You don't understand—'

Designer-man is already tapping on his hand-held. 'I'll send your replacement tomorrow.'

And he marches out the door.

***

I cry on the floor in my room, looking through a slice of the window. The park's out there, but it'll never be mine again without Possum. I wonder if the furred possum misses us. I wonder if, someday, the two of them could have been friends.

My family members visit me, one by one. First Mum, bristling with indignation and saying that the man was very rude, coming on the weekend and without warning. Then Dad comes in, his wombat lumbering after him. Dad looks away a lot when talking, because my tears make him uncomfortable. He says that what happened was unfair but, if the man's right, then maybe I can do even better with maths in the future.

'I know you're someone who gets used to things,' Dad says, scuffing my carpet with a foot. 'You're like me that way.' He glances at his wombat with affection. 'But Nik, things change. I've had my ghost for so long, but if it malfunctions then I'll get used to the new one eventually, right? Nothing lasts forever.' On his way to my door, he pauses and says, 'Well, almost nothing. The way I feel about you, Beck and your Mum will never change. You know that right, Nik?'

'Yeah, Dad.'

'Well, good,' he says gruffly, and leaves.

Hours later, Beckett slouches in with his terrier. 'Still in here, hey?'

'Go away,' I say. 'You don't understand.'

'You know what, Nik?' Beckett says, joining me on the floor. 'I really do.' He pats his terrier, who opens his mouth in a pant. 'After the first couple of months with Trick, I knew we were bonding in ways we weren't supposed to. An emotional connection wasn't part of the design.' He scratches the back of his neck. 'Whenever I go out in public by myself, I overdo the niceties. I am the most polite young man in the world. Truly. I stand up for old women on buses; I say "Good morning" or "Good afternoon" to everyone; I carry groceries for people. I use my "pleases", "after yous" and "thank yous"! And I do it so that Trick has something to report on. Something to prove that he's "working".'

I stare, and my brother sighs. I never even knew that he'd named his ghost.

'Look, Trick means the world to me so I guess that possum's probably the same to you. Did you name it?'

I nod. 'Possum.'

He struggles not to roll his eyes. 'Original, Nik. Anyway, there are times to be polite and times to screw etiquette. Remember my placement at Ghost Designs? I know for a fact that the memory chips for "faulty" ghosts are kept for study.' He looks at me intently. 'Do you want to get Possum back?'

***

We sneak in at night, using an access wrist-band Beckett says he 'accidentally-on-purpose' forgot to return. Ghost Designs is so quiet, I feel like there might be *real* ghosts hovering—the ones from old stories. Beckett repeats his instructions to hide my face. There are cameras.

'Stay outside, Trick,' Beckett murmurs as we push through the front door and, to my amazement, he does.

Heart thudding, I dash in while Beckett skirts around a desk to throw his spare jumper over a camera. I'm glad it's so dark, but who knows what kind of quality the cameras are and whether they have night-vision? I find another camera, half-hidden by a large palm in the corner. I peel off my jumper and drop it over the camera too. Then I see a third camera fitted in the wall's corner and realise that we're out of loose clothes. I've never broken into a place before.

I scramble to Beckett, back straining and hunched like an old person, and elbow him. 'Look,' I hiss, and point.

'Aw, damn, they got extra cameras,' he breathes, and then his face brightens. 'Okay, Nik. Time to go off-road, so to speak.'

I stay low to the ground as Beckett dashes to a potted lily. He drags it across the floor, steps on the pot's rim and wobbles. Then he launches into the air, arms outstretched. He crashes and hits the carpet, a black rectangle and cords dangling from his hands.

My brother—my stupid, incorrigible brother—just ripped a camera out. Heat rushes to my chest; I know at that moment that he loves me.

He stamps on the camera for good measure, cracking its lens, and lets out a whoop and the affection I feel fades. 'Cut it out,' I snap. 'You said to be quiet!'

Beckett's eyes gleam and he whispers, 'Wish Trick could've seen that. It's the weirdest thing, teaching a dog how to misbehave …'

We scan our borrowed wrist-band again and ride the elevator to floor 303. Beckett points out a row of cabinets at the back of the room and rummages through their drawers. I use my mirror-screen to shine light onto his hands and the slender, packaged chips he handles.

Finally, he draws out what looks like a tiny black square, wrapped in plastic. 'Got it.'

'That's really it?'

'Yep. They're all labelled. Which reminds me …' Beckett digs around and tears the label off my chip's plastic, stamping it over the top of another plastic sleeve. 'Let's go.'

We run through the lobby, and Beckett stops to kick a pot plant over. I tug his arm and we burst through the door into the street. He lets out a feral yell; I could hug or slap him. Trick bounds alongside us, throws back his head and howls too.

I'm trembling with nerves, but raw laughter rips out of my throat as we hurtle down one street, then another. Beckett's faster than me—always has been—but somehow I'm keeping up. We are wild things, moving shadows, rippling with the night. The wind whispers of mysteries as we sprint through the park. Before this place belonged to afternoons with Possum, or water-bomb fights with Caitlin, it was ours. Mine and Beckett's. Our feet pound the bike path's pavement, then tear through grass on our way home.

***

The next morning I wake with a heavy head. Mum and Dad watch me over breakfast, worried that I'm still upset. My cereal curdles in my stomach; I'm nervous as hell when Designer-man drops off my new Maths possum ghost. I can barely look at him or his cat but I feel sorry for them both. Because there *is* no short-cut to learning—and relying on a ghost for answers is no answer at all.

All the same, Possum did teach me. Designer-man never discovered his cat could make mistakes. He doesn't know that it might have a soul.

The new possum is not the same. It follows me but speaks without its voice rising or falling. Its tail doesn't twitch or sway, and it never falters when we recite times tables. A noisy miner lands on my window sill and ruffles its feathers, and the possum doesn't so much as glance at it.

I follow my routine of Sunday classes and wait for Beckett to sign out of his. I know we must be careful now. Once Beckett's done, I let him and Trick into my room and shut the door.

'Hey, Nik? I got up early this morning, before Trick got started, and went back to Ghost Designs. Drew some graffiti on the walls, so it looks like the bust-up was vandalism.'

I shake my head in amazement, and he shrugs, unable to hide his grin.

'Had to be done. You ready?'

I nod.

Now that the moment has come, the confidence in Beckett's expression slips. He fumbles taking the chip out of its packaging, and then scans it against my wrist-band. I feel like there's a mango pip stuck in my throat. Can I really get Possum back? Ghost updates don't normally involve anything like this, but Beckett's theory is that the two possums will meld into one during the memory-transfer. I've never so wanted Beckett to be right about something.

The ghost stands on all fours, half a pace from me. My brother holds the chip over its back and it freezes, eyes closed, as the chip dissolves. When his eyes open, they search for me.

Possum bounds forward. 'Play?'

ABOUT OUR AUTHORS

Geraldine Borella

Geraldine Borella writes stories for children and adults and has been published in magazines, online, in podcasts and anthologies. Her stories feature in *Spooktacular Stories – Thrilling Tales for Brave Kids*; *Short and Twisted*, 2016; literary magazine page seventeen, issue 11; and on Antipodean SF's website and podcast. In 2018, she won an ASA Emerging Writer's mentorship and placed second in the Buzz Words Short Story Prize for Children. She came second in the 2020 Just Write For Kids Pitch It! Competition pitching the young adult novel she is currently working on. She lives on the Atherton Tablelands in Far North Queensland.

Jennie Del Mastro

Jennie Del Mastro writes fantasy and science fiction. Her work has been published in *The Big Issue*, and the anthology *Stories of Life: The Swimmer*. She lives with her family in Gippsland, and is currently polishing her first novel.

Jonathan E. Furneaux

Jonathan E. Furneaux is a science fiction and fantasy author from Brisbane, Australia. In the second grade, his teacher let him write novels in the back of his mathematics book. As a result, he developed a joy of writing and literature, as well as an awkward pause before having to do any kind of counting.

Jonathan was awarded a High Commendation by the Fellowship of Australian Writers (QLD) for his first published short story: *The Second Father*.

He has self-published two novels: *Lessons from the Wreckage*, and *Spirits in Your Area*, both of which are available on Amazon & Kindle.

Jack Garrety

Jack is the writing name of Paul Garrety. Paul is the author of five novels and numerous other short stories (jackgarrety.com). He primarily writes urban fantasy but has strayed into fantasy, crime, and is currently working on a commercial women's fiction novel, *Middle Women*, which will be released shortly.

Paul lives high on the Blackall Ranges overlooking the Sunshine Coast with his delightful wife Annie.

In addition to writing Paul is a yoga teacher and accredited yoga therapist with Yoga Australia and has almost completed a masters in Gestalt psychotherapy. His other interests are bushwalking, reading and meditation.

Anne Hamilton

Anne Hamilton is the author of 29 books, including several multi-award winners. They range from environmental picture books to classic YA quest fantasy through to three different devotional theology series. She's also a professional editor and has worked on over 200 books and magazines, along with so many independent articles she's long ago lost count. She once taught mathematics for nearly three decades, and so all of her stories are designed using an ancient technique known as numerical literary style.

Jo Hart

Jo Hart is an award-winning speculative fiction author with a variety of short stories published in anthologies and online. She recently won the 2019 Aurealis Award for Best Young Adult Short Story for her novella *The Jindabyne Secret.* Jo lives the quiet life in rural Victoria. When she is not writing, she is busy being a mum, advocating for Autism awareness, and geeking out over all things fantasy.

Rosanne Hawke

Rosanne Hawke has authored 30 books for young people including The Tales of Jahani and the Beyond Borders series. She has been a teacher, an aid worker in Pakistan & UAE, and a lecturer in creative writing at Tabor Adelaide. Her books explore cultural and social issues, history, mystery, family and faith. She often writes of displacement, belonging and reconciliation and tells stories of children unheard. *Taj and the Great Camel Trek* won the 2012 Adelaide Festival Award for Children's Literature. Rosanne is the recipient of the 2015 Nance Donkin Award and is a bard of Cornwall.

Jennifer Horn

Jennifer Horn is a Brisbane-based freelance illustrator and emerging children's writer. Her short stories have appeared in the children's anthologies, *It's Beginning to Look A Lot Like Christmas* (2018), *Spooktacular Stories* (2019) and *Tell 'Em They're Dreaming* (2020). She draws on her love of stories and adventure to create whimsical illustrations in a Quentin-Blake-inspired squiggle style. Jen loves reading books over local radio, playing piano, and watching imaginative dystopian narratives like *Black Mirror*, in the hope of writing similar witty pieces one day.

Russell Hume

Russell's usual job these days is selling tee shirts. Before that, he was a marketer for business software. And before that, he was a neuroscience researcher, who studied how the brain processes information about our sense of touch and limb position.

He is an avid consumer of 'hard' science fiction—movies, TV series, and the written word. Russell is married, has two sons, and lives in Sydney's leafy northwest.

Penny Jaye

From picture books or young adult fiction, Penny Jaye writes to explore themes that matter. Her YA novel, *Out of the Cages* published by Rhiza Press, tackles modern day slavery. *The Other Brother* is a picture book about belonging and the power of compassion. Penny lives in western Sydney with her family and enjoys juggling a busy life with various writing commitments, including author visits. She loves family movie nights, lunch by the river and being tucked up in bed to read a new book! Penny also writes as Penny Reeve and Ella Shine.

Adele Jones

Queensland author Adele Jones writes young adult and historical novels, poems, inspirational non-fiction and short fictional works. Her writing explores issues of social justice, humanity, faith, natural beauty and meaning in life's journey, and her first YA novel *Integrate* (book one of the Blaine Colton Trilogy) was awarded the 2013 CALEB Prize for unpublished manuscript. As a speaker she seeks to present a practical and encouraging message by drawing on themes from her writing.

Emily Larkin

Emily Larkin is a Queensland author who holds a Doctorate in Creative Writing from the University of the Sunshine Coast. She is the author of *The Whirlpool*, a picture book illustrated by Helene Magisson and published by Wombat Books. Emily's dystopian YA novel *Within the Ward* is due for release with Rhiza Edge in 2021. Emily has published numerous short stories, and teaches Creative Writing and Literature at The University of Queensland and the Queensland University of Technology College. She also runs workshops for the Queensland Writers Centre. Emily loves reading and spending time with family, friends, and animals.

Stephanie Martin

Stephanie Martin, author of *Luminescent Love*, grew up on a farm near Guyra, NSW, where she fell in love with animals and nature. After completing a Bachelor of Environmental Science, Stephanie moved to sunny Coffs Harbour where she began to explore her new backyard through scuba diving and snorkelling.

With a love for all things turtle, Stephanie currently volunteers at the Dolphin Marine Conservation Park in the turtle rehab hospital outside of work. Stephanie has always been an avid reader and writer and loves getting lost in made up worlds where mystery, romance and enchantment thrive.

Catriona McKeown

Catriona spends her days hanging out with teenagers in a middle school in Southern Queensland, where she works to support and advocate for young people with special needs. Her first YA novel, *The Boy in the Hoodie*, won her the CALEB award for unpublished fiction in 2016. Her second young adult novel, *Memphis Grace*, was published in 2019 and was awarded the Older Readers category of the Australian Family Therapists' Award for Children's Literature for 2020. She also has many short stories published both online and in anthologies.

Janeen Samuel

Janeen Samuel lives in South-West Victoria surrounded by slumbering volcanoes, which may be one reason why many of her stories are speculative in nature. She has had pieces published in various magazines and anthologies, including *Award Winning Australian Writing* (Melbourne Books), *Andromeda Spaceways Inflight Magazine*, *Cicerone Journal*, and the speculative poetry anthology *The Stars Like Sand* (Interactive Press). Apart from writing and reading, her passions are walking in the bush, crawling through caves, and conserving wildlife.

R. A. Stephens

R. A. is a teacher by day, writer, editor and publisher by night. She is passionate about the written word, what stories can do to take a reader to a new world and open our eyes to love, compassion, the bigger picture and much more. When not working teaching or writing she enjoys living in the country and spending time with her kids and cats.

Lynne Stringer

Lynne Stringer has been passionate about writing all her life. She was the editor of a small newspaper (later magazine) for seven years, and currently works as a professional editor and proofreader.

Lynne wrote her YA sci-fi romance novel, *The Heir*, in 2010. *The Heir* is the first in a trilogy. Book two in the series, *The Crown*, was released in November 2013. Book three, *The Reign*, was released on 1st May 2014. *Once Confronted*, a contemporary drama set in Australia, was released in October 2016. Her latest book is *The Verindon Alliance*, which was released in May 2020. It is a prequel to her trilogy.

FUTURE SHORT STORY COLLECTIONS

This is the first Rhiza Edge themed short story collection for teens. If you are a writer and would like to contribute, please check out our submissions and themed calls for collections on our website: www.wombatrhiza.com.au.

Future short story collections coming soon!

The Opposite of Disappearing (2021)
Laura Norris and R. A. Stephens (Editors)

Dust Makers (2022)
Penny Jaye and R.A. Stephens (Editors)